I0682465

Desinence

Two Worlds Book #5

By Timothy L. Cerepaka

An Annulus Publishing Book

Annulus Publishing, Cherokee, Texas, 2015

Published by Annulus Publishing

Copyright © Timothy L. Cerepaka 2015. All rights reserved.

Formatting by Timothy L. Cerepaka

Contact: timothy@timothylcerepaka.com

Cover design by Elaina Lee of For the Muse Design

(www.forthemusedesign.com)

ISBN-13: 978-0692601938

ISBN-10: 0692601937

Acknowldgments

I would like to thank my uncle, James Wilhite, for helping me get this manuscript into publishable shape. I'd also like to thank the rest of my family for supporting me while I wrote this novel. You guys rock.

PART ONE:
ONE WORLD

Chapter I

The little girl known as Kara ran through the tall grass with glee. She had no real destination in mind, except to run and run as quickly as she could. Today, after all, was the Day of Celebration, and her parents had said that she could have the whole day off from her boring-as-paint studies.

Her plan for the rest of the afternoon was simple. She would run around in the fields around their tiny little cottage for a few hours, return home for lunch, maybe play with her older brother and her Protector if they were around, and then go with her father to the Capital City in time for the celebration itself. Father had promised to buy her whatever gifts she wanted while they were in the City, partly due to the Day, but also partly due to how hard she had worked at her studies over the last year. She fully intended on asking Father for one of those neat, skyras-powered toy jet trains that her friend, Jana, had; they were so amazing, because they resembled real jet trains down to the last detail.

If I had that, I would be the most popular girl in town, Kara thought with a smile on her small lips.

Then, without warning, her small feet tripped over something long and thick and she fell face first into the grass. She didn't break her nose or scratch her face; however, the fall did hurt, even when she put out her arms to break it.

Yet Kara was not a crybaby, like her brother always accused her of being, so she didn't make even one sound when she fell. Instead, she turned around to see what she had tripped over (thinking maybe it was a stick she could play with) but she would have been forgiven if she had screamed her head off when she saw what it was, exactly.

The thing she had tripped over was a long, deadly-looking snake with green skin the same shade as the grass. Spikes rose up from its back like the back spikes of a dragon, and it raised its large, flat head to look at her with deadly red eyes. A low, deadly-sounding hiss emitted from its mouth, while the snake itself smelled like mud and dirt.

Kara had no interest in snakes or reptiles, which was why she was unable to identify this creature's species; however, she didn't need to be an expert on reptiles to know that this snake could swallow her whole if it wanted. And considering how angry it looked, she had no doubt that it was planning to do that even as she watched it.

She scrambled to her feet and tried to walk backwards while keeping an eye on it, but she was never good at multitasking and so ended up almost falling over again. When Kara regained her balance, she just stood there in fear, staring at the snake's hypnotic red eyes as it drew closer to her.

Kara desperately wanted to cry out for her father, who she knew could kill this thing with his magic in one hit; but unfortunately, she was too paralyzed by fear to so much as whisper for help. She could only watch the monster snake draw closer and closer, its mouth opening wider and wider, revealing its fangs that looked sharper than any knife Kara had seen.

But at that moment, Kara heard someone running through the grass toward them. She did not know who it was, and neither did the snake, apparently, because it began looking around for the source of those running footsteps, which were getting closer and closer every second.

And then, without warning, a short, metal humanoid robot jumped out of the tall grass and tackled the snake to the ground. The snake hissed in anger and shock, while Kara gasped before she felt a familiar strong hand grab hers and a voice behind her say, "Come on, Kara! Let's get out of here!"

Kara looked over her shoulder and saw a boy of about ten pulling her through the tall grass. He had strawberry blonde hair and, when he glanced at her briefly, saw those natural blue eyes that she would recognize anywhere.

"Carem?" said Kara as her older brother pulled her along through the grass. "What are—"

"Vyll said he sensed you were in danger," Carem said without looking back at her. "I said he was just worrying too much about you, as usual, but he insisted we come out here and check on you anyway. Looks like he was spot on."

"That was Vyll back there?" said Kara, looking back in the direction they had came from, where she heard Vyll wrestling with the snake. "I've never seen him do *that* before."

"Well, he's supposed to be your Protector, isn't he?" said Carem. "That's what he's supposed to do, after all."

"Oh, I hope he's all right," said Kara, still glancing over her shoulder frequently. "That snake looked awfully mean."

"He'll be all right," said Carem. "He's strong. Protectors are tough."

"I hope you're right," said Kara. She felt the pockets of her dress and was relieved to feel that her picture was still folded up in there. "Because I have something special I want to share with him, something I've been meaning to give to him for a while. And I can't give it to him if the snake—"

A loud roar—with a vaguely snake-like hiss tingeing it—caused both Kara and Carem to stop in their tracks. They turned to look in the direction that the roar had come from, but they saw nothing except for the tall grass of the fields and the purplish hue of the sky above, and in the distance, the Seven Towers of Peace, but Kara could care less about the Seven Towers, because she now wondered if that roar had come from the snake, and if so, whether it was a roar of pain or a roar of victory. The roar abruptly cut off, but that did not make Kara feel any better about the fate of Vyll. She imagined the snake devouring Vyll whole, which made her stomach twist.

She and Carem watched as something made its way through the grass. It was hard to tell at first just who or what it was—indeed, for a moment, Kara almost thought that it might be the snake, having won its battle with Vyll—but soon she saw a familiar shine off a metallic head and her stomach untwisted.

"Vyll!" said Kara, waving at him as the Protector pushed his way through the grass. "Over here, boy!"

Her calling him must have encouraged him to come faster, because in seconds Vyll was right in front of Kara and Carem. He straightened up and saluted them both in that funny way he always did whenever he was reporting something to her.

"I have terminated the threat, Miss Kara," said Vyll. He gestured over his shoulder in the direction he had came. "The snake is dead. It won't be a threat to you or to brother Carem anymore."

Concerned over his well-being, Kara carefully observed Vyll's appearance. He was the same height as her and even had a similarly-shaped mouth like hers; aside from that, however, he looked completely different from her, as Protectors usually did. He had red eyes, for one (*Optics,* Kara corrected herself), and metallic skin that reflected the light of the twin suns in a pretty way. There was a weird green liquid covering his hands, but Kara knew that couldn't belong to him because Protectors like Vyll did not have blood. It was probably the blood of that snake, but she was so relieved at his survival that she didn't mind the blood on his hands.

Kara clapped her hands together excitedly. "That's great, Vyll! I was worried that you might get hurt. It was a big, mean old snake, after all, and it had really sharp teeth."

"My systems do not detect any injuries on my body," said Vyll. "Everything is functional, although I will need to oil my knee joints soon, because they are beginning to lose their nimbleness. I will also need to wash my hands of this blood."

"We can oil you when we get back to the house," said Kara. She looked up at her older brother. "Carem knows how to oil you. Right, Carem?"

"Sure do," said Carem, puffing his chest out. "Father showed me how to do it. I can do it in no time."

"Thank you for your offer, Miss Kara, Master Carem, but I do not want to inconvenience you with my maintenance," said Vyll, as humbly as always. "Your mother is preparing lunch for you, after all, and by the time we get back, she will no doubt tell you to clean up and get ready to eat and then head to the City for the celebration. I doubt she will appreciate you getting your hands oily, which will make them very hard to clean even with soap and water."

Kara put her hands behind her back. "Yeah, I guess you're right, Vyll. Mother wouldn't be happy about that. Still, I want to give you *something* in return for your help. It's only fair."

"No need, Miss Kara," said Vyll. He jerked his thumb at his chest. "I am your Protector, after all, and have been since your birth. It is my duty to protect and guide you, even as I learn with you. The only reward I need is to see that you are safe and secure from all harm."

Carem sighed and looked back in the direction of the house with a wistful glance. "Wish I had a Protector. Too bad Father didn't let me get one 'cause I'm the oldest."

"I can be your Protector as well, Master Carem," said Vyll, holding out his hand to Carem. "Not officially, of course, but—"

"Eh, forget about it," said Carem, waving off Vyll's offer. "I'm strong on my own. First born always are. That's why we don't get our own Protectors."

Kara immediately knew that Carem was lying, because she heard the jealousy in his voice. Besides, while Carem was not a weak boy by any means, he was still far more brainy than brawn; he wasn't as strong as he thought he was (although he was taking sword fighting lessons from Master Hoyan, a retired Minister of Fariah who lived just down the road from their house).

She thought about teasing Carem for his pretending not to be jealous, but then she remembered the folded up picture in her pocket and snapped her fingers. "Oh! Vyll, I have something for you."

"Something for me?" said Vyll, who, Kara was pleased to see, did not seem to guess what she was going to show him. "What is it?"

"A gift," said Kara as she reached into the pockets of her dress and grabbed the picture.

"A gift?" said Vyll. He tilted his head to the side in that way Kara always thought made him look funny. "No one has ever given me a gift before. Not even on my birthday, which is tomorrow."

"*Our* birthday, you mean," said Kara. She pulled the folded-up picture from her dress and held it out for him. "Because we were both born on the same day, remember? Anyway, that's why I drew this picture for you. I knew that no one else was going to give you a present, so I decided to make sure you got at least one; after all, you don't turn nine every year."

Vyll looked at the folded-up picture for a moment before taking it. He got some of the still-fresh green blood on it, but he wiped the picture on the grass to clean it, although Kara didn't really care, because it was his present and he was allowed to do what he wanted with it.

"Unfold it," said Kara. "Come on. Don't you want to see what it looks like?"

Vyll unfolded the picture carefully, making sure not to rip or damage it. When he finished unfolding it, he looked at it like he wasn't even sure how to react to the drawing on it.

"So?" said Kara. "Do you like it? I drew it myself."

"Hey, I helped, too," said Carem, holding up one hand. "Went and bought the art supplies myself. So it was a team effort."

Vyll looked up from the picture. His expression was hard to read, but Kara thought he looked astonished.

"I ... like it," said Vyll. He looked down at the picture again. He then began pointing at the figures that Kara had drawn on it. "That's me. And there's you, Miss Kara, and you as well, Master Carem. All three of us together."

"Of course we're together," said Kara with a smile. "I wanted to draw pictures of Mother and Father as well, but they're harder to draw, so I just went with us three. Because we're all friends."

Vyll looked up again. This time, he looked like he was close to tears, even though Kara was pretty sure that Protectors couldn't cry. "This is the best gift anyone has ever given me. Though I guess that isn't saying much; this is my very first gift, after all."

"'The first of many,' as Master Hoyan always says," said Carem. He nodded at Vyll. "I got a gift for you, too, but it's too big for me to carry around in my pockets. I was planning to give it to you tomorrow, for your birthday, but since sis here gave you yours now, I guess I can go ahead and give it to you when we get back to the house."

Vyll's mouth fell open. "That would be ... my second gift. That means I will have two gifts, even though up until now I have not even had one."

"I know!" said Kara. "Isn't that amazing? I mean, I don't really understand it all that well, because I've always gotten a gift every year for my birthday, but I'm happy that you're happy."

"Happy?" said Vyll. He held the picture closer to his chest. "Yes, I guess you could say I am happy. Is this what happiness is like? All of us being together like this?"

"Sure," said Kara. A warm breeze blew her hair around a

8

little, but she ignored it. "Everyone's happier when they're together with friends or family. I know I'm always happy whenever my parents, Carem, you, and I are together."

"Happiness is ... togetherness, then," said Vyll. "I will remember that always, Kara. That, and this gift you gave me."

Kara's smile widened even more. "That makes *me* happy."

Vyll looked at Carem. "What about you, Carem? Does that make you happy as well?"

"Sure," said Carem, jamming his hands into his pockets. "But I'll be even happier when you see the gift I got ya. It's way better than a funny little drawing."

Kara scowled at Carem. "Funny little drawing? It took me *hours* to get the colors right. I worked hard on it and even included you on it."

Carem smirked and held up his hands. "Doesn't change the fact that it's not all that great. I bet I could draw a better picture with both arms tied behind my back and Master Hoyan yelling in my ears."

"Oh, yeah?" said Kara. She pointed at the house in the distance. "Then why don't we have a drawing contest when we get home? Whoever draws the better picture wins."

Vyll stepped forward. His red optics looked concerned and he clutched the picture tighter than ever. "Why are you two going to fight? I thought we were all together."

"Fight? It's not a fight," said Carem. "Just a contest to see who's better, that's all."

"Oh," said Vyll. He stroked his chin. "Contest ... yes, I think I recall hearing that word before. You have entered sword contests before, right, Master Carem?"

"Right," said Carem, nodding. He jabbed his thumb at his chest. "Only a few so far, though, but I came in second place in the last one. Only reason I didn't win is because that kid from Jaggen used a dirty trick."

"You lost fair and square," Kara pointed out. "He didn't use any dirty trick. You just aren't as good as you think you are, that's all."

"Whatever, Kara," said Carem, rolling his eyes. "Anyway, let's go home and start that contest. If we're fast, we might be able to do it before we head into the city for the celebration. See you there!"

Carem took off through the tall grass, heading directly to the house. Kara followed as fast as she could, already forgetting about that giant monster snake that Vyll had killed. She was now more concerned with beating her older brother to the house, because she knew that if she didn't get there first, he'd gloat about winning the race all day long even if he ended up losing the picture-drawing contest.

Even so, she glanced over her shoulder at Vyll. He had not followed them yet; instead, he was still staring at the picture like it was the most valuable treasure in the world.

Although Kara hated to let Carem get any further ahead of her than he already was, she stopped for a moment and shouted, "Vyll! Are you coming or not? Remember, Carem's got a gift for you back home that he wants to give you!"

Vyll shook his head and looked at her. He raise a hand and shouted back, "I'm coming, Kara. Just give me a moment to catch up. You can go on ahead with Carem."

Kara frowned. "But—"

"Carem is going to win the race if you stay here," said Vyll. "Remember?"

Kara still wanted to make sure Vyll was coming (because she was now starting to remember the snake again and worried that there might be more hiding nearby that might harm Vyll), but then she decided that Vyll was more capable of defending himself than most adults were.

So she nodded and replied, "All right! See you later, then. Just get back before we start the contest; we need a judge and you're the best judge I know."

With that, Kara turned and resumed running after her brother. He was quite a ways ahead of her now, but Kara was certain that she would catch up with him well before they reached the house.

Even so, she could not help but look back at Vyll every now and then until he was lost from sight within the tall, scratchy grass. She was just glad that he liked her drawing. It made her so happy that she doubted even Carem winning the race or the drawing contest would be enough to put her in a bad mood for the rest of the day.

We'll be together forever, Kara thought as she ran. *Me, Carem, and Vyll. Even when we grow up, we'll still be tied together. Just like we promised.*

Chapter II

Three years later ...

V yll—now a couple of feet taller after being given an upgrade after his twelfth birthday, which was just a week ago—walked along the metal path under his feet, feeling a little awkward in his new form. Due to how recently he had received his upgrade, Vyll found it hard to adapt to. More than once over the last day or so, he had tripped over his own feet, which was not so bad when he was around Kara, who, due to her own growth spurt, was also dealing with a taller body than she was used to.

But he found it hard not to ignore the occasional stares or annoying glances he received from his fellow Protectors, who walked along the same path as he. Vyll knew none of the hundreds of Protectors that he walked along with today, which made him feel quite alone in the crowd, alone and wishing that Kara could have come with him to the Gathering, even though he knew that humans were not allowed to come to these Gatherings.

He looked around him as he walked. Wherever he looked, he saw the Protectors of other organics. Some were close in size to him, give or take a few inches, while others were as small as he had been three years ago. Most were as tall as full-grown adults and walked with such grace in their bodies that Vyll could not help but feel a little jealous at how easily they moved.

The one thing all of the Protectors had in common was their metallic skin and glowing optics. Like him, they were all robots, and each had their own human who they were bonded to for life. Of course, none of those humans were anywhere near them now, because the Gathering was not for humans, but for Protectors.

The crowd was walking inside a deep system of tunnels that went beneath the surface of Fariah, all the way down to its core— or so Vyll had been told by an adult Protector he had met when he arrived at the tunnel entrance near Capital City an hour ago. There were entrances to these tunnels all over Fariah, which allowed the billions of Protectors to travel to the Gathering place no matter where they lived on Fariah. Vyll wasn't sure how many Protectors were walking with him, but there had to be at least two or three hundred, maybe more.

Not that Vyll wanted to be here. Aside from suffering from the occasional disapproving glance from his fellow Protectors due to his awkwardness in his new body, the tunnel itself was quite claustrophobic. Vyll was so used to spending time out in the wide-open grass fields around Kara's house that he found this tunnel as confining as a jail cell. Besides, he kept worrying that an earthquake might happen and cause the ceiling to fall in on him; not an entirely unreasonable fear, considering how frequent earthquakes were nowadays.

In addition, Vyll felt like someone or something was watching him—not the other Protectors, who aside from their occasional disapproving glances barely paid him any attention otherwise, but the tunnel itself. Lights in a variety of colors shone across the ceiling, providing enough illumination by which to see the tunnel's interior, but Vyll thought of those lights as eyes, watching his every movement and making notes of everything he did.

"Disturbed?" said a voice to his right, above him. "Don't worry, little one. Everyone is when they go to their first Gathering."

Vyll looked up when he heard the voice. A large Protector with a round belly—an adult, probably—was walking a little behind him to his right. Unlike the other Protectors, this one wore a friendly smile on his face and didn't seem at all judgmental of Vyll's awkward attempts to keep pace with the rest. He had a red bandanna tied around his neck and yellow eyes, although Vyll had no idea who he was or which human he belonged to.

"How did you know this is my first Gathering?" Vyll asked, feeling a little awkward keeping an eye on the path while also talking with the adult. "I didn't tell anyone that."

"Because I've never seen you around here before," said the adult Protector with a chuckle. "And you seem uncomfortable, which is the typical reaction of young Protectors like yourself when they come to their first Gathering. But don't worry; the Rock won't judge you. There are billions of young Protectors just like you out there. The Rock is used to dealing with younglings like you. It won't single you out for any reason."

Despite the adult Protector's friendly tone, Vyll still had a hard time relaxing. He never trusted strangers quite as much as he trusted his family, but he decided he could afford to be a little friendly to this stranger, who seemed like a kind Protector to him. Besides, Vyll wanted someone to talk to and an experienced adult

Protector who had clearly been to multiple Gatherings in the past was certainly a good person with whom to speak.

"How rude of me," said the adult Protector. He jerked a thumb at his chest. "Call me Xalon. What's your name, youngling?"

"V-Vyll," said Vyll, rubbing his hands together anxiously, though he managed to raise his voice to be heard above the other conversations held by the other Protectors all around them, which echoed off the tunnel walls slightly.

"Vyll, huh?" said Xalon. "I like it. Short, sweet, and to the point. The Rock gave you a good name."

Vyll looked up at Xalon again in surprise. "The Rock? But I thought it was my human's parents who named me."

Xalon shook his head. "Nah. When a new Protector is born, it's the Rock's job to grant them life and a name. Don't feel bad about not knowing that, though. Most young Protectors don't really know or understand much about the Rock until their first Gathering or until they meet an older Protector willing to explain it to them."

"Oh," said Vyll. He frowned. "Does that mean that my human and I aren't real family, then?"

Xalon shrugged. "You and your human are whatever you want to be, youngling. The Rock is our guiding force and creator, but it ain't the end-all, be-all of everything, okay?"

Vyll nodded, although he wasn't entirely convinced about that. "Is that why I came here? Because it was about a week ago that I felt someone summoning me here. I had to leave Kara, my human, quickly because I couldn't resist it. I didn't even get a chance to say good bye. She thought I was being rude, but that's only because I couldn't explain my behavior myself."

15

"Yep," said Xalon. He gestured at the tunnel around them. "The Rock draws all Protectors to itself when it calls a new Gathering so that everyone can hear its announcements. These Gatherings are pretty rare, though; the last one was about twenty-five years ago, I think, well before you were even an idea in the Rock's mind."

"Why is the Rock calling this Gathering now?" said Vyll, who was starting to feel more comfortable speaking with Xalon, who seemed like a kind person. "Do you know why?"

Xalon shrugged again. "Nope. The Rock usually only calls these Gatherings when there's a great emergency on the horizon—something so bad that it requires all of us Protectors to know about it so we can protect our humans."

Vyll put one hand over his mouth. "Do you think something really bad is about to happen? Will my human's life be at risk?"

"Relax," said Xalon. "I doubt it's anything we Protectors can't fix by working together with our humans. That's why we Protectors and humans are allies, after all, because by working together as one, we are stronger and smarter than we would be by working apart."

Although Xalon spoke encouraging, upbeat words, Vyll noticed that Xalon didn't sound quite like he believed them. His yellow optics kept glancing away at the Protectors around them, which made Vyll wonder if Xalon actually knew what the Rock was gathering them for and if he would explain it to Vyll.

No, he probably won't, Vyll thought. *Kara's Father rarely explains things to Kara when she doesn't understand. He always says that she doesn't need to worry about it or that she'll understand when she's older. Xalon will probably do the same, just like most adults.*

So Vyll decided to change the subject. He said to Xalon, "Who is your human?"

"A skyras gatherer who sells skyras in Capital City," said Xalon. "Been with him ever since he was young. We don't make a lot of money, but we have a fun time anyway and generally get by all right. Who's your human?"

"A young girl who lives in the countryside with her parents," said Vyll. He opened the compartment in his chest and pulled out the folded-up picture that Kara had given him three years ago, which he then unfolded carefully. "Look. She gave me this three years ago, for my ninth birthday. It was the first gift that anyone gave to me."

Xalon took the unfolded drawing and looked at it as carefully as Vyll had unfolded it, which pleased Vyll greatly. "That's really nice of her. My human doesn't usually give me gifts, but sometimes he'll give me a cut of the profits of his business. Not that I really need the money; I don't even know what to do with it half the time, because I can't use it to protect him better. I just use it to buy him food and clothes, mostly, whenever he needs some."

Xalon handed the drawing back to Vyll, who quickly folded it up again and slipped it back into his chest compartment where it would be safe. He smiled when he felt the folded-up drawing land in his chest, because having that drawing there made him feel like Kara was right next to him, even though he knew that she was miles away at the moment.

"Your human must really like you if she went to all of that trouble to draw that picture for you," said Xalon. He smiled wistfully. "Sometimes, I wish my human would give me a gift

17

like that. But I guess it's not a big deal; he treats me well and I protect him. That's all that I ask."

Again, despite Xalon's tone, Vyll was certain Xalon was not as happy as he appeared. The adult Protector did not meet Vyll's optics and Vyll thought he heard a hint of jealousy in the older robot's voice. Of course, Vyll might have been imagining things —he had been told more than once by Kara that he had a pretty active imagination—but somehow he didn't think that he was imagining anything right now.

In any case, Vyll and Xalon talked about a variety of subjects on their way down to the Rock. Mostly, they talked about their humans, which was nice because Vyll had always wondered how different adult humans were from young humans and what kind of responsibilities that being the Protector of an adult human entailed versus being the Protector of a young human.

In fact, Vyll became so engrossed in their conversations that he almost didn't notice the massive archway coming up until Xalon pointed ahead and said, "Looks like the archway is coming up."

Curious, Vyll looked in the direction that Xalon was pointing. Unfortunately, he was too short to see over the heads of the taller Protectors, so he couldn't see what Xalon was pointing at. "Xalon, I can't see the archway. I'm too short."

"Let me help you up for a moment, then," said Xalon.

He bent over and grabbed Vyll around his waist. He then lifted up Vyll with no problem, raising him above the heads of the other Protectors (who paid no attention to this, because their attention was fixated solely on what Xalon had seen ahead).

Not far down the tunnel was a wide and absolutely massive

metallic archway that was the biggest archway that Vyll had ever seen in his life. It was wide enough for the entire crowd of Protectors to walk under with plenty of room for at least a thousand more Protectors. Although the archway had no doors or gates, Vyll did notice a thin, transparent red barrier covering the archway, which he figured that all of them would have to go through if they were going to reach the Gathering spot.

Xalon lowered Vyll to the ground and let go of the smaller robot, allowing Vyll to continue walking alongside him. "Well, youngling? What do you think?"

"It's huge," said Vyll, spreading his short arms as widely as he could to emphasize the width of the archway. "What is it?"

"The Arch of Truth," said Xalon. "It's how the Rock determines who we are. When you pass through the Arch of Truth, the skyras energy running through it scans your body and mind to make sure that you are not a deceiver trying to get inside for bad reasons."

Vyll looked up at Xalon again. "Why would anyone try to fool the Rock?"

"Sadly, not everyone on Fariah likes the Rock," said Xalon, shaking his head. "Some people want to control its power. The Rock doesn't serve anyone, however, and doesn't *want* to serve anyone, either. That's why the Arch of Truth exists; otherwise, anyone would be able to come down there and use the Rock's power for their own selfish ends."

"Oh," said Vyll. He looked back in the direction of the Arch; now that they were closer, he could see the top of the arch connected to the ceiling, though it was still too high to see in any great detail. "What happens to deceivers who attempt to pass under the Arch?"

Xalon shuddered. "You don't want to know. Let's just leave it at that."

Actually, Vyll *did* want to know, but he could tell that Xalon was not going to answer his questions about it. He decided that he would learn later; maybe he would ask another adult Protector who would be willing to tell him.

Soon, the whole crowd of Protectors passed under the Arch. Vyll kept walking, even though the Arch of Truth now terrified him. He knew it wouldn't harm him, because he had no intention whatsoever of harming the Rock, but he still found the idea of passing under the Arch disturbing.

When he passed through the thin, transparent red wall he had seen before, he felt … *something* scan his whole body. It felt like the scrutinizing eye of Kara's Father, who always had a way of appearing to read your mind when you were in trouble. Yet this something—maybe the Rock—felt far more alien than Kara's Father, although familiar at the same time, too, like Vyll had felt this presence before but had forgotten about it a long time ago.

In any case, Vyll was thankful when he passed through it and did not suffer any negative consequences. In fact, none of the Protectors with him were harmed or punished in any way, which told Vyll that these Protectors had no ill intentions for the Rock. That made him feel safer, although he continued to stick close to Xalon because he still didn't trust or know any of the others very well.

One hour later, the crowd of Protectors emerged out onto a massive balcony, with a rock railing on the other end, that jutted out over what was probably a large, deep hole. Vyll could not see much of it, however, because his height prevented him from seeing over the heads of the other, much taller adult Protectors, who were now looking at something ahead, but what it was, he didn't know. There was a large, dull green light glowing from the front of the group, but Vyll could not see what the source of the light was.

"Hey, youngling," said Xalon, causing Vyll to look up at him. "Want to see the Rock itself?"

Vyll nodded eagerly. "Is that what everyone is looking at?"

"Yep," said Xalon. "We're here. Let me put you on my shoulders so you can get a better look at this place."

In one smooth motion, Xalon lifted up Vyll and placed him on his shoulders. Xalon then gripped Vyll's short legs with his big hands, which made Vyll feel safe and secure on Xalon's shoulders. Still, he grabbed the back of Xalon's head for extra safety and looked around the large cavern they had entered.

His attention was first drawn to the size of the cavern. It was enormous; in fact, 'enormous' was an understatement. It was so huge, so wide-open, that Vyll felt less like he was underground and more like he was standing out in the open with the sky above him. It was even larger than the Coliseum in Capital City, which surprised him, because he thought the Coliseum was the largest building in all of Fariah. He figured you could fit ten Coliseums in here, with room for an extra Coliseum or two to spare.

Along the walls, Vyll spotted hundreds—no, thousands—of similar mega balconies like the one he and the others stood on. In fact, there were so many balconies full of so many Protectors that he could not count even half of them. The balconies in the distance looked like waves of metallic gray, with red, blue, yellow, green, and other colored dots disrupting the thick grayness of the other Protectors.

But what truly captured his attention was the titanic rock in the center of the cavern. It was absolutely gigantic and shaped like a square; in fact, it was so huge that Vyll couldn't even see half of its immense surface. It glowed a soft, friendly, strangely familiar green, the same light Vyll had noticed before, yet Vyll sensed within it an intelligence that was not to be questioned or treated with familiarity.

"Wow," said Vyll. He was surprised he could speak, because he was certain that he had lost his voice upon seeing the massive rock in the center. "What is *that*?"

"The Rock in the flesh," said Xalon. He chuckled. "Well, actually, it's in the stone, but you know what I mean. It's also known as the Core of the World, the Foundation Upon Which Our World Rests, and a bunch of other names as well, but you can just call it the Rock."

"It is so ... pretty," said Vyll, unable to take his eyes off its glowing, massive surface. "Where did it come from?"

"The Rock has always been and always will be," said Xalon. "You know how the humans worship their Gods? Well, think of the Rock as *our* god, although in my opinion, the Rock is way better than their Gods, if only because we know it exists."

"God ..." Vyll repeated. "Do we worship it?"

"Not in the way humans worship *their* Gods," said Xalon. "We worship it by protecting our humans. That's all it asks of us."

"Amazing," said Vyll. Then he looked around at the massive balconies built into the walls of the cavern again. "And are these other Protectors?"

"Yep," said Xalon. "All eight billion or so should be present. You can't see them all—quite a few are on the other side of the Rock and some are underneath us, while others are above us—but they're there. They have to be, because the Rock wills it."

Vyll had always known that the human population of Fariah was about eight billion, but until today, he had not comprehended what that number might look like in real life. Yet even that did not compare to the majesty and mystery of the Rock itself, which he thought was the most beautiful thing he had ever seen in his life.

Next to Kara, that is, Vyll thought. *I will still have to tell her about the Rock, though, when I go home. She will definitely want to hear about it.*

"Can the Rock talk?" asked Vyll, looking down at Xalon when he said that.

"Yep," said Xalon.

"But how?" said Vyll, glancing up at the Rock again. "It doesn't seem to have a mouth anywhere."

"It just can," said Xalon. "Like I said, the Rock has always been and always will be. It can do almost anything. If it wants to talk without a mouth, it can talk without a mouth; although, in truth, it actually speaks to us in our minds. But it can speak aloud, too; it just doesn't usually need to do so because it is connected to all of us."

"Is it going to speak to us?" said Vyll.

"Probably," said Xalon. He gestured at the Protectors standing around them. "That's why it gathered us all here. It has something important to tell us, something so important that everyone has to be here. It will probably start to speak as soon as everyone arrives and settles in."

Vyll nodded and looked at the Rock again. He couldn't even imagine something so huge, so ancient, so intelligent. It looked big enough to crush the entirety of Capital City underneath it, maybe even big enough to reach the twin moons in the sky if it was taken out of its cavern and placed on the surface.

And I came from it, Vyll thought with awe. *It created me, like it created every other Protector here. I wish Kara was here with me so she could also see it. There is no way I will be able to describe it to her in a way that makes it sound as awesome as it looks.*

But then Vyll noticed something off about the Rock. His optics zoomed in closer to the Rock's surface and noticed what appeared to be minute cracks running along it. They were barely noticeable, even when he zoomed in one hundred percent, but they were there. He wondered where they came from.

Returning his vision to normal, Vyll said, "Xalon, why are there cracks on the Rock's surface?"

"Cracks?" Xalon repeated. "What cracks? The Rock's surface is supposed to be smooth and uninterrupted. The Rock is made of the hardest substance in the world anyway; how could anyone or anything ever hope to crack it?"

"But I see cracks on it," said Vyll, pointing at the Rock. "If you don't believe me, look for yourself. You'll need to zoom in your vision to see them, but they are there."

Xalon clearly did not believe Vyll's claims; nonetheless, he leaned forward slightly, fixating his optics on the Rock. Vyll clung to Xalon's head tighter than ever to avoid falling off, but that precaution was unnecessary, because Xalon then returned to

24

his original height.

"You're right," said Xalon, his voice full of disbelief. "Those are cracks, all right. Almost invisible, but they are there."

Xalon didn't say that very loudly. He spoke in a whisper, so low that Vyll had to raise the volume of his audio receptors in order to hear him. The other Protectors did not seem to hear him at all, which made Vyll wonder if Xalon was intentionally whispering so that none of the other Protectors would hear his words.

"What does that mean, Xalon?" Vyll asked, keeping his voice to a whisper as well.

"Not sure, youngling," said Xalon. "Not sure. But I doubt it means anything good for the Rock. Or for us."

Vyll wanted to ask Xalon more questions, but before he could, an irresistible force drew his attention to the Rock. He didn't even really think about questioning the force; it was just like Kara's Father telling her to come and listen to him when she was playing.

Although Vyll was not looking at the other Protectors, he knew that they, too, had ceased speaking among each other and were now focused entirely on the Rock. In fact, he sensed that every single Protector in this massive chamber—from the youngest child to the oldest adult—were now staring at the Rock, awaiting to hear it speak. How he sensed that, he wasn't sure, but he suspected it was because of the Rock connecting them all together, so that he could sense the collective movements of his fellow Protectors all at once.

And then, the Rock did speak. It spoke in a deep and ancient, yet quite clear, voice. It was completely unlike any voice Vyll had heard in his life. Even in his youthfulness, he could sense an authority and power behind that voice that was not to be treated lightly. It made the voice of the Grand Chancellor of Capital City —always so booming and commanding—sound like the voice of a small, arrogant child.

My children, said the Rock. The whole cavern seemed to shudder when he spoke. *I am glad to see that all of you made it. I remember each and every one of you, even though it has been some time since I last spoke with all of you like this.*

Though the Rock's voice was commanding and without doubt, Vyll noticed a definite hint of weakness behind it. It reminded him of Master Hoyan. The old swordsman, due to having been a high-ranking general in the Capital City Army in his younger years, always spoke like he was still commanding an army, yet was never able to completely hide the hints of old age and sickness that had ravaged his body over the years.

That made Vyll wonder if the Rock was sick and trying to hide it. He dismissed the thought as silly, because there was no way that the Rock, easily the strongest entity Vyll had ever seen in his life, could ever get sick.

But this is no time for happy reunions or reminiscences, said the Rock. *This Gathering will not be a time of celebration, but perhaps our next one will be, if all goes well. Although I will admit that even I am uncertain of what the future holds in store for this world and for myself.*

Vyll didn't understand the Rock's words, and based on Xalon's puzzled expression, neither did he. In fact, when Vyll looked around at the other Protectors in his vicinity, he saw that none of them seemed to understand what the Rock meant. That all of these older and wiser Protectors were as clueless as he was about the Rock's meaning made him feel very afraid indeed.

You are all wondering why I summoned you here today, said the Rock. *For many of you, this is your first Gathering, and I wish it had not even been that. But what I have summoned you all here for is exactly why I created the concept of the Gathering eons ago—when I created the first Protectors to protect the first humans.*

Vyll was again starting to wish that Kara was here with him. He found the Rock's words strange and opaque, hardly comforting. He wondered if the Rock often spoke like this or if some recent turn of events had forced him to speak like this. Based on how puzzled and disturbed the older Protectors seemed, Vyll decided that the Rock normally did not speak so frighteningly.

I do not know how to say this without creating fear and panic in all of you, said the Rock. *But I have always believed in speaking to my children as frankly as I can, so I will not beat around the bush: I am dying, and with me, Fariah.*

Pure terror—stronger than any fear Vyll had ever felt in his life—began to rise within him like lava within a volcano. His limbs became heavy, his joints felt stiff, and his optics's vision became blurrier. He almost fell off Xalon's shoulders, but Xalon redoubled his grip on Vyll's legs. Even so, Vyll barely noticed, so focused was he on what the Rock had just said.

But he did notice all of the billions and billions of Protectors around them, talking among themselves loudly and confusedly. He couldn't hear the words of any individual Protectors in the racket that had erupted after the Rock's words, but he didn't need

27

to, because he already knew what everyone was talking about.

Please calm down, my children, said the Rock. *I understand your distress and fear. It is something I underwent myself when I first understood that my death is near. The quakes that have been shaking the world above have been due to my own fear of death, though I have since reined in that fear and have thus made the quakes less frequent than they were for a while there.*

The other Protectors stopped talking, and Vyll did feel a little less afraid, but only a little. Deep down, the dread that overwhelmed his heart was as terrible as the constricting tentacles of some mysterious sea monster. He wanted to escape it, but even he, in his immaturity, knew that there was nowhere he could run to escape from this fear.

As for why I am dying, I am not certain, said the Rock. *My great wisdom, accumulated over the countless years of my existence, has failed to show me why I die. All I know is that, as the years go on, these cracks will become thicker and thicker, until I shatter completely into a million pieces.*

"Shatter?" Vyll whispered to Xalon, but Xalon didn't even seem to hear Vyll, because he was looking at the Rock with his mouth hanging open. "What does that mean?"

I do not know what will happen to me after I die, said the Rock. *But I do know this: The resulting destruction will kill billions of innocent lives all over Fariah. Humans, dwarves, elves, Jikorians, the wild beasts of the air and the fish of the sea ... all of it will die. The planet itself may be completely destroyed; although I again do not know for sure.*

Panic. That was the word Vyll was looking for. That was what he felt in the air of the chamber. Panic was in the hearts and minds of every Protector in the area. This sense of dread was so powerful that Vyll just wanted to leave and go home and forget everything that the Rock had just said.

But even worse were the Rock's words, that billions of innocent lives would die along with him. And he said human lives, too, and Kara was a human as well, which meant that Kara would—

How many years I have left, I do not know, said the Rock. *I believe that I have at least a decade of life left, but it might be even less. All I know is that there is no way to save me, no way to prevent death from taking me. Believe me, I have searched and searched for a cure of some sort, but to no avail.*

Vyll held up his wrist to his mouth, hoping to contact Kara through his built-in communicator, but unfortunately, the signal was blocked. He supposed that the Rock was preventing them from contacting the outside world, but that hardly comforted him, because all he wanted to do was talk to Kara and find out if she was okay. He needed her voice to calm him, even though he knew that there was nothing she could do to help the Rock or anyone else in this situation.

This may very well be the end of Fariah as we know it, said the Rock. *But, despite this grave situation, not all is lost. I believe there is a way that you, my children, can survive, even after I die.*

The panic in the chamber subsided for a moment, making Vyll feel a little better. He still wanted to call Kara and hear her voice, but not as much anymore. Instead, he popped open his chest compartment and felt the drawing within. The sensation of the paper against his fingers calmed him down immeasurably, making it easier to listen to the Rock's plan, whatever it was.

But in order to survive, you will need to change, said the Rock. *For eons, I have allowed you, my children, to live alongside humans in peace. It was an arrangement that I made with the humans' Gods so long ago that even I cannot remember how many ages have passed since that day; but I believe that in order to ensure the survival of every individual Protector here, we must end the partnership prematurely.*

Vyll looked down at Xalon and whispered, "What is the Rock talking about? What does he mean by 'ending the partnership prematurely'? Does that mean I won't get to see my human anymore?"

"Shh, youngling," said Xalon, his eyes still fixed on the Rock. "The Rock is still speaking."

I know how close you Protectors are to your humans, but if this partnership continues, it will only result in the end of both species, said the Rock. *The humans will not be able to survive the coming cataclysm that will result due to my death; however, you Protectors might, due to your more resilient physical forms. Even if only a minority of you survive the cataclysm, at least then you will be able to go on and rebuild Fariah and whatever else survives my death.*

Vyll didn't like what he was hearing at all. He held Kara's drawing tighter than before, but without ripping it. He wished this was all some horrible nightmare, that none of it was true, but there was no getting around the fact that all of this was happening and that every word that the Rock spoke was the absolute, awful truth.

Yet we cannot do this right away, said the Rock. *To forcibly sever your connection with the humans immediately would be disastrous. No; I will slowly aid you in separating from the humans, setting up your own societies, forming your own cultures and creating your own laws. It will have to be subtle yet quick, because with only a decade of life left in me, I cannot afford to take as long to do this as I would have liked.*

Vyll did not even know what the Rock meant by that. He didn't understand why they needed their own societies and cultures and laws separate from the humans'. He liked human society and human culture and human laws; why did they need to abandon it? Why did they need to abandon the humans at all? Why did he need to abandon Kara?

You must not tell any *human of this, or any of the other intelligent species on Fariah,* said the Rock, in a much sterner voice than before. *Tell not even your own human about our plans. If humans became aware of our plans, they would demand that we help them, which we cannot. Or worse, they will turn against us and begin slaughtering us like lambs. It is not something I wish for any of my children to undergo.*

Humans? Slaughter them? Vyll wasn't sure he believed that. Why would humans slaughter him and the other Protectors? Sure, there were a few bad humans who didn't like Protectors, but the vast majority of humans loved them, didn't they? There were even laws in certain human countries that made killing a Protector as bad as killing a human. That's what Kara had told Vyll once, and he believed Kara because she always told him the truth.

When you return to your humans, you must tell them that the Gathering was only to discuss with all of you how to best protect and serve your humans, the Rock continued. *Do not let them even suspect that this Gathering was for anything else. As your father and creator, I demand it.*

Vyll did not sense any dissent or disagreement among the other Protectors; in fact, he did not sense even any discomfort about the Rock's commands. Hiding secrets from their humans was considered a difficult thing by most Protectors, even looked down upon in certain circles. Yet Vyll knew beyond with certainty that none of the Protectors present would have any issue with keeping the true purpose of this Gathering a secret from their humans.

Even worse, Vyll knew he would not tell Kara the truth, either. He would lie to her face if he had to, because he understood that the Rock was ultimately superior than Kara in the hierarchy of life.

The rate at which new Protectors are born in the next decade will slow so gradually that humans will not notice until it is too late, said the Rock. *But I will impart the secrets to creating more new Protectors to a select few here, who I will make the leaders of the new society that will exist after I pass. This way, you will be able to keep the Protector legacy going even long after I have passed.*

Vyll didn't want to listen to anything more that the Rock said. He just wanted to go back home, back to Kara's house, and play with her again. He didn't want to be here, in this big, dark scary cave listening to these terrifying words that held no comfort in them.

But he didn't run. He just grabbed the back of Xalon's head even tighter as he listened further to the Rock's words.

Over the coming months and years, I will subtly aid all of you in separating from humanity, said the Rock. *I will give you more details about the exact process you will undergo to fully separate from your humans; but for now, this Gathering is over. Each one of you may return to your homes now, but remember: Tell* no one *about the true purposes of this meeting, no matter what.*

Every head that Vyll could see was nodding in affirmation, including Xalon and Vyll himself. Vyll couldn't control the movement of his head; it was like instinct, and he wasn't even aware he was doing it until he noticed everyone else doing it.

Then, all around him, the other Protectors turned and began to leave back the way they had came. Xalon lifted Vyll off his shoulders and gently placed him on the ground before grabbing Vyll's hand and pulling him along behind him.

"Come on, youngling," said Xalon, in a much more subdued voice than before. "We have to leave now. The Rock said so, so we mustn't stay around longer than he wants us to."

Vyll looked over his shoulder at the Rock. He knew that Xalon was right, but he was so worried sick about Kara that he didn't want to leave just yet.

He wrenched his hand out of Xalon's and—ignoring Xalon's shouting to come back—ran up to the stone railing of the balcony. Vyll reached out with one hand toward the Rock, but his arm was so short that he couldn't even scrape the Rock's surface with the tip of his longest finger.

"Rock!" said Vyll, waving his arm as hard as he could in order to catch the Rock's attention. "Rock! Please listen to me! I have a question only you can answer!"

"Youngling!" said Xalon behind him. "What are you doing? Come along now. The Rock is finished speaking. He does not want to be bothered by a youngling such as yourself."

Xalon grabbed Vyll's other arm and began pulling him again, but Vyll wrapped his free arm around the stone railing and continued to shout, "Rock! Please listen to me! I'm sorry if I'm bothering you, but I need an answer and I need it right away."

The Rock was as silent as a corpse as it glowed as brightly as ever. Although it seemed to Vyll that maybe its glow was dimming, which made sense if it was dying.

And then, quite without warning, Vyll heard the Rock in his head saying, *What question do you wish to ask of me, youngling?*

Xalon must have heard the Rock's voice, too, because he immediately stopped trying to pull Vyll away from the railing. Vyll glanced over his shoulder and saw Xalon standing there with his mouth hanging open, looking as shocked as if he had been electrocuted.

Then Vyll looked back at the Rock and asked, "What will happen to my human, Kara? Can she come and live with us, even if the other humans can't? Can she?"

Again, the Rock was silent; this time, it was so silent that Vyll was certain that he had asked a stupid question that the Rock was not going to answer at all.

But then the Rock said, *If she is human, then she will die.*

"What about her brother, Carem?" said Vyll. He barely finished that sentence without allowing his emotions to overcome him. "Will he—"

If he is human, then he will die.

"And their par—"

If they are human, then they will die, said the Rock. There was no kindness or understanding in its voice. *As I said,* all *humans will die. They will not be able to survive my death. You must forget those humans you just mentioned and be prepared to abandon them at a moment's notice.*

"But I …" Vyll fought back the despair creeping into his voice. "But Kara is *my* human. I—"

I have already answered your question, youngling, and with a definitive answer that will not change no matter how much you badger me with your words, said the Rock in irritation. *Xalon, take the youngling away. He will understand when he is older.*

"All right, youngling," said Xalon, who seemed to have gotten over his shock by now. "You gotta come with me. I'll even take you back to your humans, if you'd like."

"No!" Vyll shouted, shaking his head and clinging to the railing even tighter than before. "I want to convince the Rock to spare them. I want him to spare my humans; to spare Kara."

"Youngling, you can't convince the Rock to do anything," said Xalon. "I know it is hard, I know it is difficult, but what the Rock says, goes. He is our father and creator; we cannot go against his wishes or convince him to do something else when he has set his mind to do something. We can only obey him to the best of our abilities"

Xalon is correct, youngling, said the Rock. *But I can tell that you are a stubborn one who will not leave even if I tell you to. Therefore, I will cast you into a deep sleep, so that Xalon may take you out of here without trouble.*

"I don't *want* to sleep," Vyll said. "I want to stay awake. I want to be with Kara. I want to be with my humans … forever …"

Even as he spoke those words, a strong tiredness came over him unlike anything he had ever felt before. His systems were shutting off, his vision was blurring, and he was starting to lose strength in his limbs. He let go of the railings and fell to the floor of the balcony, unable to even lift his head on his own.

Sleep, youngling, said the Rock. *And when you wake up, you will understand why this must be done.*

Vyll wanted to argue that point, but then he fell into unconsciousness and neither spoke nor thought anything else.

Chapter III

Five years later ...

Kara walked along the streets of Capital City, brushing away the stray strands of her hair that the nice cool breeze had blown into her eyes. The twin suns were shining in the sky above, but it wasn't a terribly hot day despite that. She wore her favorite blue summer dress—a gift from Father when she left home to study in the city—and smiled at the colorful birds chirping and singing in one of the tall heart trees planted along the street.

All around Kara, humans, Protectors, dwarves, elves, and other species bustled about. She saw a couple of handsome, sharply dressed young men who might have been going to an important business meeting, based on the way the two spoke to each other as they walked while comparing holographic plans that projected from their hands; walked past an elfish street performer singing a beautiful song in a language she didn't really recognize but which she loved the tune of anyway (so much so that she dropped five Farian notes into the collection bowl at his feet, which prompted a nod of thanks from him); saw a Jikorian lady with her two young children apologizing profusely to an elderly, angry-looking dwarfish man, apparently for one of her kids who had accidentally splattered the dignified dwarf's pants with snow cream; and even saw the Grand Chancellor himself zoom by in his personal travel hover car, although he drove by too fast for her to see him very well.

Not only that, but the buildings all around Kara looked particularly beautiful today. Their glass windows seemed to be made out of the finest crystal, reflecting the warm rays of the sun. The royal purple color of many of the buildings contrasted in a beautiful way with the clear blue sky above, while the green vines that grew along their surfaces were arranged in wonderfully strange patterns today that Kara just couldn't describe easily.

Perhaps Kara noticed how nice today was because of how stressful things had been over the past five years. The ground, for example, was stable today and, according to the weathermen, was in no danger of shaking at all for the rest of the week. It was like those sudden quakes that had been shaking the whole planet in recent years had decided to take the day off due to the beautiful weather, although Kara knew that was a rather silly thing to think.

Guess I'm a rather silly girl, Kara thought with a chuckle.

She stopped when she noticed one of the gigantic telescreens on the buildings. It showed a news report of what appeared to be a riot of some sort breaking out in Nohans, one of the northern cities, but Kara turned her face away from it and kept walking down the street, trying instead to focus on the pleasant, rose-like scent coming from the heart trees planted along the avenue.

Today, Kara didn't want to think about negativity or about any of the bad news reports that seemed to come in every day. She was a young lady of seventeen now, with a bright future as a student of magitek at Unity University—the best university in all of Fariah—ahead of her.

Of course, graduation was four years off, but Kara had some good short term things to look forward to as well.

Such as lunch with Vyll and Carem, Kara thought with a smile. *This is the first time we've all been able to get together like this since I started going to Unity. I wish that Father and Mother could be here with us as well, but Father is always too sick to leave the house nowadays and Mother is always looking after him. I wonder if I will ever become as good a wife to my future husband, whoever he is, as Mother is to Father.*

According to the message Kara had received from Vyll, the three of them were supposed to meet at the Protector Cafe on North Sixth Street. Kara had only lived in Capital City for a few months now, but she had never been to this particular Cafe, which Vyll claimed was the only Protector-run cafe in the entire city. He said that their customer service was the best and that they made the best coffee and smoked soup.

Kara didn't doubt for a second that Protector Cafe was the best. Not because she had been there before, but because she trusted Vyll's opinion more than the opinion of anyone else. If he said that something was the best ever, then Kara always agreed with him.

Carem probably doesn't, Kara thought with a chuckle. *He's always so opposite and contrary. That's what makes him so great.*

Thinking about her older brother did make her smile falter a little. While she loved Carem as much as any sister loved her brother, she had to admit that she wasn't entirely supportive of some of his recent career choices. He had just returned from a six-month trip around the world in which he hunted down criminals as a bounty hunter. She didn't like him doing that because it was so dangerous, but Carem was good with a sword, thanks to his training with the late Master Hoyan, and he had come back alive, after all, so maybe she was worrying about nothing. Still, she knew that most bounty hunter careers—and their lives—were short-lived for obvious reasons, so she felt justified in worrying about Carem's career choices, even if he didn't.

In any case, soon Kara found herself on North Sixth Street. She then spotted the Protector Cafe, which was easy to see, because a large Protector that she didn't recognize stood in front of the outdoor cafe, projecting a large, glowing sign from his hand that read *PROTECTOR CAFE* in large, easy-to-read letters.

That was when she spotted two familiar people sitting at one of the tables at the outdoor cafe. One of them was Carem; there was no mistaking his rugged face with stubble anywhere, nor the long, rough-looking sword leaning against his seat. He wore a dark traveling cloak that looked like it hadn't been washed in months, which was probably true, considering how Carem usually didn't take very good care of himself.

Carem also seemed to have some trouble moving. Whenever he raised his cup of coffee to his lips, he had to do it carefully, which made Kara wonder if Carem had sustained some kind of injury during his trip around the world, and if so, how serious it was. She hoped it was only minor, but something told her it wasn't.

Sitting on the right side of the table was Vyll. He was much taller now; in fact, he was almost taller than Carem. In contrast to Carem's unkempt appearance, Vyll's metallic skin practically shone in the sun and he appeared to move without any issue. Of course, Vyll had taken after her, which explained why he took care of himself so well; still, Kara was pleased to see that only one of the two boys looked homeless today.

Waving at Carem and Vyll, Kara called out, "Hey, you guys!"

Carem and Vyll both looked in her direction. A large smile broke over Carem's lips and he waved back at her just as hard as she waved at him, while Vyll only waved for a moment before resting his hand back onto the table.

Kara had come to expect that subdued response from Vyll, although she didn't really like it. Ever since he had come back from that last Gathering of the Protectors five years ago, Vyll had not been as friendly or playful towards her as he used to be. He had assured her multiple times that he still thought of her as a friend and of course still loved her, but he had never been very good at faking his emotions. She knew him well enough to know when he had changed, and he had definitely changed since then, though why that was, she did not know.

Maybe I will get to find out today, Kara thought. Then she shook her head. *No. I shouldn't bring up such a subject right now. I want to make this lunch as positive as possible, so I'll focus on the positive things we've all got going on in our lives.*

As Kara approached the outdoor cafe, the Protector she had noticed projecting the holographic sign earlier glanced at her. It was a brief glance—so brief that she almost missed it—but there was no mistaking it for what it was: A glare.

It was something that Kara had been noticing over the last five years. Aside from Vyll, most Protectors seemed to treat her with disdain or distrust. And it wasn't just her, either; Kara had heard from her friends that most of the Protectors treated them far less

41

kindly than they usually did. Mother, for example, had even been outright insulted by a Protector who had come to Kara's parents' house to perform some minor repairs on the roof two years ago. The Protector had been forced to apologize by the company he worked for, but that insult had been so rude and unexpected that Mother still talked about it sometime even years later.

Even worse was what she heard on the news almost every day. It seemed like every time Kara watched the news, there was a report of a Protector assaulting yet another human. There were even reports of criminal gangs composed entirely of Protectors assaulting random civilians—always humans, though sometimes elves and dwarves suffered attacks as well—at night, often when the civilians were alone and unarmed.

It was at least partially why Kara now carried a skyras blaster under her clothes. She had not yet been assaulted by any Protectors or Protector criminal gangs, but that did not mean that it could not happen to her at some point. Better to be safe than sorry, in her opinion, even though she utterly detested violence of all sorts.

But Kara pushed that out of her mind. Today, she was going to enjoy this lunch with her brother and her Protector, her Protector who would never harm her. She always tried to look on the bright side of life, no matter how grim everything else was.

Besides, look at how sunny and bright everything is, Kara thought, glancing up at the beautiful blue sky again. *What are the chances of some random criminals assaulting me in broad daylight? Close to zero, I imagine. Therefore, I have nothing to worry about.*

Thus, when Kara sat down at the table at which Carem and

Vyll were sitting, she had already put those depressing and scary thoughts out of her mind. Maybe she would think about them later; or better yet, never think about them at all.

"Good to see you again, Kara," said Vyll, nodding at her. "How have you adapted to city life?"

Kara smiled and shrugged. "I'm doing all right. It's pretty crazy and different from the country, but I think I'll survive."

Of course, Vyll already knew how Kara was doing. While the two of them didn't hang out all day together like they did in their younger years, Vyll was still her Protector and so wrote to her regularly. Kara didn't find this behavior unusual; Father had told her that it was common for a human and her Protector to grow somewhat distant and more independent from each other as they aged.

But that still doesn't really explain why he's been acting so distant towards me ever since the Gathering, Kara thought. But then she scolded herself. *Stop thinking those negative thoughts. Enjoy this time with your brother and your Protector. Worry about Vyll's behavior later, if you must.*

Carem—who had been taking a drink from his emerald cup— slammed the cup down on the table and said, "You think Capital City is crazy? You should go to Gigas. Thirty-one million people of every race, species, color, religion, and gender you can think of. Buildings packed together like dirt. Capital City is like a rural backwater in comparison to Gigas. There's a reason it's called the Behemoth of Fariah, you know."

"You went to Gigas on your travels?" said Kara. "Wow. How did you survive?"

"Luck, mostly," said Carem with a shrug. "That, and most

43

Timothy L. Cerepaka

people there are so busy and in a hurry all the time that they really don't pay much attention to a country bumpkin like me. Anyway, tracking down the criminal I was looking for there was like searching for a needle in a haystack; that city is practically crawling with criminals, and am pretty sure is run by a few as well."

He shuddered at the thought, which impressed Kara, because Carem had always been extremely tough. If even he found Gigas a difficult place to survive, then Kara would have to avoid traveling there for a while.

"And after this, I am heading out to the Eastern Frontier," Carem continued, gesturing in a generally easterly direction. "Gonna travel with another group of bounty hunters heading the same way. It's dangerous out that way, so we figure that we'll all be a lot safer if we stick together until we get there."

"Who are you looking for?" asked Kara. She tried to ignore the smell of dirt and sweat coming off of Carem's body.

Carem pulled out a rolled up piece of paper and unfurled it. He then placed it on the table face up and, stabbing a finger at the face depicted on it, said, "This guy."

Kara and Vyll leaned forward to get a better look at the face on the wanted poster. It showed a rather scary-looking Protector with soul-less black eyes and thick, sharp teeth. Underneath the portrait was the name 'RYFA THE CRUSHER,' along with his bounty, which was so high that Kara thought that it must be a misprint of some sort.

"Who is Ryfa the Crusher?" said Kara, looking up at Carem with a puzzled expression. "I've never heard of him."

"A Protector gone wild," said Carem. "Wanted for the murder

44

of a dozen humans, and that's just in the last year. Some say that he even eats the humans he kills, which doesn't make a lick of sense to me, since Protectors don't eat anything, much less humans, but that's the rumor and I've seen some evidence that supports it."

"That's awful," said Kara. "How do you plan to stop him?"

Carem shrugged. "No idea at this point. All I know is that sixty thousand notes is a lot of money and would be more than enough to help fund the rest of my travels around the world until next year. He was last seen at the Eastern Frontier, which is why I am heading there to catch him."

Kara shuddered and hugged her body, even though it was quite warm out today. "I don't know if you should, Carem. If this Ryfa the Crusher kills and even eats humans, then I think you should leave his arrest to the law enforcement or to the more experienced bounty hunters at least."

Carem rolled his eyes. "Come on, Kara. You know I'm tougher and smarter than any stupid Protector."

"Carem!" Kara said. She glared at him and gestured at Vyll. "Stupid Protector, really?"

Carem held up his hands defensively. "Don't be so sensitive. I wasn't calling *Vyll* stupid. Vyll's great. Vyll's really smart. I was just referring to Ryfa, who I have heard isn't all that smart, despite evading law enforcement and bounty hunters alike for years. You understand, right, Vyll?"

He said that while looking at Vyll. Vyll had not even acted offended about what Carem said, but Kara was worried that he was anyway. She didn't like anyone offending or insulting Vyll, even if that person was her one and only brother. Especially since

45

Vyll had become so introverted over the last five years; she was worried that even unintentional insults might end up isolating him from them even more than he currently was.

But Vyll simply shrugged and said, "I see nothing to be offended by. Ryfa does indeed look like quite the idiot. But thank you for your concern, Kara. I appreciate it."

Kara saw through Vyll's lie right away. Again, he was never that good at keeping his true feelings or thoughts hidden for very long, at least from her. She heard the reluctance in his voice, saw the way he did not meet either of their eyes, and paid attention to the way he rubbed his hands together, making a tiny, squeaking metal sound between them as he did so.

Carem, on the other hand, didn't seem to notice, because he leaned back in his chair and said, "See, Kara? Vyll knows he's not like the other Protectors, so of course he doesn't feel offended when I say things like that. Besides, he's known me at least as long as he's known you, so he knows I don't mean any ill will by my jokes."

Kara pursed her lips. While Carem did not in any way hate the Protectors, his opinion of them had grown more and more antagonistic over the years, or so it seemed to Kara. He made quips like that, claiming that Vyll was 'smarter' than the other Protectors, how he didn't trust the Protectors much anymore, and so on.

Part of this Kara understood as due to the fact that Carem never had his own Protector growing up. 'Protector-less,' as people like him were usually called, rarely understood the deep connection and bonds that formed between humans and their Protectors. Even though Carem had grown up with Kara and Vyll and in some ways treated Vyll like the younger brother he never had, she had always known that he never truly understood her connection with Vyll.

Though she also worried that his insensitivity was part of this broader movement that had been growing among humans ever since the Gathering five years ago. Due to the sudden increase in violence and crime from the Protectors, quite a few humans—including several members of the Capital City Council—were starting to say that humans did not need Protectors at all and in fact that the Protectors were causing more harm than good. The benevolent of them simply suggested that all Protectors be rounded up and shipped to the Eastern Frontier to form their own country independent of any human country; the most malicious suggested instead denying the Protectors their rights and treating them like second class citizens.

As far as Kara knew, Carem was not part of that movement and had no real interest in it. For that, she was thankful, because she was certain that the members of that movement would eventually find themselves at odds with the Protectors. And if that happened …

Stop thinking about it, Kara told herself. *Think positive. Focus on the good stuff, like how you and Carem and Vyll are together again for the first time in a long time. Thinking about depressing world events will only spoil your best chance to have a great time with the two people you are closest to in the whole world.*

"I am not a particularly special Protector," Vyll said. He gestured at himself. "I am quite ordinary, in fact. So I don't consider myself all that 'better' than my comrades or peers, to be honest."

"Well, you know what I mean anyway, right, Vyll?" said Carem. He slapped Vyll on the shoulder. "Come on, now. No need to be so serious."

For a moment, Kara thought she saw a terrible anger in Vyll's optics. It filled her with terror, because she had never seen Vyll get that angry before.

But then Vyll's optics returned to normal and, turning to look at Carem, said, "Yes, I know what you mean. I simply do not like the insinuation that my species is somehow inferior while I am, for some reason, better than them, simply because you know me."

Kara heard movement behind her and looked over her shoulder. She thought she had heard the Protector projecting the cafe's sign looking at her, but when she looked, he was still facing the street, his holographic sign spinning in a circle above his head.

Must have been my imagination, Kara thought, shaking her head as she turned to look at Carem and Vyll again.

"But you *are* smarter than the rest of 'em," said Carem. He gestured at the Protector projecting the cafe's sign. "See that one? He's probably not all that smart, considering all he does is stand in front of this cafe all day projecting that sign. You're not doing that sort of work, so of course that makes you smart."

Again, Kara looked at the Protector. The sign-projecting Protector still wasn't looking at them, but Kara had a feeling that he was listening to their every word.

"You don't know him," said Vyll, folding his arms across his chest. "How do you know he doesn't have a good reason for taking this job? Maybe he needs the money to help support his human. Or maybe he lost his human and doesn't have anything else to do."

"Eh, maybe," said Carem. "Still, it's a pretty simple job, wouldn't you say? Not the kind of job you'd do, but the kind of job pretty much every other Protector I've known would do without even thinking about it."

"You speak as if most Protectors are a bunch of a bumbling simpletons who can't handle complex jobs," said Vyll. "And I find that to be quite inaccurate. More than inaccurate, in fact; downright incorrect."

"Uh, guys?" said Kara, waving her hand in an attempt to get them both to look at her, but she unfortunately failed to grab their attention. "Why don't we talk about something else? I saw this really cute puppy the other day that—"

"I'm not going back on what I just said," Carem snapped, glaring at Vyll. He pointed at the sign-projecting Protector again. "I've been all over the world over the last six months and all I ever see are dumb Protectors wherever I go. Most of them can't even spell their own names, much less study something like magitek. And what's even weirder is how many of them have popped up over the last few years; like a mass malfunction or something."

"There is nothing wrong with my fellow Protectors," said Vyll. "If anything, I think you humans are the ones who are causing us problems. I am well aware of those members of your species who want us either to leave all human countries or die. I wonder if they play a role in why we Protectors do not always meet your standards of excellence."

Vyll's tone was surprisingly calm despite the heated argument, but Kara knew Vyll well enough to know that he was probably even angrier than Carem at the moment. Carem reached for his sword, which alarmed Kara greatly.

"Come on, you two," said Kara, putting on a happy smile. "There's no need to argue and fight right now. Why don't we go back to talking about nicer things than whatever conflicts exist between humans and Protectors? I mean, it's bad enough that we have to hear about it on the news every day; why do we have to bring it into our personal conversations, too?"

"I'm not bringing anything into anything," said Carem, still glaring at Vyll. "I'm just stating the facts as I see them. If Vyll has a problem with that, then I'll fight him about it right here and now."

Carem now gripped the handle of his blade. It was still sheathed, but Kara had seen Carem draw his sword before, and he could do it faster than anyone else Kara knew.

"Carem!" Kara said in shock. "What are you saying? Fight Vyll? He's your friend. He'd never—"

"I accept."

Kara looked at Vyll, uncertain that she had heard him correctly. Surely he had not just accepted Carem's offer. He didn't even look like he had opened his mouth recently. It must have been her ears playing tricks on her, but she had to know anyway just to be safe.

"What?" said Carem, staring at Vyll uncomprehendingly. "What did you just say?"

"I said, I accept your offer for a fight," said Vyll. He still spoke in a monotone voice. "Unless you don't think you can beat a Protector. I mean, I recall you bragging just a few minutes ago about how you could beat Ryfa the Crusher easily, and I am by no means as strong or big or vicious as he."

"Whoa now, Vyll," said Carem, looking around as if to make sure no one was watching (although there was no one else sitting at the tables in the outdoors cafe besides them). "I was just—"

"Joking?" Vyll finished for him. "Of course. You always did tell jokes pretty often. I understand if you would rather not have to actually prove that you're as good as you say you are; it's much easier to continue to *think* that you're good and strong than to prove it."

Though Vyll's tone was hardly antagonistic, Kara could tell that each and every one of his words cut through Carem like a knife. She saw Carem grinding his teeth, saw his grip on the hilt of his sword tighten so much that his knuckles became white, but she hoped that he would not actually attempt to fight Vyll here and now. In fact, she didn't want them to fight at all anywhere ever.

Finally, Carem said, "All right, Vyll. Glad to see you took up my offer. I'll fight you just as if you were my enemy."

"Excellent," said Vyll. "When shall we do it? Right now?"

Carem grabbed his cup, drained it in one gulp, and then slammed it down on the table again. "Tonight. At midnight. Meet me in the Public Housing District behind House Number Forty-Four."

"Very well," said Vyll. "Any restrictions on weapons or—"

"Take what you want," said Carem. "Swords, guns, iron knuckles, skyras-powered weapons, whatever. Anything and everything is permitted."

Kara reached over and grabbed Vyll's arm, prompting him to look at her in surprise.

"Kara, what are you doing?" said Vyll. "Why did you grab my arm like that?"

"Because I don't want you to fight Carem tonight, that's why," said Kara. She looked at Carem. "And I don't want you fighting Vyll, either. This was *supposed* to be a friendly lunch, not a time to discuss a good time and place for you two to fight."

"What are you worried about, Kara?" said Carem with a snort. "I'll be fine. Vyll will, too, probably. You just don't understand that two men have to go at each other sometimes when they disagree about something."

"Besides, we've fought before," said Vyll. "Remember when we were children? Carem was bullying you once. I tried to stop him, and then we began to fight each other. It was broken up by your father, so we never found out who would have won, but it was a good fight nonetheless."

"But you two were *kids* back then," said Kara. "Now you're adults. Carem's a bounty hunter, for the Gods' sake! You two could seriously injure, even kill, each other."

"There won't be any killing tonight," Carem said. He chuckled. "But I can't guarantee that I won't cause Vyll here to take an extended vacation at the shop for a while."

"I agree with Carem," said Vyll. "This is not about killing; it is simply about resolving our differences with violence. It is not a hard concept to grasp."

Kara stood up, pushing her seat back as she did so, and snapped, "You know what? Fine. Go ahead and be idiots. I won't even tell the police what you're going to do. I'm going back to my apartment and I will spend the rest of the day there. Don't come crying back to me when you two idiots get caught for fighting illegally after dark."

Before either Carem or Vyll could respond to that, Kara stomped off. She passed the large sign-projecting Protector on her way out, but she barely acknowledged his presence. She was just so annoyed by Carem and Vyll's stupidity that she didn't want anything to do with either of them anymore, or at least for a while.

I'll just sleep through the entire night, Kara thought as she stomped her feet against the pavement. *Won't even think about them. And when I get up in the morning tomorrow for class, I won't even have time to wonder how the fight turned out. Idiots.*

She decided then and there not to think about the fight for the rest of the day. She had much better and more constructive things to do than worry about her brother and her Protector's combined stupidity.

Chapter IV

That night, Kara found herself in the Public Housing District (which she had found by carefully studying the map of Capital City that all residents of the City were given upon moving there) all by herself. She was looking for House Forty-Four, where Carem and Vyll's fight was supposed to take place. It was hard to see because the Public Housing District was not as well-lit as the rest of the city (mostly due to the strict curfew that the government enforced on the people who lived here, which resulted in the lights going out usually after sunset), but she knew she should find it soon, because she had already passed House Thirty-Nine a block back and was coming upon House Forty next. She flashed her light—a tiny metal stick that glowed from one end—across each street and House sign that she passed, while occasionally flicking the light across the street to make sure there wasn't anything that could trip her.

The Public Housing District was not a very nice part of the city in comparison to the rest. The Houses—six hundred in all, according to what her research had shown her, though they were large enough to hold five hundred people each—made up this District. It was where the poor and those who had fallen on hard times came for shelter when things got tough, but Kara didn't envy them, because the Houses had boarded up or broken windows, cracked front steps, and few working or active street lamps at night.

Not to mention it smelled like smoke and burned rock most of the time, which made Kara cover her nose to keep her nostrils safe from the foul smell. Why it smelled that way, she wasn't sure, although she had heard that most of the District's inhabitants smoked a variety of different less-than-legal substances when they weren't working. There were also a few magicians around here who used the District's relatively quiet atmosphere to study magic away from the rest of the city, although she did not see any tonight.

Kara did not come here unarmed. She had her laser blaster in a holster on her hip. She did not expect to use it, but she had heard stories about how some of the inhabitants of this part of the city were a little less-than-kind toward young university women like her and that it was usually advisable not to go out here after dark without some sort of protection.

Or Protector, for that matter, Kara thought.

Yes, she had said that she was not going to watch Carem and Vyll's fight. Yes, she had said that she didn't care if the police busted them. Yes, she had said that she was just going to get a good night's rest tonight and maybe find out what happened in the morning. Yes, she was aware of all of that, and more, but she still managed to rationalize her decision to come here.

Just because I said all of that doesn't mean I actually meant it, Kara thought as she walked along in her comfortable, silky shoes across the hard, cracked concrete. *I was hoping that they would listen to me and decide that angering me wasn't worth fighting each other for, but I guess they're even bigger idiots than I thought.*

Kara had not told anyone—not her roommate, not her parents, not the landlord of the apartment she was staying in—where she was going tonight. Assuming all went well, then she would never need to tell anyone just what she, Vyll, and Carem were doing out here tonight.

Knowing those two, though, I might just have to fight them myself to get them to stop this nonsense, Kara thought, scowling at the thought. *Those two can be so pig-headed sometimes. It's ridiculous. And Carem is supposed to be my* older *brother. With the way he acts sometimes, he sure seems like the younger brother to me.*

That was when a sudden, pained—and far too familiar—cry pierced the air. It was horrible, like the sound of someone being tortured; in fact, it was so horrible that it caused Kara to stop in her tracks and break out into a sweat, even though the night was not very warm.

Then the cry cut off abruptly and the night was silent again, save for the distant sounds of hover vehicles soaring through the air in the rest of the city and what sounded like an argument between a husband and wife in one of the Houses (although their argument was too muted for her to make out the specifics of their disagreement).

That cry ... Kara's eyes widened. *Oh my gods. Was that Carem? Was he hurt? Was he hurt by—?*

Kara didn't allow herself to finish that thought. She just ran down the street, heedless of whatever danger lay waiting in the darkness around her, searching for House Forty-Four. Her whole focus was on getting to that House as fast as possible, so she didn't even allow herself to slow down as she passed House Forty-One ... House Forty-Two ... House Forty-Three ...

And soon, there it was: House Forty-Four. It looked exactly like the rest of the Houses in the District, aside from the sign hanging above the entrance reading *HOUSE FORTY-FOUR*. Kara recalled Carem telling Vyll to meet him behind House Forty-Four tonight, so she dashed down the alleyway between House Forty-Three and House Forty-Four, drawing her laser blaster from her holster. She now thought she was going to need to use it tonight.

At the end of the alleyway, Kara saw a light shining. It wasn't as bright as the streetlamps, but it was bright enough to let her know that there were people over there. She could even hear voices, although their low tones combined with the foreign language they spoke meant that Kara couldn't understand a word they were saying.

In any case, the rays of the light showed her a fallen trash can in her path, which Kara jumped over with ease. As she burst out of the alleyway, she shouted, "Carem! Vyll! It's me, Kara! Are you—"

She paused, both in speech and in action, when she saw a scene she would never have expected to see even in her worst nightmares.

Carem was lying in a pool of blood—*His* blood, Kara thought with a twist of her stomach—on the street. His sword was broken in half and covered with his blood as well. He wasn't moving, not even breathing. She could smell his blood, smell its metallic stink, the smell alone nearly enough to drive her insane. She couldn't even feel the firm handle of the blaster in her hands anymore; in fact, she couldn't feel anything at all. It was like a dream, a nightmare, but this was worse than any nightmare she had ever had, because she knew this was real.

Carem's lifeless body was not the only thing present in this back alley. Standing around the body were four Protectors; one was the large, sign-projecting Protector from the Protector Cafe, while the other two she did not recognize, though both were female from what she could tell.

But the fourth … she recognized him without trouble. It was Vyll. He looked up when she appeared, a startled expression on his face. He did not have any blood on his hands, but Kara knew that he had to have taken part in this horrid mess that she saw.

"Kara?" said Vyll. He sounded astonished to see her here. "Kara, I thought you were going to be in bed to—"

"What did you do?" said Kara. She pointed at Carem, although when she saw her finger pointing at him, it was like looking at the finger of someone else, as if she was a spirit floating outside her body. "What did you do to Carem?"

Kara had expected herself to scream, but oddly she spoke so quietly that she almost whispered. The shock in her system might have numbed her vocal chords. Or maybe this was just the way she naturally reacted to this kind of shock; this was the first time she had experienced this sort of thing before, after all, so she didn't really know what to expect.

"It's not what it looks like," Vyll said. He gestured at the other Protectors standing nearby. "My fellow Protectors and I—"

"No need to dance around like a headless chicken, Vyll," said the sign-projecting Protector from earlier, his voice wolfish. He shook his head. "She's not going to live much longer anyway, so why make up some crap about what 'really' happened? Just be straight with her."

"Wait," said Kara. Sweat rolled down the side of her head, though she ignored it. "Are you saying—"

"Yep," said the sign-projecting Protector, nodding. He gestured at Carem. "We killed him. Or technically, *I* killed him. These two helped."

He gestured at the two female Protectors, who had not uttered a word since Kara had come here. She could tell, however, that they were not even slightly apologetic about their helping to murder Carem. That thought would have made Kara raise her blaster and start shooting, but her arms and legs were so weak that she found it hard, almost impossible, to stand, much less aim and fire her gun at them.

"Vyll, on the other hand, didn't do a thing to help us," the murderer continued. "Just stood there and watched as we beat the pulp out of this kid's body. Your brother fought back like a cornered animal, but there was no way he could ever beat us. It was a quick fight."

No tears ran down Kara's face. She just stared at the corpse of her brother, stared at it, and said, "But why? Why did you kill him? What did my brother ever do to you?"

"He insulted me," said the murderer, jerking his thumb at his chest. He chuckled. "I heard every word he said about me and the other Protectors earlier. And then he said that he was going to go and capture me and get my bounty, as if a kid like him could ever even hope to do that."

"Capture you?" said Kara. She stepped back, even though she

wasn't really intending on running away. "Wait, are you—"

"Ryfa the Crusher, as some call me," said the murderer. He grinned, revealing row upon row of sharp teeth, just like in the wanted poster. "Though to be frank, I only earned that name because I crushed my first human victim. I've killed humans in a variety of ways since then, so it's kind of annoying to be remembered for that one thing I did years ago, but—"

"C-Carem said you were in the Eastern Frontier," said Kara. "How can you be here? And how come no one has found you out?"

"That's a rumor I spread to make sure that everyone was looking for me in all of the wrong places," said Ryfa. He gestured at his face. "I had my face altered by a couple of friends of mine so no one would recognize me. As for why I came to Capital City, that's easy. Who would expect one of the most wanted criminals in the country to be hiding right under the noses of this country's best law enforcers? Even better, I got a job at that Cafe, so I'm basically hiding in plain sight. Brilliant, isn't it?"

Ryfa chuckled at his own cleverness. "Everything thinks I'm dumb because I'm so big, but they're the dumb ones for judging me based solely on my appearance. It's how I've managed to retain my freedom for as long as I have. If I was even half as stupid as everyone says I am, I—"

"How dare you," Kara cut him off. She didn't raise her voice; she was still so shocked that she doubted she would ever be able to speak loudly again.

Ryfa scowled. "Hey, I wasn't finished speaking."

"I don't care," said Kara. "All I care about is the fact that you killed my brother. Murdered him in cold blood."

Ryfa shrugged. "So what? He was going to die anyway. I actually did him a favor, if you think about it. This world doesn't have much longer, so why let him die in agony in the coming apocalypse when he can die in peace here?"

"Apocalypse? Peace?" said Kara. "I have no idea what you're talking about at all. And I have no idea why Vyll is with you. I thought you were *better* than that, Vyll."

Vyll cringed at Kara's words, but said, "Kara, please understand, I didn't approve of what Ryfa and his friends did. I —"

"But you stood by and let him kill Carem anyway!" Kara's voice suddenly rose and the tears finally began to flow from her eyes. "You as good as killed him, you … you monster!"

Vyll looked shocked by Kara calling him a 'monster,' but she didn't care. She didn't care if she offended him, which was light in comparison to Carem's fate.

"She's got a point, youngling," said Ryfa, nodding. "What's the point in denying it? Anyway, it doesn't matter, because she's not got long to live. She'll be joining her brother in a few short years, so why do you care if she gets angry at you over such a petty thing?"

"Because—" Vyll said, but Kara didn't let him speak because she still had a lot to say.

"I thought I could trust you, Vyll," Kara continued. She was finding it harder and harder to speak clearly, due to the immense emotion that was starting to overtake her. "We grew up together; you, me, and Carem. We were basically *siblings*, a *family*. My parents treated you like me and Carem. We loved each other. We supported each other. But now you go ahead and do *this*?"

Vyll raised his hands. "Please, Kara, calm down and listen to me. I—"

"I don't care what your stupid excuse is," Kara snapped. She wiped the tears from her eyes, but it was pointless because she was still crying. "Carem is dead and you let him die. You let these monsters kill him. That makes you no better than them."

Vyll said nothing in response to that, which was good, because Kara didn't want to hear another word from his stupid mouth. She just wanted him to shut up and listen and feel awful for what he did.

"I used to love you like a brother," Kara said. "And I always loved you, even after you came back from that Gathering a different person. I thought you were my friend, thought we would always be friends, but now … now I can see that you are nothing more than a disgusting monster who I want nothing to do with anymore."

Kara tried to say more, but her emotion kept choking her up. She wiped the tears from her eyes and then turned and ran back the way she had came. She didn't look back, didn't slow down. She was going to tell the police about what she saw, and if that ended in Vyll's arrest and even execution, then so be it. She did not care if he was killed, because he clearly did not care about her.

Chapter V

Vyll watched Kara go. He wanted to call her to come back so he could explain himself, but he knew that she was not going to listen to another word he said ever again. He might as well be dead to her.

"Harsh words from such a small thing," said Ryfa, stroking his chin with his blood-stained fingers. "Very harsh. If she wasn't so scrawny, I would have been afraid of her. But humans— especially ones like her—can really only shout and yell at us. Can't do much else unless they're armed with something more potent than a skyras blaster."

Vyll's shoulders slumped. "You don't understand. That girl was my human. We were closer than siblings."

"So?" said Ryfa. "My human and I were plenty close before I killed him. You're better off without her, anyway; remember what the Rock said, about how humanity isn't going to survive his death?"

Vyll nodded, though without any enthusiasm. "Yes, I do. That still does not change the fact that Kara and I share a link that we do not share with anyone else. And that I feel her hatred of me as much as I feel my own emotions."

"There's nothing you can do to make her like you again, if that's what you're thinking," said Ryfa. He shook his head. "Whatever. I'm getting out of here. Unless you want to stop me, that is. I mean, killing me to avenge this human—" and here he gestured at Carem like Carem was nothing more than garbage on the street, "—might make her like you again, but I know you won't, and you want to know why?"

Vyll looked up at Ryfa. He tried to avoid looking at Carem's corpse. That was much more difficult to do than it seemed, because Carem's body was between him and Ryfa. "Why?"

"Because we're both Protectors," said Ryfa, jerking his thumb at his chest. "You and me both. The Rock wants us all united and working together in preparation for the day of his death. You can't 'redeem' yourself because the Rock will not allow it. I didn't do anything wrong, if you think about it."

"You could at least *sound* a little disturbed by the fact that you murdered an innocent human being," said Vyll.

Ryfa laughed. "Me? Disturbed? I am Ryfa the Crusher. Murder is what I do. I really could not care less about who I kill, especially if they're human. Not like it makes any difference in the long run."

"What are you going to do now?" asked Vyll. "Go and kill someone else?"

Ryfa scratched his chin. "Eh, maybe sometime, but probably not anytime soon. That human girl is going to go and tell the police. Once they find out that I'm here, they'll be on my behind faster than a chatter snake on a hog. Think I'm going to lay low for a few months, maybe actually head out to the Eastern Frontier, since the news of this murder will undoubtedly reach out that way soon enough and then all of those bounty hunters will come here in search of me. Then I'll go and rejoin the other Protectors in time for the Rock's death."

Vyll looked at the two female Protectors who seemed incapable of speaking. He found it hard to read them, even though they were fellow Protectors, which disturbed him, although that may have been because they were female and he was male.

"What about those two?" said Vyll, looking back at Ryfa.

"My girls?" said Ryfa. He smiled. "Coming with me, of course. They got nowhere else to go. Besides, one of the reasons I've lasted as long as I have is thanks to their help. Don't know where I'd be without them. They're way better than my old human, that's for sure."

"I see," said Vyll. He still avoided looking at Carem. "Then why haven't you left?"

Ryfa held out one of his bloody hands. "Because I wanted to offer you a chance to join my crew. The City police will probably drag you in for questioning, and I can tell you that you've broken at least three dozen different City laws just by being here, not counting the fact that you are technically an accomplice in the murder of this dumb human here."

Ryfa gestured at Carem's corpse when he said that, but Vyll again kept his gaze firmly on Ryfa. Vyll then said, "You seem awfully knowledgeable about the laws of this city."

"My human was a lawyer who let me read his law books when I got bored," said Ryfa. "So I know more about law than even most human lawyers. Anyway, what do you say? Want to come with me? We're brothers, after all, connected by our father the Rock."

65

Vyll looked away, back in the direction that Kara had been standing in not long ago. In his mind, he still saw her standing there, staring at Carem's corpse in horror. He doubted he'd ever forget that image for as long as he lived.

"No," said Vyll at last. He looked at Ryfa again, whose face was half-hidden in the shadows cast by the dim street lights. "I must decline your offer. I will figure out how to evade the police on my own."

"Are you sure?" said Ryfa. "'Cause the City police force are some of the best in the nation. They don't take prisoners; quite literally, in some cases."

"I said I will be fine," said Vyll. He gestured in a random direction. "Just go. I don't want to see your face ever again."

Ryfa shrugged his large shoulders. "If you say so. But don't come crying back to me when you get caught and thrown into prison. Come on, girls."

Ryfa turned and went walking down the street. His two friends followed him without so much as looking at Vyll. Not that Vyll cared; right now, he would have been quite happy if those three forgot about him and left him alone for good.

Then he heard a moan of pain and he started. Looking down, Vyll thought at first that he had been hearing things, because there was no way that Carem could have survived being stabbed in the ground by his own sword or having his face beaten in by Ryfa.

Much to his astonishment, however, that was exactly what he saw. Carem was moving and moaning; granted, his movements were weak and his moans were low, but he was clearly and obviously still alive.

How did he survive that? Vyll thought in horror, stepping

back. *He should be dead. He can't be that tough.*

"Vyll ..." Carem said. His voice was so weak that it was like he was whispering. "Vyll ..."

Vyll looked down the street in the direction that Ryfa and his friends had gone. The three of them were nowhere to be seen, which made Vyll relieved and afraid at the same time. Relieved that Ryfa was not going to come back and finish the job; frightened that Carem would remember how Vyll had not stopped Ryfa from trying to kill him and thus hate him for it.

And if the police come in time, they will be able to take Carem to the hospital where he will be healed, Vyll thought. *Even if Ryfa beat Carem so badly that Carem doesn't remember all of the details, he probably remembers enough to put me behind bars for life. Or simply get executed.*

Of course, even if Vyll was put behind bars, that didn't mean a thing, because the world was going to end in five years anyway. Still, Vyll had no intention of remaining locked up in prison for the next half decade, not when there was still so much to do in preparation for the Rock's death.

I need to get Carem out of here, Vyll thought. *Ryfa mentioned that House Eighty-Eight—the one behind House Forty-Four—is currently unoccupied. I should drag Carem into there.*

So Vyll grabbed Carem by the shoulders and began dragging him toward House Eighty-Eight. He hoped that Ryfa had been right when he said that the House was unoccupied, because Vyll was in no mood to kill more people just to save his own skin.

It took Vyll approximately five minutes to find the back door of House Eighty-Eight. It took him only a minute to hack the lock and open the door into the dark building, into which he quickly dragged Carem. Once they were inside, he closed the door, although he soon realized that Carem's body had left behind a trail of blood that led all the way up to the House's back door.

Damn it, Vyll thought. *But not much I can do about it. If I try to wash it off, the police will notice the wet street. Looks like I'm going to get caught anyway.*

House Eighty-Eight was dark, almost too dark to see in, but Vyll had night vision built into his optics. This allowed him to see that he had dragged Carem into some kind of kitchen; there was a sink in one corner, plus an empty dish rack, and white tiled floor. An old-fashioned wooden table stood in the center, with six chairs arranged around it, but there was a thick layer of dust on all of the furniture, which made it look like this place hadn't been lived in for quite some time.

That was not too surprising. Many of the Public Houses were not well-maintained due to how few poor people actually lived in them. No doubt there were other parts of the building in even worse condition, which meant that Vyll would have to leave here soon in search of better and less obvious places to hide.

But I can't just leave Carem here, where anyone can find him, Vyll thought, glancing at Carem, who was not moaning anymore but was clearly still breathing. *I need to take a moment to sit and think.*

So Vyll pulled up one of the chairs at the table and sat down on it. The chair creaked under his weight, but it thankfully held steady. He then rested his chin in his hands and stared at the floor, still unwilling to look at or treat Carem's wounds.

I can't believe how horrible things have gotten, Vyll thought.

68

DESINENCE

And in just one night, too. I was always told that things can change quickly, but I never really understood that until tonight.

He could not imagine how things could get any worse. Carem was nearly dead. Kara hated him, the police would be here any minute, and the Rock was going to die. Granted, he had known that last one for a while now, but he still felt depressed every time he thought about it.

I'll have to live a life on the run now, Vyll thought. *Stupid, stupid, stupid me. I just stood there and let Carem get himself beaten almost to death. And there is almost certainly no way I can save his life now. I am no doctor and the nearest hospital is miles away. If Ryfa's beating didn't kill him, then those wounds will, and I'll be blamed for his death no matter what happens.*

Vyll popped open his chest compartment and took out the drawing that Kara had given to him when she was nine. He unfolded it and looked at it again. It had been months since he had last looked at it, mostly because he had been so busy and distracted by the work the Rock had put him to that he simply hadn't had a chance to look at it as much as he wanted.

The drawing showed him, Kara, and Carem, all young and childish, standing together arm-in-arm in the fields around Kara's parents' house. It had only been eight years ago, but it seemed like a lifetime ago to him now. It even still had the green stains from the blood of that giant snake that Vyll had saved Kara from; in fact, he hadn't done much to clean the drawing since those days, because he was too afraid of accidentally ruining it forever.

I'm not deserving of this drawing anymore, Vyll thought. *Kara gave it to me to symbolize that all three of us will always be together, but I can see now that the Rock was right: We*

Protectors must separate from the humans now. It is our only option.

Together … separate … until tonight, Vyll had never truly understood the concepts. When he lowered the drawing and looked at Carem's bloody body, he no longer saw a brother of another species. Instead, he saw a foreign creature, one he did not understand and one which did not understand him.

Wait, what am I thinking? Vyll thought, shaking his head. *Of course I know him. He is Kara's brother. I have known him since the day I met Kara. We don't have to be separate, even if the Rock decrees that it must be so.*

Don't have to be separate … never have to be separate … can be together forever … one species, one people, one destiny …

Those thoughts echoed in his head, but they weren't his thoughts. They were the Rock's, but they were weak due to how close the Rock was to death. It didn't help that Vyll barely understood them or even why the Rock was contacting him specifically; they seemed as incomprehensible as an elfish riddle.

But then, something clicked in Vyll's head and he stood up. He folded up the drawing as carefully as he always did and deposited it into his chest compartment, which he then closed.

Maybe we don't *have to be separate,* Vyll thought. *I now understand. I* must *get Carem to the Rock. That is what he is trying to tell me. I must, and I must do it quickly, before Carem dies.*

Vyll looked at Carem again. No longer did he see a product of his own failure to stop a vicious murderer; now, he saw a way to save the bloodied, almost dead person before him. And he already knew how to do it, too.

DESINENCE

It will be hard, but I think I can do it because I know of a tunnel near here that will take me down to the Rock's chamber, one that none of the humans, even the human police, will be able to find, thought Vyll. *All right, Carem. After I clean up the blood, you and me are going to be the start of a new race, one that will end this suffering and bring about a healing between our two species. You just don't know it yet.*

Chapter VI

Five years later ...

Kara could not remember what it was like to live on a world that did not shake anymore. Not that it was particularly important; as she and her fellow magitek warriors traversed down the tunnels that, according to a captured Protector, would take them directly to the Rock, she had to keep her eyes and ears open for even the slightest hint of danger.

Even though she had already checked her magitek several times in the past hour or so, Kara checked them again. Her gauntlets—each one fitted with a jewel capable of containing skyras energy—were in working order, as was her crescent blade that was specially designed to cut through Protector skin. Her blue-and-black armor—made of magnified metal, the strongest metal in the world—fit well over her more muscular body, which she had worked hard to get in preparation for this day.

Even so, Kara did not feel entirely safe, despite traveling with four other magitek warriors wearing armor and wielding weapons similar to hers. The tunnel—while wide-open—was still too dark for her tastes; she never knew if there was something lying in wait in the shadows just outside of the reach of Captain Arol's light at the front of the group.

So far, the team called the Secret Squad had not run into any Protectors. This in spite of the all-out war that had erupted between the humans and the Protectors in the last five years. It had actually been Carem's death that had led to it; when Kara reported his murder to the police, it seemed like every news reporter in Fariah was intent on writing the story that the days of peace and togetherness between the two species was over. Kara had seen battles waged across Fariah on the telescreens; even the other species, such as the dwarves and elves, had joined the war, picking one side or another in an effort to avoid being caught in the middle of what had turned out to be the bloodiest and largest conflict in the recorded history of the world.

How many people had died so far? Kara didn't know. Despite having joined the Capital City Army after graduation from Unity University, Kara kept herself ignorant about the true number of deaths on both sides. All she knew was that both the humans and the Protectors had lost many lives, but that the two sides were still going at it as viciously as ever and the conflict did not seem to have an end in sight.

But that's why we're going down to see the Rock, Kara thought. *If we can find him and talk to him, maybe we can end this terrible war before it destroys us all.*

Kara looked around at her allies. There was Captain Arol, the middle-aged leader, who walked in the front of the group, using the light of his sword to guide their path through the darkness; then there was Faya and Gahan, the brother and sister duo who were only five years Kara's senior yet seemed so much older than her already; Kagyan, a woman similar in statue to her, though far more efficient at killing Protectors; and finally, Haran, the kindhearted but tough second-in-command of the Squad.

Each one of them was a trained magitek warrior, just like she was. Almost all of them were more experienced than her—Arol, for example, had been a general in the war before the current one about thirty years ago—but the Grand Chancellor had still assigned her to the Secret Squad due to her deep connection with and understanding of the Protectors.

The plan was to find the Rock—the god-like being said to live beneath Fariah's surface, who had created all of the Protectors on Fariah, but who no human had ever actually seen—and convince him to tell the Protectors to end this war. Because it was becoming rapidly clear that the war was not going to end with either one side or the other emerging victorious; if it did end, Kara knew, it would end with both sides utterly annihilating each other from existence and maybe destroying the planet between them in the process.

The hope was that the Rock would be reasonable enough to listen to the Secret Squad's demands and would call off the war before the Protectors and humans killed each other. Whether or not the Rock would listen, whether it even cared about ending the war, and many other questions aside, were questions that no one knew the answer to. And of course, there was the ever-popular theory that the Rock had in fact ordered the war in the first place, but again, no one knew for sure.

If it did order the war, then I doubt any of us will ever come out of here alive, Kara thought, her eyes looking around at her companions. *It's been nice knowing everyone, I guess.*

Perhaps Kara should have had more positive thoughts, but

ever since Carem's death, Kara had found it hard to be positive about anything. So many people she knew had already died in the war; her former classmate, Jakar, who had been burned alive by a group of Protectors with flamethrowers built into their hands; her friend, Camey, who had attempted to infiltrate enemy ranks, only to end up being found out and torn to shreds by the Protectors who discovered her; and even her parents, who had attempted to move out of their old home in the country, but were not fast enough to escape the army of Protectors that had razed the countryside in an attempt to slaughter as many humans as possible.

I just want this damn war to end, Kara thought. *I'm sick of it. I don't even care anymore if we humans kill all of those Protector bastards or not. Even Vyll could die, and I wouldn't care.*

Thinking of Vyll did not help her mood. After Carem's death, Vyll had vanished from the face of the earth, or so it seemed. The police had been unable to find him when they went to the Public Housing District on Kara's report; even when they followed the trail of Carem's blood into House Eighty-Eight, they had found no sign of where Vyll or Carem might have gone. And with five years having come and gone since that day, with no sign or hint at all of where they might be, Kara no longer felt any feelings of warmth or positivity toward Vyll at all.

Damn idiot stole Carem's body, Kara thought. *What did he do with it? Take it to his friends as a trophy to show off? Maybe tossed in a hole somewhere where no one can find it. I can't even give Carem a proper funeral, and never will, all because of Vyll.*

In fact, that was why Kara had trained so hard to become a magitek warrior and why she had worked to earn her spot on the

Secret Squad, which was made up of elite magitek warriors appointed by the Grand Chancellor himself. She wanted to kill Vyll the next time she saw him; or better yet, let the others kill him, while she stood by and watched, just as he stood by and watched Ryfa kill Carem.

Speaking of Ryfa, Kara had heard a report that Ryfa had been killed in a recent struggle near the Seven Towers of Peace. She had even seen pictures to prove it; pictures that showed Ryfa's old, rusty corpse with a thick spear stabbed straight through his head. It was an image she enjoyed, one that she hoped to repeat with Vyll, next time she saw him.

"Wait," said Arol ahead, his tone tense, causing Kara to break out of her thoughts. He was holding up his other hand, the one that didn't hold the light. "Do you see that?"

The rest of the Squad stopped and looked around Arol at what was ahead. Kara saw a gigantic archway—the fabled Arch of Truth, according to the captured Protectors—ahead of them. It had no gateway to speak of, although there was a red, transparent wall that allowed her to see the rest of the tunnel on the other side. The red energy wall kept flickering in and out of existence, but Kara felt no desire to try walking through it, despite its weakening appearance.

"Huh," said Haran, a squat, bulky man who Kara always thought was half-dwarf. "Looks like those stupid machines were telling the truth."

"Then they were probably also telling the truth when they said that the Arch will destroy any non-Protectors who pass underneath it," said Arol. "We keep walking nonetheless."

"Keep walking?" Kara spoke up, staring at the back of Arol's head in disbelief. "And get killed? Are you even listening to your own words?"

Arol didn't look over his shoulder at Kara. He just started walking again, saying, "Trust me. We'll be perfectly fine."

Kara knew that Arol was a highly experienced soldier and combat veteran, but she figured he had to be losing his marbles if he thought that walking under the Arch—and by extension, through the flickering red barrier—was a smart move. She thought they were going to use some sort of device to disrupt it long enough for them to pass through, but apparently Arol had not thought that far ahead.

I hope Arol isn't actually suicidal, Kara thought as she and the other members of the Squad started following Arol. *But maybe he knows what he's doing. I* hope *he knows what he's doing.*

With every step closer to the Arch, Kara just wanted to turn and leave. She did not know what it would be like to get killed by the Arch, but she doubted it would be a pleasant experience. She could already imagine her skin burning away or her brain exploding; she doubted that either of those two methods would actually be how the Arch killed her, but she couldn't think of two more horrible ways to die than those, so she imagined them. She did, however, stop herself from imagining both of them happening at the same time.

It wasn't long before Arol passed through the Arch's red energy barrier without hesitation. He was followed by Faya and then Haran and the others; none of them so much as cringed when they passed through. None of them had their skin burned away, nor did anyone's brains explode; still, Kara did not want to walk under that Arch.

But because she wanted to end this war and going through that barrier was the only way to do it, Kara continued walking forward anyway, but she closed her eyes so she wouldn't have to see her own inevitable—and likely gruesome—death. When she passed through the wall, she felt some kind of presence pass over her, but it was a weak presence and it lasted only for a second; when she reached the other side, she no longer felt the presence.

Opening her eyes, Kara saw that all of her fellow Squad mates were all right. They did not look like they were dead or about to die; in fact, everyone looked as well as they had just seconds ago. She looked down at her own hands and body, but did not see or feel anything out of the ordinary.

"See?" said Arol, causing Kara to look up at his helmeted face. "We're all fine. I told you we would be."

Kara looked over her shoulder at the flickering red energy wall. "But … why? None of us are Protectors."

"You're right," said Arol, nodding. He patted his chest plate. "But our armor is made of Protector skin."

Kara looked down at her armor so fast that she hurt her neck. "What do you mean, 'Protector skin'?"

"What Arol means, Kara, is that our magitek armor was created from the melted down corpses of Protectors killed during the war, of course," said Faya. She did not sound even slightly disturbed about it; in fact, she spoke of it like she was talking about the weather. She raised her armored hand and waved at Kara as if to demonstrate. "The heads of the Capital City government were aware that the Arch of Truth kills any non-Protectors that try to pass through it. It was a problem without a solution until one of the government's top magicians hypothesized that cladding us Squad members in Protector skin would trick the Arch into thinking we were Protectors and thus let us through when we passed underneath it."

"Hypothesized?" Kara repeated. "You mean no one knew if it would *actually* work until just now?"

"Yep," said Arol, nodding. He was smiling, though it was a rather nervous one. "If that wizard had been wrong, all five of us would have been dead right off the bat, and you would never have learned about that theory."

Kara put a hand over her heart. She felt dizzy and sick at the thought of how closely they had avoided death, and at the thought that she was essentially wearing a corpse. Just seconds ago, she had felt very safe and secure in her armor, but now all she wanted to do was throw it off and take a nice, long shower back in the City, even though neither was a realistic option for her at the moment.

"The captives said this was the only obstacle between us and the Rock, so we just need to keep walking forward until we find it," said Arol. He closed the visor on his helmet, turned around, and walked down the tunnel. "Come on, guys. The quicker we do this, the quicker we can end this damn war."

The other three warriors followed Arol. Kara followed as well, but she hung at the back, still looking over her shoulder every now and then at the flickering red energy barrier that was becoming smaller behind them the farther down the tunnel they walked.

Oh my god, Kara thought, shuddering every now and then. *Can't believe I almost died. But I didn't, thanks to the dead Protector protecting me.*

Despite Kara's feelings of revulsion, she had to smile at that thought. Even in death, this Protector—whoever he or she had been—still protected a human. It reminded her of how safe she had felt when Vyll had been her Protector, but she ignored those feelings, because she could not allow nostalgia for a long-gone past to distract her from what she needed to do.

Even so, Kara didn't like the idea of wearing Protector skin. It made her feel wrong, like she had taken the skin of another human being and wore it as clothes. But her rational side said that she was likely to continue to need the armor until they reached the Rock at least, and probably on the return trip as well.

Yet Kara could not shake the feelings of unease and dirtiness that followed her as she walked. The other Squad members did not seem even half as disturbed as she was; then again, all four of them had been in war before, and had likely had to do far worse things than wear armor made from the melted down bodies of deceased Protectors.

Just another reason to want this war over, Kara thought. *Then I won't have to wear the skin of my enemies anymore.*

About an hour after they passed underneath the barrier, a dim, teal light shone at the end of the tunnel. Rather than making Kara feel relieved, she drew her magitek sword and made sure that her gauntlets were ready, while her fellow Squad members did the same. This was supposed to be a peace mission, but Arol had said that peace missions often had a bad habit of turning into war missions, which was why all of them were armed to the teeth. They had not yet seen any Protectors even after the Arch, but there could still be some hiding nearby, ready to kill Kara and her teammates the second they let their guard down.

DESINENCE

In another few minutes, Kara and the Secret Squad emerged out of the tunnel into the most massive chamber that Kara had ever stepped foot in. Standing upon a wide balcony that stretched out over a deep hole, Kara saw dozens upon hundreds upon thousands of similar balconies everywhere she looked, although all of them were completely empty at the moment. The ceiling was so high that she could not see it, even when she activated the zoom-in feature built into the visor of her helmet and zoomed in as much as the visor allowed.

But what was most impressive about this place was the massive, square rock in the very center of it all. The gigantic rock was the source of that dim teal light, but she could tell that its light had once been much brighter than it was today. Now the square rock looked sick, like it had come down with a cold, although Kara knew that that was a silly thought. Huge cracks ran all over its surface; in fact, there were so many cracks that Kara believed that it was a miracle that it hadn't split into pieces yet.

It must be the Rock, Kara thought, with more than a bit of awe. *It's even bigger than Vyll said it was. Something that big must have enough power to wipe an entire city off the map, yet it instead spends all of its time down here, away from the surface, and has its children doing its work for it. Simply amazing.*

"Hey, you!" Arol called out suddenly, causing Kara to jump. "Who are you? Identify yourself!"

Kara looked in the direction that Arol was pointing in. A tall, humanoid person wearing golden robes, with a hood pulled over his head, stood at the very end of the balcony, near the stone railings. The figure had not so much as moved a muscle when Arol shouted at him, which made Kara wonder if the robed figure

81

Timothy L. Cerepaka

had heard Arol at all.

"I'm talking to you," said Arol, pointing his sword at the figure, which glowed slightly dimmer now due to the light of the Rock providing sufficient illumination. "Are you listening to me? Or are you just going to ignore me? Are you a Protector?"

"No," said the robed figure. His voice sounded like deep and masculine, but with a tinge of that metallic accent most Protectors spoke with. It immediately made Kara uneasy. "I am not."

"Are you a human, then?" said Arol. "A traitor to the human race?"

"I am neither human, nor Protector, nor elfish, nor dwarfish, nor Jikorian," said the robed figure. "I belong to no race known to Fariah, nor one known to the Gods that you worship. I am a unique individual, the founder of a new race that will emerge from the ruins of the old world after this terrible war is ended."

The robed figure's voice now sounded familiar to Kara, but she did not know where she might have heard it before. It reminded her of Vyll, but also of Carem, but she dismissed it as her mind playing tricks on her. This figure, whoever he was, was clearly different from either of those two.

"Unique, eh?" said Arol. "Buddy, *everyone* thinks they're unique. 'Start of a new race' … yeah, right. Only the Gods can create a new race, and I know for a fact that you aren't a creation of the Gods."

"You are correct," said the robed figure. He raised one hand, causing his sleeve to fall down and reveal a completely mechanical, Protector-like hand. "I am a product of the Rock, his chosen vessel to create a new race that will succeed both the human and Protector races."

"Then why don't you show us your face?" said Arol. "If you're so great, then surely you can do that much, at least."

"Very well," said the robed figure. "But be warned; my appearance may frighten you greatly."

The robed figure turned around, but his face was still hidden in the shadows of his hood. But Kara could see his eyes: His left eye was blue—the same shade as Carem's eyes—and the right eye was red, the same shade as Vyll's optics.

Kara stepped back. *No. It can't be. He can't—*

The robe figure then reached up with both of his hands and lowered his hood, allowing Kara and the Secret Squad to see his full face.

It was an abomination; that was the word Kara would have used to describe it, if the shock of his appearance had not completely taken her tongue away from her. It was half-organic, half-mechanical, and she recognized both halves with no problem. The organic half was Carem's face; she recognized his chin and stubble. The mechanical half was Vyll's face; there was no mistaking that red optic or those metallic lips for the features of any other Protector.

"By the Gods," said Arol. He tapped the side of his helmet, causing his visor to flip open, showing his stunned face. "Just what the hell *are* you, freak?"

The robed figure raised both of his hands to the ceiling. "I was once a Protector named Vyll; I was once a human named Carem. When my human side was dying five years ago, Vyll brought the dying human to the Rock … and the Rock brought them together into one whole. Now there only exists I, the new being, who is neither Vyll nor Carem, but a new creation superior to both."

Kara shook her head and flipped open the visor of her helmet with a tap of her helmet. She stepped forward to the front of the group and said, gesturing at her face, "Vyll … Carem … whoever is in there, it's me, Kara. Do you remember me?"

Vyll or Carem or whatever that thing was, lowered his hands and looked at her more closely. Then recognition dawned in his eyes and he said, in a voice that sounded very much like Vyll and Carem's voices combined, "Kara? Is that you?"

Kara's heart almost broke when she heard both of their voices at once like that, but she kept up a strong face for her Squad mates and said, "Yes, it's me. Is there anything left of Vyll or Carem in there? Anything at all? Please tell me."

For a moment, the robed figure looked like he was going to answer in the affirmative, but then he shook his head and a scowl crossed his features. When he spoke, he no longer sounded exactly like Vyll or Carem. "Vyll and Carem are no more. They became one, brought together to create a whole greater than their individual selves. Now only I, the Founder, exist, and no one else."

Kara didn't believe that. She saw how the Founder had recognized her. Vyll and Carem were still in there somewhere, or at least their memories were. She just had to figure out how to bring those memories back.

Arol then stepped forward and, resting a hand on Kara's shoulder, said, "Kara, stand down. We don't know what this guy is capable of. Let me speak with him."

"But I—"

"That is an order, soldier," said Arol, in a much more authoritative tone than before. "Understand?"

Kara bit her lower lip, but then nodded and said, "Understood, sir."

"Then do as you're told," said Arol, taking his hand off her shoulder and gesturing at her to stand back. "I'm in charge of this mission, so it's my duty to speak with this freak even if you know the people who this thing used to be."

Kara nodded again and stepped back. She watched the Founder more closely than ever as Arol stepped out in front of the group, his sword in his hands, though he had lowered it, perhaps to show that he was not a threat.

The Founder, meanwhile, had not uttered even one word during that short conversation. He looked like he was waiting for them to speak to him, which made Kara wonder what he was thinking. Despite having known Carem and Vyll since childhood, the Founder truly did seem like a completely different individual, despite clearly retaining some memories from both. That made it harder for her to guess at what was going through his mind at the moment.

"So you say you are a fusion of a human and a Protector?" said Arol. "How is that even possible?"

"Through the power of the Rock, of course," said the Founder. He gestured at the massive, dimly glowing stone behind him. "Five years ago, I was summoned by the Rock to this place, to be the first of a brand new race of people. The Rock believed that combining us together would help show the Protectors and humanity a third way, one in which they can live in peace by becoming one people."

"What if we don't want to become a new race?" asked Arol. "What if we just want to remain separate? Because frankly, I don't want to be fused with Protector scum."

"You do not understand," said the Founder. "In separation, there is pain and even death; in togetherness, there is only life. And it is my duty to bring the Protectors and the humans together. Even the other sentient species of Fariah can become one with us, if they so wish."

"The only 'life' I see is you, freak," said Arol. "No way am I going to give up my individuality in favor of union with my enemies."

The Founder placed one hand on his chest. "But the Protectors and humanity are not enemies. We have been friends for eons; it is only recently that the two peoples have become enemies. It is this union between the races that was intended all along, by the both the Gods and the Rock. It is the next step in our evolutionary paths; by becoming one, we can walk among the stars as gods ourselves."

The Founder spoke so passionately about this that Kara almost wanted to believe him. But then she remembered that Vyll—the one who betrayed her—was still in there and her cold, hard rational mind grounded her back into reality and the facts, which were that the Founder was not her friend and never would be as far as she was concerned.

"I don't recall the Gods ever saying that this was the next step in the evolution of humanity or even the Protectors," said Arol. "Just sounds like an excuse by a madman to strip away our individuality in the name of *your* pathetic excuse for a god. Anyway, if what you say is so true, then why is this war even happening? Why didn't the Rock come out and tell us that this is what he wanted in the first place?"

DESINENCE

"The war happened because the Rock is dying," said the Founder. He gestured at the ceiling that was too far above their heads for any of them to see. "He is losing control over his children, who have decided that the only way to survive the coming apocalypse is to kill humanity, mostly due to humanity refusing to give us our independence. It was supposed to be my mission to go among the humans and the Protectors and preach this good news, but I have stayed down here to keep the Rock alive with my own powers as long as I can."

"The Rock is dying?" Arol said. His eyes flickered up at the Rock over the Founder's head. "What 'apocalypse' are you talking about?"

"The Rock is what keeps the world together," said the Founder. "When Fariah was born ages ago, the Rock was born within its core, where he has acted as the planet's heart and anchor. But the Rock is dying, and once he does, Fariah will go with him, the same way that a human cannot survive if his heart fails. Once that happens, everyone on this world will die."

"But the Gods will save us," said Arol. He nodded at the ceiling, although Kara knew he was referring to the sky. "The Gods won't let Fariah die. Right?"

The Founder shook his head. "Have you seen any hint of the Gods anywhere? I suspect that the Gods fled this world or are at least watching from a distance. They have no way of stopping it; despite all of their power, it was not the Gods who brought Fariah into existence ages ago. They control Fariah's domains and elements, but Fariah is much greater than its sum, and it is that greater whole that the Rock sustains."

"Well, if that's the case, then it seems like we need to heal the

Rock," said Arol. "How do we do that?"

"We don't," said the Founder. "Or, to put it more accurately, we can't. There is no known cure for the illness afflicting the Rock. We Protectors have been searching for a cure for a decade now, but without knowing what caused the Rock's sickness, it has been a fruitless effort. The Rock will die, and Fariah will go with it."

"No, no, no, no," said Arol. He pointed his sword at the Founder. "This isn't right. If there's no way to save the world, then why do anything? We all might as well slit our throats here and now. At least then we can avoid the apocalypse that will kill off everyone else."

"Not all hope is lost," said the Founder. "The Rock believed that the Protectors would survive the coming apocalypse. That is why he started to separate the Protectors from humanity, but he fell into a coma before he could finish the job, which is partly why the war between the humans and the Protectors has broken out on the surface. He would never have approved of this war, but without his guidance, the Protectors have gone astray."

The Founder sounded genuinely sorrowful about the war. That made Kara wonder briefly if there was still something of the old Vyll in there, or if this was simply part of the Founder's own personality. She hated that she could not know for sure.

"How could anyone survive an apocalypse?" said Arol. "Your Rock doesn't sound like it understands what an apocalypse is, to be frank."

"The Rock understands more than any of us could ever hope to," said the Founder. "That is why I trusted him when he said that. Perhaps a new world will emerge from the ashes of the world, and in this new world, the Protectors, if they survive, will be dominant, not the humans."

"I don't like the sound of that," said Arol. "If this apocalypse is really going to happen, then I will survive so I can ensure humanity's survival. Count on it."

"Your tenacity is admirable, but ultimately fruitless," said the Founder. "Once the Rock dies ... and that will be soon, because he is in the throes of death even as we speak ... then it won't matter how much tenacity you have. Humanity will die, the Protectors will die, but I will survive as the founder of the new race that will dominate the new world that is born of the Rock's death."

"Right," said Arol. "I can see that you and I are running out of conversation material. So why don't we skip to the part where we take you out and drag you before the Capital City Council for your aid in the murder of Carem?"

The Founder tilted his head to the side, reminding Kara far too much of Vyll when he did that. "Despite everything I said, you want to *fight* me? What good will that accomplish? The world is dying and our species are fighting, yet you think fighting me is the next logical step?"

"Because I don't believe you, you sad, insane idiot," said Arol. He looked around the cavern. "I don't see any evidence for what you just said. All I hear is a bunch of wild claims about a 'new race' and the 'next step in evolution' and all that crap. Personally, I believe that you and the Rock are trying to win this war via assimilation; by making humanity part of you, you're hoping to end the war without having to actually wipe us out the good old fashioned way."

"You shortsighted fool," the Founder said, a hint of anger sneaking through his voice. "This is not about 'winning' any war. It is about unity. It is about ending all conflict. It is about healing the frayed bonds between humanity and the Protectors. But I understand that you humans do not have the insight I do, and perhaps cannot even comprehend it in your current forms."

"The only thing I need to comprehend is how to beat you," said Arol. "And because you are clearly not much of a fighter, I think taking you down will be ridiculously easy."

"Do not attempt to fight me, Arol," said the Founder. He held up one hand in warning. "Or I will be forced to destroy you."

"Make all of the empty threats you want," said Arol. "Doesn't change the fact that we're gonna kick your ass and haul you to prison, where you belong."

Arol looked over his shoulder at the other Squad members and, pointing at the Founder, said, "Attack! Don't let him get away. Hit him with everything you've got!"

With that, Arol charged forward, and so did the rest of the Squad. Even Kara joined in, but only with great reluctance, and she had to avoid looking directly at the Founder's face as she ran at him, because if she looked at it too closely, then she would see both Vyll and Carem, and she did not want to see either of them right now.

The Founder did not move an inch from where he stood. He didn't even look like he was going to try to run away from them. He simply stood there, still holding his hand up, as the Squad members came closer and closer to him, their swords aimed directly at him.

Then the Founder sighed. "Very well. I suppose not everyone

DESINENCE

is destined to understand the necessity of the Rock's actions."

The Founder jerked his hand to the side.

As soon as he did that, Kara went flying off her feet. She landed hard on the ground, the impact so hard that it cracked the visor of her helmet and caused her head to bang against the helmet's interior. The side of her head started bleeding and she saw lights in her eyes, but she managed to raise her head high enough to see what was happening to everyone else.

She saw Faya go flying over the railing, screaming in fear, before disappearing over the other side; watched Haran let out a strangled cry and fall to the ground and not get up; witnessed the Protector armor of Kagyan crush around her body like a tin can; and saw Gahan explode, sending bits of armor and blood-covered organs flying everywhere. She raised her arms to avoid the worst of it, but some of Gahan's blood got through and landed on her cheek anyway.

Only Captain Arol had avoided getting harmed in the attack somehow. He continued to charge at the Founder, his sword glowing white with charged skyras energy, and slashed his blade at the Founder's body.

But the Founder raised his hand and caught the blade, which immediately shattered in his hands. He then reared back and punched Arol in the face, smashing through Arol's visor and sending the Captain of the Squad flying through the air. Arol crashed into the wall over the entrance to the balcony and then fell—with a sickening *crunch*—onto the ground. He did not move again.

"Arol! Faya! Kagyan! Gahan! Haran!" Kara cried out. She pushed herself up, but the impact had rattled every bone in her body, making even the simplest movements difficult. "No!"

Despite the pain, Kara managed to struggle to her feet. She picked up her sword, which she had dropped upon falling to the ground, and turned to face the Founder again. The Founder's right hand, the one with which he had punched in Arol's face, was bloody, bits of Arol's visor gleaming in the dim glow of the Rock. The sight only served to enrage her.

The Founder turned his attention to her. There was no mistaking it: Kara saw Vyll and Carem's eyes looking back at her. Yet at the same time, it was like they weren't looking at her at all. It was like some distorted version of both was looking at her, trying and failing to resemble both.

"You survived," said the Founder, "because I wanted you to."

"Why?" said Kara, trying to ignore the blood running down the side of her face. She struggled to raise her sword, which seemed heavier to her now than it did before. "Is it because there's still something left of Vyll and Carem in there?"

The Founder simply stared at her. "Vyll and Carem no longer exist. I spared you because I did not want to turn this into a complete massacre. I believe you may be willing to help me in bringing peace to the war, by uniting the species into one, just as the Rock intended."

"Why would I ever do that?" said Kara. She gestured at the corpses all around her. "You killed my teammates, and now you expect me to be your friend? You must be totally deluded if you think that makes any sense."

The Founder stepped forward, but he did not seem like he was going to harm Kara. "But Kara, aren't you glad that Vyll and Carem's deaths did not go to waste? While they may no longer exist as individuals, they are now part of a greater whole that even you can be a part of, if you want."

"I *don't* want to be part of it, though," said Kara. "Why do you think I would? I only want my best friend and my brother back, not some hodgepodge of a freak like you."

"But they *cannot* come back," said the Founder. He put one hand on his chest. "They are gone. I have stated that several times already. They will never return. Only I exist. Besides, I know how much you hated Vyll, so why would you want him back? Just to kill him yourself?"

There was a deep sense of betrayal and anger in the Founder's voice. He must have been accessing Vyll's memories or feelings. Maybe the Founder was only expressing how Vyll had felt after Kara started to hate him ... or maybe it was a trick to make Kara agree to his insane plan. The latter option seemed far more likely to her.

"Because I don't think Vyll deserved the fate he got," said Kara. "Or Carem, for that matter. You not only look like a monster, but act like one as well by killing my teammates in cold blood."

"I killed them only out of self-defense," said the Founder. "And I find it funny how you claim I am a monster when you are wearing the skin of a dead Protector. I can think of little that is more monstrous than wearing the skin of your dead enemies as armor, personally."

Those feelings of revulsion from before, which had made Kara want to take off her armor, returned in full force. She ignored them, however, because she could not afford to be distracted at this point. The Founder was a dangerous being, so she could not allow him to distract her.

"So what?" said Kara. "Because of you, my brother and best friend no longer exist. They died because of you. It's all your fault."

"My fault?" said the Founder. There was hurt in his voice, before it was replaced by anger. "Just like your deceased teammates, you do not understand. There is no death to be found in this unity; only new and superior life. You would understand that if you would only listen."

Kara shook her head. "The only thing I understand is that you are delusional. I will never support you, no matter what you offer me."

"Then how do you intend to save the world, Kara?" said the Founder. He pointed at the Rock behind him, its cracked surface as ugly as a corpse. "Look. Even you can tell, with your limited human eyes, that the Rock is dying. His death will result in the deaths of countless billions of individuals. Is that what you want, Kara? The deaths of billions on your hands? Will you wash your hands with the blood of humans and Protectors alike?"

Kara wanted to say, like Arol had, that the Founder was lying, but she could not. Deep down, she understood that the Founder was telling the truth: The Rock was indeed dying, and when it finally did, untold catastrophe would engulf the whole world. How she knew that, even she couldn't explain, but maybe it was her old connection to Vyll that helped her to understand this truth.

So Kara said, "I don't know. Maybe it's impossible to save the world. Maybe we just have to wait for the Rock to die and then try to survive afterward."

"Try to survive?" said the Founder. He brought his fist up to his chest, a wild look in his eyes. "No! I will save the world. I will. And when I do, everyone will acknowledge it and follow me on the path to a higher plane of existence, one where war and conflict and separation do not exist!"

"How can you guarantee *any* of that, Founder?" said Kara. "You can't. No one can. You're babbling like a lunatic."

The Founder stomped his foot on the ground so hard that the floor cracked under his feet. "No! You have not seen what I have seen. The Rock showed me a world where nothing is impossible, where the highest and purest ideals can become reality, where no one—*no one*—is ever separate from another."

"It sounds to me like the Rock is just as delusional as you are, then," said Kara. She wiped some of the blood off the side of her face, because it was starting to distract her. "If that world is full of people like you, there will still be problems, maybe even worse than the problems we have now."

"No, there will not," said the Founder. He held out a hand toward her and she saw pleading mixed with insanity in his eyes. "Please come with me, Kara. Despite what I said before, there is still a little bit of the Vyll who you loved left in me. Let me prove it to you."

The Founder plunged his hand into the pockets of his robes and pulled out a folded, ragged-looking piece of paper that Kara recognized even before he unfolded it and held it out before her.

It was the drawing that Kara had made for Vyll ten years ago. It was old and faded, but Kara had no trouble recognizing her old art, if you could call it that. Despite its age, it wasn't even torn, though she spotted the little bit of green blood from that giant lizard creature that had attacked her on the day she had given Vyll

95

that drawing on its surface.

"See?" said the Founder, holding out the drawing for her to see. "See? Vyll kept it all these years, and then I received it when he and Carem became one. I kept it because it is a symbol of the world I hope to build, the one where we can all be together forever in peace and love. Why can't you see that world as well?"

Tears started to stream from Kara's eyes, mixing with the blood leaking from the side of her head. "It's been years since I last saw that drawing. I thought Vyll had lost it or thrown it away at some point."

"But he never," said the Founder. "And I never will, either. Now, is this proof enough that I am, in some ways, still Vyll? Don't you want to be with Vyll, just like this drawing shows? And Carem, as well, parts of whom also still exist within me? We can still make this drawing a reality, if you would only give up your foolish desire for revenge and stand by me."

Old memories of the day Kara had given that drawing to Vyll flowed into her mind. She remembered how nervous she had been about giving Vyll that drawing, how happy she had been when he declared that he liked it, even recalled how hot it had been that day. She had not thought about that drawing in a long time, but her memories of the day she had given it to Vyll were as clear as if it had happened yesterday.

He held onto that drawing even after I rejected him, Kara thought. *Even after I told him I wanted nothing more to do with him. He treasured it even after I stopped treasuring him.*

Kara wanted to cry, because she now realized how foolish she had been earlier, blaming Vyll for Carem's death. She had thought he had gone over the edge, that he was irredeemable, but now, she knew that Vyll had been the same Vyll that she had always known and loved. And she had been a fool for treating him with such contempt.

"Yes," said the Founder. "Yes, I can tell you are starting to rethink your earlier foolishness. You are starting to see the truth of my words. All you need to do is walk over to me and—"

"No."

The Founder froze. "What?"

"No," said Kara. She wiped the tears out of her eyes to clear her vision, allowing her to see just how shocked the Founder looked. "I will not join you."

"But why not?" said the Founder. He pointed at the drawing again. "Don't you want this image to become a reality? Don't you want us to be together again?"

"Not in your sense of being together," said Kara. "You keep talking about losing our individuality, about how we must all be together as one, but that's not what I meant all those years ago, when I first gave Vyll that drawing. I meant that we could be individuals, yet still enjoy each other's presence and be together as friends. That is what I meant and that is what I believe. Not your twisted view of 'unity.' Besides, despite having that drawing, you *aren't* Vyll or Carem, and you never will be."

The Founder stared at her with a lack of comprehension in his eyes. He seemed at a complete loss for words at what Kara had said, as if he had not anticipated this reaction of hers.

But then the Founder scowled and said, "Very well, then. If you will not stand by me, then I will be forced to—"

Crack.

That lone sound echoed through the whole cavern, causing the

Founder and Kara to look at the Rock. And unless Kara's eyes were deceiving her, there was now a massive crack—larger than the rest—running down the very center of the Rock. Its light had dimmed darker than ever and was rapidly fading even as Kara watched.

"No," said the Founder, his voice a whisper of despair. "I am too late."

The next moment, the Rock split cleanly in half, and a massive gust of wind exploded from within. The gust struck the Founder first, knocking him off his feet and causing him to let go of the drawing, which swirled through the air toward Kara.

In the seconds before the gust hit her, Kara snatched the drawing out of the air. She turned to run, but as soon as the gust hit her, she went flying through the air uncontrollably. She slammed into the ground again, the impact knocking her breath out of her lungs. She clung to the drawing as tightly as she could, not loosening her grip on it even slightly.

The gust of wind soon ended, but Kara felt the world shifting under her body. It was like feeling the last final spasms of a dying animal, which made Kara feel awful.

And before she even realized it, a massive, blinding white light swallowed her entire vision and she soon lost consciousness entirely.

Chapter VII

Kara awoke with a start, her heart beaing wildly. "Vyll! Carem!"

She blinked several times, however, before realizing that neither Vyll nor Carem were anywhere near her. Even worse, she knew they never would be again.

She felt her head. Her helmet was missing; however, the wound she had received back in the Rock's chamber seemed to have healed, because it was not bleeding anymore. Still, her head throbbed and her throat was dry. She needed water, but she did not know where to find any.

Sitting up, Kara looked around at her surroundings. She had expected to still be in the Rock's chamber, where she was surrounded by the corpses of her teammates, but to her surprise, she was not in that chamber at all. She wasn't even underground.

All around her, for as far the eye could see, rolled green fields. One sun shone above; yes, that was correct, just one sun, not the two suns that she had grown up under in Fariah. It made the field much cooler than it should have been, but Kara was still covered in sweat.

Kara rose to her feet, despite a stabbing pain in her hips that made her want to sit down. She still wore her Squad team armor and spotted the helmet lying only a couple of feet away from her, but Kara was too disoriented by this new environment to even think about putting it back on.

Kara looked around the area. She saw mountains in the distance; large, snow-capped mountains, by the look of things. Yet they did not look like the Arctic Mountains of Fariah, but a completely different range, one she did not recognize at all.

That still did not answer *where* she was, though. The last thing she remembered was a bright white light enveloping her, but that was a useless memory.

Then Kara heard some paper fluttering in the wind and looked down at her feet. The drawing—with her, Vyll, and Carem on it— lay at her feet, but she did not hesitate to snatch it up and hold it close to her armored chest. She stared at it for a moment before folding it up and depositing it in the chest compartment of her own armor. It was the only familiar thing in this world, so she intended to keep it safe with her for as long as she could.

How did the drawing even survive that explosion? Kara thought. *It should have been destroyed. I should have been destroyed. Why wasn't it? Why wasn't I?*

Kara suddenly felt a great pain in her back. It felt like there was something growing from her back that was trying to break free. It was so horrible that she not only tossed off her chest armor, but her blue shirt underneath as well, because even that held the thing on her chest that demanded freedom. Her shirt fell onto the soft grass on top of her heavy chest plate.

As soon as she removed her top, Kara heard a loud *fwhoop* sound and looked over her shoulder. She was shocked by what she saw.

Extending from her back—as white as snow—were massive

wings, wings she had never seen before in her life. She tried to turn around to look at them better, but that was before she realized that they were indeed attached to her back. They didn't feel particularly heavy, but just the sight of them was enough to make Kara question her own sanity.

What ... where did these come from? Kara thought, reaching back to touch one of her wings, which felt as soft as a pillow under her touch. *Is this the Rock's work? But why did I gain wings?*

Deciding to solve this mystery later, Kara looked around, wondering if there was anyone else nearby. Kara saw no other people in any direction. She didn't even see any birds in the sky. She felt like the last being in the world.

I don't even see Vyll or Carem or the Founder or whoever he is, Kara thought, shivering slightly at the cold breeze that blew over her shirtless body, causing her to cover her body with her wings to keep it warm. *Did he ... die? But if so, why didn't I die, too?*

This didn't make any sense. The Founder had claimed that if the Rock died (which had happened), then all of Fariah would die. Yet Kara was clearly not dead. And this world ... it didn't look like Fariah, not exactly, but it certainly wasn't the dead wasteland she had envisioned when the Founder had told her that apocalypse would happen when the Rock died.

Kara looked up at the sky again. *Why is there only one sun? What happened to the other? And are there any other survivors? If so, where are they?*

Her stomach growled with hunger, making Kara decide to worry about the nature of this world later. For now, she would start looking for other people. Maybe someone else would be able to explain to her what happened; at the very least, another survivor might have food, and she really needed to eat because it felt like she hadn't eaten in years.

The Founder is probably dead, Kara thought as she picked up her chest plate and shirt, even though she could no longer wear either due to her new wings. *He took the brunt of the explosion, I bet, because he was right there in front of the Rock when it exploded. I'd be shocked if he didn't.*

So Kara, her shirt slung over her shoulder and her chest plate under her arm, walked toward the mountains in the distance. She thought she saw a forest at the base of the mountains, which might be where other survivors congregated. At the very least, there would be animals there, animals she could hunt and eat, as well as shelter for when the weather turned bad later, though she knew nothing about this new world's weather or wildlife and therefore wasn't entirely sure what to expect.

Still, Kara could not help but wonder about the Founder's fate. Part of her would be thrilled if he died; another part of her, however, caused her eyes to water at the thought. She wiped the tears out of her eyes with her wings, but that did little to comfort her mourning heart.

The Founder stood on top of a tall cliff that jutted out over a long drop. In every direction he looked, he saw nothing but endless sand, canyons cut into the earth, and rocks and boulders that covered the landscape like a bunch of thrown dice. He saw no people; no humans, no Protectors, no elves or dwarves or Jikorians or any other species. Nothing but lifeless waste wherever his eyes traveled.

In the sky above was a single sun, when there should have been two. This sun beat down hotly on him, but the Founder did not remove his robes or move from his perch. He simply stood there, looking at the desolate world around him, searching for Kara, even though he knew she wasn't here, or anywhere else on this world, for that matter, because the Founder's connection to the Rock had revealed to him that Fariah had split into two. Somewhere out there, beyond the sky, was this world's twin, but he did not know how to reach it right now, if it was even possible to reach it at all. The two worlds might have been separated forever, thus preventing them from ever reuniting. It was a sobering thought.

What is my purpose now? the Founder thought. He wiped the sweat off the human side of his face. *The Rock is dead, my people are also dead, and Fariah is now two. Am I destined to live on this dead world for eternity, forever wandering its empty wastes, waiting for the day when my human and Protector halves break down, leaving my corpse to decompose under this harsh sun?*

But it was then that the Founder felt movement under his feet. Bending over, he pressed the tips of the fingers on his right hand over the harsh, hot sand. He sensed something underneath him, but he did not believe it at first. He thought his senses were playing tricks on him, but when he felt that same pulse again, he knew that his senses were working just fine.

Skyras energy, the Founder thought. A smile appeared on his lips. *The life force of the Rock. It is still here. But what does—*

That was when he felt something else. All over the world, he felt a pain and fear in the earth that he had not sensed on Fariah. It

103

was the combined pain and fear of the peoples of this new world, as well as the pain and fear of the world itself. They were crying out for reprieve from the Gods, but the Founder knew that the Gods would not—perhaps could not—hear their cries.

They will die unless someone corrects this terrible condition as quickly as possible, the Founder thought. *And I imagine that this world's twin is in pain as well. Someone needs to heal the worlds. But who?*

The Founder then stood up. A thought was brewing in his mind, one he had not considered before. It seemed like an impossible thought, but the more he considered it, the more logical and even possible it seemed.

I know now my true purpose, the Founder thought. He looked up at the single sun in the sky again. *I must heal the worlds. This is my Mission. I must find the separate halves of the Rock and reunite them. This is why the Rock chose me; this is my purpose.*

At this point, the Founder no longer cared if Kara was alive or dead. His mind full of his purpose, the Founder turned and walked down the back of the cliff to the bottom. He did not know for sure what he needed to do next; however, he was confident that the Rock—despite being dead—would reveal that to him in due time.

PART TWO:
THE PRESENT

Chapter Eight

Ten thousand years later ...

'Twas awakened by the tremors 'neath mine body, causing me to sit up, despite the searing pain in mine back. Actually, I now wondered exactly how I had slept at all; though the pain was just barely tolerable, it still hurt and I still found it hard to think about much else aside from that pain.

I saw nothing because of the immense darkness which reigned all around. It seemed like I had been thrown into a deep, dark pit, from which I could not escape. It even smelled like a pit; bloody and slimy, along with a staleness that told me that this place had not been exposed to clean air for years.

And then there were the tremors again. They were not quite as frequent as I supposed; however, I still felt them. They came at a regular pace, like the heartbeat of a god, but I feared that they would cause the ceiling to fall in on me. That did seem perhaps like an unfounded fear, for the tremors were not bad; however, I still gripped the edge of the cot that I lay upon every time I felt the tremor.

Still, I did not intend to spend the rest of mine life down here. I needed to find out where I was and how I had gotten here. I recalled being stabbed in the back—far more literally than I would have liked—by my sister, Kiriah, shortly after I had attempted to kill the villainous Founder. I had lost consciousness after that, but how long had it been since I lost consciousness? Where was I? How close were the Founder and my sister to completing the Mission?

Mine throat was sore and scratchy, while I could feel a stubble starting to grow out of my chin due to the fact that I had not shaved in some days. My clothes felt sweaty and dirty, whilst my feet were shoe-less, much to my frustration. When I rested my feet on the floor, it felt cold, hard, and grimy; nonetheless, I stood up. 'Twas hard, however, because the pain in my back—right in the spot where my sister had stabbed me—was almost overwhelming, but I did not allow it to control me, for I needed to find out where I was and how to escape, if possible.

The tremors that shook the floor did make my progress across the room more difficult than it ought to have been. Still, I did make my way across the floor, until I bumped into what felt like cold, metal bars, which told me that I was in the dungeons 'neath Reunification's Xeeonite headquarters. I wrapped both of mine hands around the bars and pulled and pushed, but they were built as firmly into the ground as a mountain; thus, I made no progress whatsoever.

Then a familiar voice in the darkness called out, "Apakerec? Are you awake?"

"Resita?" I said. Mine voice sounded awful due to my scratchy throat, but 'twould have to ignore it for now until I could get some water to moisten it. "Ye are still there?"

"Yep," said Resita. "I'm still here. Managed to survive getting tortured by Assassin."

"How long have I been out?" I asked. "Where is the Founder? Kiriah? And Sura?"

"Can't answer any of those questions, sorry," said Resita. "I've been down here for so long I don't even know what day it is. All I know is that some of Reunification's agents dragged you down here and put you in that cell a while ago. I have no idea where they are now or what they are doing currently."

"What of the tremors?"

"Just started pretty recently," said Resita. "But the Dead Lands are known for their tremors and earthquakes, so I'm not that worried about them."

"These seem far too steady to be natural," I said. "I think that they were created by the Founder. He must be closer than ever to completing the Mission now. They were making great progress on digging out the Unification Stone last I saw; if they were working as hard as they were before, then 'twould not surprise me if they had fully unearthed it by now."

"Unification Stone?" said Resita. "What's that?"

"'Tis what Reunification has been in search of for centuries," I said. "There is one on Dela as well, in the Winterlands, I believe. They are attempting to use the Stones to reunite Xeeo and Dela."

"So *that's* how they intend to do it," said Resita. "How big are they?"

"Enormous, based on what I saw of the one here on Xeeo," I said. "But it matters not how big they are. What matters is that Reunification cannot be allowed to reunite them, for if they do, billions will die."

"I already know that," said Resita. "But I don't see how we can stop them. We're both trapped down here in these cells. I barely have even enough strength in my legs to stand, much less break through these bars."

"Quickly, we must search our cells for anything we can use to escape," I said. The pain in my back shot up out of nowhere, making me grab at my back before the pain subsided like the waves of the ocean. "I recollect how you hacked the speaker system. Can ye do something similar to that again, except possibly hacking the rest of the headquarters's systems to free us?"

"These cells aren't controlled electronically," said Resita. "And even if they were, Assassin took away anything on me I could possibly use to hack into anything. He even took away my food bowl; I have to lick my dinner off the floor now." He said that while sounding quite disgusted about it.

I cursed, but then said, "It does not matter. With the aid of the Old Gods, we will escape and stop the Founder's vile plans for the two worlds. This, I swear on the holy name of the Divine Books."

"Good luck with that," said Resita. "I am pretty sure that the only way we could get out of here is if one of Reunification's agents came and freed us. That's not very likely to happen, though, considering how they're the whole reason we are even down here to begin with."

"Then I shall search mine cell for anything I can use to escape," I said. "I shall look for spoons, forks, knives, loose stones in the floor that might reveal a secret exit, anything … there must be some way out of here."

With that, I began to feel along the floor and walls for any tools I could use. The floor and walls were grimy and dirty, which felt awful, but something in my instincts told me I had dealt with much worse—and much dirtier—than this before. Unfortunately, when I tried to remember when that 'twas, the back of my head ached again, which told me it was yet another memory that the Founder had erased from mine mind.

But mine cell was not very large, and thus in only a few minutes, I had checked the entire thing. I had even looked under mine cot, but there was nothing under there, either. Of course, I should not have been surprised, because it would have been sheer idiocy for the members of Reunification to leave me with any tools I could use to escape.

In frustration, I returned to mine cot and sat there. It creaked under my weight, but held, which 'twas good, because if it had broken and dropped me on the floor, that would have only added to my anger.

"Couldn't find anything?" came Resita's voice from out of the darkness.

"Yea," I said, not bothering to hide the frustration in mine voice. "My former allies were quite thorough in making certain that I had no tools with which to escape this prison cell. The curs."

"I expected as much," said Resita with a sigh. "They really don't want us to escape."

"Let us wait, then, until the jailer comes down with the key," I said. "Then we can jump him and use the key to escape."

"Not likely to happen," said Resita. "I overheard the Reunification agents who brought you here saying that they were going to block off the exit. So I doubt they'll be coming back down here soon, if ever."

"I call a thousand curses from the Old Gods down upon these

villains," I said. "But why would they block off the exit? 'Tis makes no sense to me."

"Maybe they just want to make sure we don't escape," said Resita. "After all, if they complete their plan, I sincerely doubt that either of us will survive it. They probably hope that the reunification of the worlds will kill us."

"Murderers and deceivers, that is all they are," I said, slamming my fist down upon mine knee. "Fools, the whole lot of them are." Then I paused. "But why would they spare me? I recollect being stabbed in the back—" here I said not a word of my sister's betrayal, which I didst not think was what Resita needed to know at the moment, "—but my wound has clearly been healed."

"One of the agents who dragged you down here was wondering the same thing," said Resita. "The other agent claimed that your sister had your wound healed so you wouldn't bleed to death down here. Guess your sister must have thought that would be too cruel or something."

I considered that. The old Kiriah would have done that, because the old Kiriah was a kind and gentle woman and sister who never harmed others. Not like the new Kiriah, who cared only for obeying the dictates of a madman whose goals are in direct contradiction to all that which is good and noble and holy. Perhaps there was still some of the old Kiriah left in the new Kiriah.

Whatever the case may be, I said, "Regardless, we must find a way to escape and stop Reunification. We must."

"Well, it's not like there's much we can do to stop them," said Resita. I could just imagine him shrugging, even though I could not see him in the darkness. "Might as well sit back and wait for whatever happens to happen. It's about all we can do now."

I folded mine arms across my chest. "Nay, brother Resita. I shall not sit back and let them win. I shall figure out a way to get us both out of here, one way or another."

"All right," said Resita. "But don't expect me to help. I've pretty much given up on escape. I just hope that our deaths aren't too painful, at least."

After that, Resita went silent. I did not tell him to help, because I could tell that he was indeed resigned to our fate. 'Twas a cowardly way to behave in our current situation, but I knew better than to waste mine time convincing a coward to become a hero, so I instead spent mine time more productively on figuring out an escape plan.

Unfortunately, my knowledge of the dungeons 'twas quite limited, for as an agent of Reunification I had never journeyed down here much and thus knew little about them. Breaking down the bars that separated us from freedom did seem a necessity to me, but without a weapon or magic to accomplish that task with, I felt quite powerless.

I prayed to the Old Gods for guidance. I asked them to give me clarity of mind so I could think of a way to get us both out of here alive. Again, I knew not whether they heard my prayers, but I asked for their guidance nonetheless, for there was nothing else I could do here.

Verily, however, I did not actually believe that the Old Gods would listen to my prayers, even if they could hear them. I had already sinned against them by allying with Reunification, a wicked organization that idolized its own leader. I wondered if I had yet strayed beyond the forgiving and safe light of the Old Gods or not.

The only one who would know for certain would be Sura. But of course, Sura was dead, killed by the Founder. I did not even get to see mine older brother's body. I wondered what Reunification was doing with it; though to be honest, I had a feeling that they would simply feed it to the Lizard-men. 'Twas the sort of vile thing that villains like them would do to a wise and righteous man like mine brother.

And it would be Kiriah who would feed his body to them. Mine blood boiled in righteous anger when I thought about my sister's betrayal. I had always known she was loyal to the Founder, but I had never expected her to go out of her way to harm me in order to save *his* life. That told me that she truly had been brainwashed so completely and utterly that she was not even the same Kiriah I had grown up with anymore. Nay; she was a vicious woman, as unpredictable and dangerous as a Delan ghost dragon, and to be trusted as such.

A part of me wished to take my sister and beat her just as she deserved. She was no family of mine anymore. She was nothing more than a mindless, sycophantic servant of the Founder. Were she to die right now, I would not even shed one tear of sadness for her passing.

But another part of me was horrified at the thoughts I was having. After all, I had spent six years searching for Kiriah, traveling from the Fertile Plains to the fire pits of Cargana and everywhere in betwixt, just to ensure she was still alive. Even if she was brainwashed, perhaps there was some way I could still save her from the Founder's evil influence.

Or was there? Kiriah never showed any doubts about the Founder's plans. She treated him as a god, perhaps even greater than the Old Gods. She would never treat me even half as kindly or gently as she did in the olden days. If the Founder told her to come down here and slit mine throat and leave my corpse to rot, I am certain that she would do it without question.

'Twas a sobering thought indeed, knowing how far my sister had fallen. She did not even seem angry about Sura's death. Nay, she likely continued to think that Sura deserved it for his refusal to join Reunification. That she healed me before I was tossed into this dungeon did not endear me to her; nay, for it had been she who had harmed me to the point where I needed that aid in the first place.

But Kiriah was nothing in comparison to the Founder himself. What a vile, wicked man he was. How did I ever think him a noble or kind soul? He was the farthest thing. He was a monster, one who did not listen to reason and who could not tolerate dissent. He would kill every last person on both Dela and Xeeo if it meant achieving his wicked ends. I trusted him even less than I trusted Kiriah.

Even the Red Ring Smugglers were not as bad as this man. Yet I did not know how to defeat him; not only did he have his legions of Lizard-men and his loyal Reunification agents to protect him, but he himself wielded a great power that no one could match. Likely he'd kill me himself if I got in his way again, for I knew now that the Founder had gone over to the side of darkness and insanity and no longer tolerated any obstacles, no matter how minor, between him and the completion of his Mission.

But again, I returned to the simple fact that I could not escape from mine cell. It mattered not whether I hated the Founder and Kiriah or not; what mattered was that I was still stuck in here, and would be forever (or until the Founder's wicked plans came to fruition) unless a miracle happened.

I had no time for miracles, however, so I stood up and began feeling the bars of my cell again, searching for any sign of weakness that I could take advantage of. The bars felt as solid as ever under my grasp, but I knew better than to give up. To give up now would be to allow the Founder and Kiriah to win, and I could not allow that.

However, I found no weaknesses in the bars at all. They were too well-made. I had no idea who might have built them, but whoever did had certainly done a good job on them. Far too good a job, in mine opinion, though that thought did nothing to help me escape.

Scowling, I kicked the bars, but succeeded only in hurting my large toe. Cursing, I grabbed my toe and sat back down on my cot, not caring if Resita could hear my curses. Then again, I could not hear him at all; he was probably sleeping, which made sense, seeing as he had already given up. That did not endear me to him much.

When the pain in my toe subsided, I placed my foot back on the floor and rested my chin in my hands. This was it, then. There was nothing I could do to escape. Perhaps I should have taken a leaf from Resita's book and given up. 'Twould have been just as effective as my current efforts, and far less tiring. It may have even been my destiny; the Old Gods had not tried to intervene, so perhaps I was meant to die here after all.

Just as that thought passed through mine head, a large, cold hand wrapped around my abdomen. Before I could cry out in surprise, the hand jerked me back and I found myself hurtling through a darkness that was even blacker than the darkness of mine jail cell.

'Twas like falling down a cliff, but unlike a cliff, I could not see the bottom, and I could still feel the hand pulling me along. Nor could I scream; mine mouth was sealed shut, thus making this entire experience that much worse.

Then, without warning, I landed on hard-packed sand and groaned loudly from the impact. I lay on my back, panting, my whole body shaking uncontrollably. I could see the sky above, which was darker than it should have been due to the absence of clouds, though I barely noticed that.

A second later, a massive shadow hand emerged from the shadows of a nearby cliff and deposited Resita right next to me. Resita looked as awful as he did when I first saw him not long ago, although he was missing even more feathers than before. Still, he at least seemed to be in one piece and 'twas coughing, so I believed he would be better later after he was healed and rested.

"Apakerec?" Resita said, blinking when he saw me. "What … what happened? How did we get out here?"

"Why, I saved ye, of course," said a familiar voice above and behind us.

This did prompt me to sit up and look over mine shoulder. I could not believe what I saw, yet there was no mistaking those pure white robes or that familiar kind face for the robes and face of anyone but mine older brother, Sura.

"Sura?" I said, rising to my feet, although that 'twas a difficult

118

move because of how weak and tired I was. "I thought ye were dead!"

Sura smirked. "How little faith ye have in the gifts of the Old Gods, younger brother. Ye should have known better than to assume that the gifts of the Old Gods would not have saved me. 'Twas saved at the last minute by mine shadow hands; not a difficult feat by any means, though I had to retreat to avoid the Founder discovering that and coming down into that pit in order to finish the job."

"Sura?" said Resita, who still lay on the ground. He was looking up at him with wide eyes. "Your brother?"

"Indeed," said Sura, before I could respond. "But call me Kapalteek. 'Tis the name I use when introducing mine self to non-humans such as yourself, Resita."

I helped Resita to his feet. The Checrom smelled like grime and dirt, a disgusting stink, and he felt so fragile under my arm that I thought I would break him if I was not careful. Still I helped him up, for though I could not remember all of our adventures together, I still knew that he and I had been friends at one point and were allies now.

As I helped him up, I looked around at our surroundings. As far as I could tell, we were somewhere in the Dead Lands, for I saw tall cliffs, sand dunes, and rocks wherever I looked. I had sand in mine hair from where I had fallen, while Resita, too, looked sandier than normal. 'Twas not a big issue for me, however, because I inhaled the clean outdoors air deeply, for it was superior to the stale and dank air of the dungeons in every way possible.

Then I looked at Sura again and said, "Brother, how did you

know that Resita and I were in the dungeons? Why did ye save us?"

"The shadows told me," said Sura. He nodded at the shadows of a nearby cliff. "The shadows show me everything. They are the most reliable informant that I have worked with in a long time. A better informant cannot be found in all of the two worlds."

"Well, I am glad that ye survived, at least," I said, for I did not quite know what else to say to that. I looked around again. "But where is Reunification's Xeeonite base? I see it naught anywhere."

"We are far from it at the moment," said Sura. "I took us away from it because I did not want us to be seen by Reunification's agents or their vile Lizard-men. 'Tis too dangerous, especially when both of ye are so weak."

"But we must stop Reunification right away," I said as another tremor shook the earth 'neath our feet. "Do ye even know how close they are to completing the Mission? We must strike now, while we have the element of surprise on our side. With your powers, we can defeat them once and for all."

Sura shook his head. "Nay, brother. As much as I would like to aid in that way, the Founder has cast some strange magic on the Xeeonite base which keeps my shadows from entering the pit. I doubt he knows I have survived; however, he must be quite prudent if he cast such a spell to keep mine shadow hands out like that."

I cursed again. "But we can still get in there, can we not? Or are ye suggesting that we run and hide like scared little children?"

"I suggested nothing of the sort, brother," said Sura. "Nay, the Old Gods have revealed to me a different way to stop him."

I raised an eyebrow. "The Old Gods? They spoke to ye?"

"Of course," said Sura. He gestured at the sky. "Though the Old Gods are trapped in the moon, still they can communicate with their faithful lambs. As I have been faithful to them since my youngest years, 'tis only appropriate that they speak to me. Anyway, this plan of mine will require that we head back to Dela."

"Back to Dela?" I said. I brushed mine sticky hair off my forehead. "Brother, why should we go to Dela? The Founder is *here*, on Xeeo. So is Kiriah, for that matter."

"Yea, 'tis true," said Sura. "But the Old Gods have revealed to me that the Founder's vile scheme can only work if he has both Unification Stones in his grasp. If we can access the one on Dela and remove it from the hands of their agents over there, then we can stop Reunification's plans for good."

"That's actually a pretty brilliant plan," said Resita, who I had almost forgotten about during my conversation with mine brother, despite having to support him like this. "Reunification's Xeeonite base is well fortified due to the fact that the Founder spends most of his time there. Their Delanian base, on the other hand, is probably not as well protected due to the fact that he isn't there, though I doubt attacking it will be a walk in the park."

"A challenge awaits us either way," said Sura. "But I believe that returning to Dela would be the simpler challenge; yet even if it were not, we would have to go anyway, because the Old Gods demand it."

"Well, brother, if that is indeed what the Old Gods want, then I suppose I cannot argue against it," I said. "Yet how do we get from here to there? I see no Portals we could take. Can your shadow hands take us there, brother?"

"Nay, mine shadows hands cannot cross the divide that keeps the two worlds separate," said Sura. "But I have found us an unusual ally in this wasteland who claims that he can help us. The Old Gods led me to him, so I trust him, although I must admit that if the Old Gods had not led me to him, I would probably have avoided him entirely."

"An ally?" Resita and I exchanged puzzled looks. "What ally? There is no living thing out here in the Dead Lands that would ally with us."

"He ought to be here any minute now," said Sura, glancing at the sun in the sky. "He did say that he needed a little bit of time to get us a Portal, but never fear, for he said that he would retrieve one for us nonetheless."

"What is the name of this—" I asked, before being interrupted by the sound of heavy metal footsteps crunching against the sand from behind me, causing me and Resita to turn around to look at what was approaching us.

By the Old Gods' names! A titanic, metallic creature—with twin green optics and a head that was almost entirely sharp metal teeth that looked capable of cutting through human bone like paper—was approaching us. Its rust-covered, sand-encrusted skin did not gleam in the sun, which made it look like it shouldn't have been able to function at all.

It carried on its back a large, odd-looking Portal that I had never seen before. The Portal looked to have been thrown together hastily, for its colors were irregular and its parts uneven. It did not even look like it would function even if activated; then again, the massive robot walking toward us should not have been

DESINENCE

able to function, either, based on its appearance, so perhaps 'twas a lesson for me not to judge so hastily.

Resita grabbed me more tightly when he saw the machine. Despite his thin, weak hands, his talons cut into my robes, though I did not bleed and it did not hurt very much in comparison to being stabbed in the back by mine sister.

"What's this, what's this, what's this," said the robot, its toothy maw twisting upwards into a smile when it saw Resita and me. "I recognize you two. I tried to kill you a couple of weeks ago, didn't I?"

'Twas something eerily familiar about this machine, though I could not place it right away. The back of mine head ached when I heard its voice; and then, without warning, I suddenly remembered what this thing was and where I had seen it before. Mine memories of my last encounter with it flooded mine mind, allowing me to understand Resita's fear.

"Brother!" I said, looking over my shoulder at Sura, who did not seem at all alarmed by the appearance of this foul machine. "Is *this* the ally ye spoke of? The Destroyer?"

"Of course, brother," said Sura. "Why else would he be carrying a Portal on his back if he were not intending to aid us?"

"But that behemoth attempted to *kill* me the last time I saw it," I said. I looked at Resita, who continued to cling to me like a fearful bird. "Do ye remember that, Resita?"

Resita nodded, but he seemed too frightened to speak.

"Only because you insulted me," said the Destroyer. It rested the Portal on the sandy earth. "And I thought you were an agent of Reunification, but I see that I was wrong. I hope that the Old Gods will forgive me for my mistake."

123

I looked back at the Destroyer again. "Ye worship the Old Gods as well? What strange alternate reality have I stepped into? Or is this instead some kind of nightmare sent onto me by the Old Gods, perhaps as punishment for mine actions in Reunification?"

"'Tis neither, younger brother," said Sura with a laugh. "The Destroyer is indeed a servant of the Old Gods, same as I. The Old Gods led me to him and the two of us talked for quite some time. He is not nearly as fearsome as he appears."

"But he is the Destroyer!" I said. "He has killed innocent people and has caused so much death and destruction! How can a monster such as that ever be a servant of the Old Gods?"

"I am hurt by your cruel words," said the Destroyer. He patted the Portal. "But I understand why you say what you do. I did say I wanted to dissect you the last time I saw you, didn't I?"

"Yea, ye did," I said, though without a hint of friendliness in mine voice. "Ye wanted to learn the difference betwixt Delanian humans and Xeeonite humans, if I recall correctly."

"I still don't know the answer to that, biologically-speaking," said the Destroyer, nodding. "But I can see that I probably will not be learning that anytime soon."

Sura walked around me and Resita until he was in front of us, although I noticed that he kept his distance from the Destroyer. "I should probably explain the true nature of the Destroyer. It is quite an unusual story, but ye must know it if ye are going to trust him."

"Then explain," I said, keeping mine eyes on the Destroyer, though it didn't look as though it was going to attack. "But quickly; my tolerance for that foul creature grows weaker and weaker by the second."

124

"All right," said Sura. "As I understand, based on what both the Old Gods and the Destroyer have told me, the Destroyer was once a machine stolen by Reunification to keep people out of the Dead Lands. Its existence gave the Xeeonian government justification for banning travel to the Dead Lands, which was in fact nothing more than a ruse to prevent any non-agents from discovering Reunification's dig site."

The Destroyer nodded along as Sura spoke, as if confirming every word he said. Whilst I trusted Sura, I was not so certain that I trusted the Destroyer.

"That was how it lived most of its life for the past six years or so," said Sura. "Until, that is, the Old Gods granted him a soul. 'Twas only recently that they did so; for ye see, the Old Gods needed a servant to keep an eye on Reunification, so they used the Destroyer, which, due to its ties to that organization, was able to keep an eye on it by pretending to be nothing more than a mindless machine controlled by them."

"So the Old Gods placed a soul inside the Destroyer?" said Resita, the skepticism in his voice matching the skepticism in mine mind. "I gotta admit, I don't know much if anything about these Old Gods, but that sounds far-fetched to me."

"Anything is possible with the Old Gods," said Sura. "Anything at all. Anyway, as I said, 'twas only recently that they did so, for it was when the Old Gods realized how close Reunification was to achieving its vile Mission that they brought the two of us together. Hence why I consider the Destroyer an ally, despite its terrifying appearance and history."

"I must admit, brother, that, like Resita, I find your tale a difficult one to believe," I said. "Yet ye say that the Old Gods told you this, correct?"

"Correct," said Sura, nodding. "The Old Gods told me that I could trust the Destroyer, so I did. 'Tis not as simple as it seems, I admit, for the Destroyer is a terrifying-looking creature, especially once I learned of its unsavory past."

"But the Old Gods do not judge their servants based on their appearances or their past," said the Destroyer. "That is why they are so great."

I looked at the Destroyer, though not without some hesitation. "If Sura's story is true—and I cannot honestly doubt it, for he is a truthful man—then whose soul do ye have? If ye are not the Destroyer, then ye must be someone else."

The Destroyer smiled. "That is not something you need to know. What's important is that you three go to Dela and stop Reunification's plans here."

"Using this Portal?" I said, gesturing at the Portal that the Destroyer had brought. "Where did you get this Portal from?"

"I discovered it in the wastes of the Dead Lands," said the Destroyer, gesturing vaguely behind himself. "I believe it is an old Portal dumped out here by Reunification at some point in the past, probably after it broke down, though I managed to repair it easily enough. It has a twin in the Winterlands that leads to the organization's pit there, which is how I knew that it must have belonged to Reunification."

That did not surprise me much, because I had once seen Arn and Lauz take a broken Portal and throw it out into the wastes because the Founder had deemed it too costly to fix. Kiriah had even told me that 'twas a fairly regular thing, so I accepted the Destroyer's explanation without question.

"And what of ye?" I asked. "Will ye come with us?"

"No," said the Destroyer, shaking its head. "I will stay here in the Dead Lands. The Old Gods have another plan for me, so I cannot come with you, unfortunately."

"I'd love to go to Dela and help and all," said Resita, causing us to look at him, "but look at Apakerec and me: We're both very badly beaten-up, not to mention hungry and thirsty. I can barely even stand."

"'Tis a problem, I agree," said Sura. "Hence why I used my shadow hands to gather these things."

Sura gestured toward the shadows of the cliffs. Two shadow hands emerged from the darkness, their fingers closed tightly around some large objects that I could not immediately identify. 'Twas unnerving to watch the hands in action, even though I knew I could trust them; when they drew close to us, I stepped back instinctively.

The hands then deposited a couple of large crates on the earth. After they did that, the hands retreated into the shadows, where they vanished without another sound.

"There," said Sura, gesturing at the crates. "There ought to be enough food and water in there for both of ye. As well, brother, I managed to get you something ye will need if ye are going to fight Reunification on Dela."

Puzzled, I said, "Well, I shall go check their contents. Resita, ye can sit here."

Resita did not protest when I sat him on the earth, though I felt his eyes following me as I walked over to the crates. They were large, almost as large as I, and made of metal; however, their lids were not locked, a thing which I discovered as soon as I pushed open the lid of the first crate.

Inside the first crate—which smelled like disinfectant—was a dazzling variety of foodstuffs in brightly-colored packaging, though the packages themselves lacked any sort of identifying words or logos on them. There were also bottles of water, plus what appeared to be a medical kit of sorts.

I looked over mine shoulder at Sura, who was smiling. "Brother, where did you get all of this food and water and medicine? Does looks like ye went shopping in one of Xeeon's large markets."

"The crates are a gift from a fellow servant of the Old Gods," said Sura. He stroked his chin as if in thought. "His name is Mackar, if I am not mistaken. He is a Jikorian merchant who claimed to have met ye once and, after hearing of your plight, agreed to send me supplies that I could give to ye."

"Mackar?" I repeated. "Doth he run a business called Mackar's Miscellaneous Stand of Treasures and Antiques?"

"I believe that that is what he called his business, yea," said Sura, nodding. "Have ye visited it before?"

"Nay," I said, shaking mine head. "But he does sound like the same Mackar who met with me in Xeeon to discuss the photographs of Kiriah on mine first day in Xeeo. He did not mention that he was a servant of the Old Gods as well."

"How curious," said Sura. "Perhaps he did not think he needed to. In any event, he told me that he was giving me these supplies for the low price of six hundred delanes, though he told me he would let me pay later."

I frowned. "If Mackar is a fellow servant of the Old Gods, then why did he charge me for that information about Kiriah?"

"Well, he told me, in his words, that he 'had to make a living,'" said Sura. "He is yet another figure whose choice has made me question the wisdom of the Old Gods; but then, I have made a point of not questioning the sometimes odd decisions that the Old Gods make. Better to trust that they know what they are doing than to doubt their goodness."

"Indeed, brother," I said. "But how did ye get into contact with Mackar at all? He is all the way in Xeeon, is he not?"

"Through their own mysterious ways, the Old Gods brought us together," said Sura. "I spoke with him through a damaged machine I found in the wastes of the Dead Lands, which somehow, through the miraculous powers of the Old Gods, connected to his own machine. I was thus able to explain to him our predicament, which caused him to give us these supplies full of food and other necessities, which I took and kept safe with my shadow hands until I rescued you two."

"There's food in there?" said Resita. He was craning his neck trying to look in, though due to the fact he was sitting down, I doubted he saw much. "Why don't we eat now?"

"Certainly, but not yet," I said. "Whilst I appreciate the food, Sura, I still see that one thing is missing; namely, weapons. How are we supposed to fight Reunification in Dela without any weapons?"

"Open the second crate," said Sura, pointing at the crate to the right of the first one. "That should hopefully answer your question about equipment."

Again puzzled, I walked over to the second crate and flipped open its lid, which flipped open as easily as the lid of the first. Peering inside, I was amazed by what I saw.

129

'Twas a full suit of metalligick armor, the kind of armor that the Knights of Se-Dela wore. Not only that, but it appeared brand new, for it reflected the light of the sun above as beautifully as a clear lake in the summer. There was even a skyras-powered silver sword, the kind that was best used for killing vampires.

I looked over mine shoulder again at Sura. "Did Mackar also provide this suit of armor?"

"Yea," said Sura. "He did. How he got his hands on that suit, I know not. But I can confirm that that is indeed a genuine suit of metalligick armor; in fact, Mackar assured me that it will fit ye perfectly."

"Amazing," I said. "Perhaps I should rethink my opinion of Mackar, although I still think he is a greedy man, or Jikorian, as the case may be."

"Mackar also said there were weapons for the rest of us, if we should need them," said Sura. "Such as a—what did he call it? —'paralyzing repulser blaster,' or PRB for short. Quite an odd name for a weapon, though I have been told that it is typical equipment for the J bots that patrol Xeeon."

"Well, that solves that problem, I guess," said Resita. "What do we do now?"

I reached for the helmet of the suit of armor and looked at it. I could see mine own face—dirty and grimy—reflected in it, as well as the sun above.

"We eat, drink, and suit up for battle," I said, without looking at Resita or the others. "But we must do it quickly, for we have no idea how much time we have before Reunification completes the Mission."

Chapter Nine

The Xeeonite food was mostly rectangle-shaped, rather chewy bars that, according to Resita, were known as 'protein bars' on Xeeo. He said they were quite popular among the inhabitants of Xeeon, especially among those who were too busy to cook a real meal. He also said that the bars would provide us with enough energy to help us focus on our mission.

I was skeptical about the goodness of these bars before I had my first one. Oh! How wonderfully it tasted. How it crunched in mine mouth in a satisfying way. Perhaps it had been because I had not eaten in several hours, but even so, I found the bars as delicious as any food on Dela. They were a humble little food, but a delicious one nonetheless. 'Twas perhaps the only thing on Xeeo that I truly liked.

But we did not linger in our meal. Resita and I ate and drank quickly, and after we did that, I suited up in mine metalligick armor, though I did not do it very comfortably, for having abandoned the Knighthood, I was not certain that it was right of me to wear this armor.

Nonetheless, I managed to put it on quickly. As Mackar had promised, it fit me well, like mine own suit of armor. However, I had to adjust the straps of mine helmet slightly in order to prevent it from clinging to my head too tightly; even so, that was the only issue I faced in putting this armor on.

Once I did, I felt too hot. The armor covered me from head to toe, which was good for combat, but poor for the hot desert sun of the Dead Lands. I had to readjusted the dials and switches on mine armor to make the skyras energy within cool me down, though I still sweated even after the armor began to cool down.

Resita, too, armed himself. He took the PRB that Sura had mentioned, which he said he knew how to use because he had practiced using the gun prior to joining the Foundation. And despite his weakness, he did indeed hold it like an expert and showed no hesitation in using it.

After we were all armed and ready to go, the Destroyer activated the Portal. Although I was at first skeptical that it would work, all of my skepticism melted away when I saw the blue vortex appear within it, which looked as strong as the vortex of any other Portal connecting the two worlds.

"Just step into this Portal and you will emerge into the Winterlands," said the Destroyer, gesturing at the Portal's vortex. "It will be freezing cold, but your metalligick armor should protect you and keep you warm."

I did not appreciate the Destroyer treating us with such concern. That might have seemed an odd thing to think, but it was true. I still recalled how the Destroyer had tried to kill us not too long ago, so I kept expecting the machine to betray us when we least expected it.

Resita, on the other hand, said, "Hold on. How am I going to survive in the Winterlands without my feathers or a coat?"

"That is a valid concern, Resita," said Sura. He placed his fist under his chin before snapping his fingers. "I know. Ye can remain here with the Destroyer while Rii and I head to the Winterlands. The two of us ought to be more than enough to stop Reunification's operations there."

"Stay here?" said Resita. He sounded disappointed. "But I want to help. I thought I'd get to see some actions after being in that dungeon."

"Nay, Resita, I believe that my brother is right," I said. "Despite the meal we just had, ye are still quite weak. There is no way ye could survive in the Winterlands, much less fight against Reunification. Ye would be safer here, where ye can rest until ye get better."

Resita glanced at the Destroyer and gulped. "But staying here means staying with the Destroyer."

"The Destroyer is on our side," said Sura. "He will not harm ye."

Resita looked at the Destroyer again, but he did not seem much assured by mine brother's words. The Destroyer, on the other hand, merely smiled in response; 'twas perhaps its attempt to make itself appear kindly, but to me it looked more like the evil grin of a predator about to eat its prey.

"Fear not, Resita," I said, placing one hand on his thin shoulder. "Sura and I will return before ye know it. Reunification's Delanian agents shall not be able to stand before our united might."

"I hope so," said Resita. "Well, good bye, then. Just make sure to come back as soon as you can, all right?"

"Yea, we shall be back in an instant," I said, nodding.

Thus, Sura and I passed through the Portal, which felt somewhat like walking through a wall of water. Still, I was so used to the sensation by now that I barely registered it, for mine attention was instead on whatever lay on the other side, which would undoubtedly require mine full attention.

A second later I stepped out into the snowy wastes of the Winterlands and blinked rapidly to end the Portal sight effect that afflicted me. When it passed, I saw that the sky above was dark, mostly because of the thick and gray clouds that blanketed the sky. I had only ever been to the Winterlands once before; 'twas why I shivered greatly when a gust of icy wind blew through mine armor, forcing me to readjust the temperature on mine armor to a warmer temperature.

Sura stepped out next to me. Though he wore the pale priestly robes of the Old Gods, he barely seemed concerned with the gelid wind which tore at his robes like the claws of a wild beast. Instead, his eyes were on something in the distance, so I looked in the same direction as his eyes in order to see what he saw.

Down below us was a wide, deep, black pit identical to the one back on Xeeo. There were even cranes and other assorted construction equipment built around it, but I saw no workers at all. I did, however, spot what appeared to be an office building, hastily constructed atop what looked like a patch of blackened earth, as if an explosion had happened there recently. Not only that, but I also spotted the remains of a destroyed crane half-buried in the snow on the pit's perimeter, which made me wonder how that happened. Had someone else already been through and thwarted Reunification's plans here?

I looked over mine shoulder. The Portal behind us was closing rapidly, until soon it resembled nothing more than a large stone ring embedded in the earth. I did not see a control panel on it, which made me wonder if it would be possible to return to Xeeo using it.

"Fret not over the Portal, brother," said Sura, causing me to look at him in surprise. "As it is of the Old Gods, we will use it when we have need of it. Our current plan is still the same, which is to say that we must head down there and stop Reunification's agents here before they can succeed."

"But I see no agents of Reunification anywhere," I said, gesturing at the area. "'Tis appears to have been abandoned some time ago. Mayhaps it be a trap?"

"Possibly, though I see no way they could have known we were coming," said Sura. "In any case, we must go forward. For the Old Gods chose us to save our world from these wretched villains, and who are we to back down in fear? Nay, we must move on, as the Divine Books say."

Sura spoke far more confidently than I had ever heard him speak before. That convinced me that he had indeed spoken with the Old Gods and that they had indeed given him this mission; even so, I could not help but feel uneasy whenever I looked down at the abandoned pit. Where were the Reunification agents?

"But it would perhaps be wise for us not to head down there too quickly," said Sura. He placed a hand on his forehead. "For if this is indeed a trap, 'twould be foolish to run headlong into it. Let's see if my shadow hands can discover anything out of the ordinary down there."

Mine brother closed his eyes. I looked back down into the pit, the area as still as always. But I knew that if anyone could find out what was going on down here, then it would be Sura, who with his mystical powers could uncover any hidden traps or trickery.

But as Sura stood there, so still that he was like a statue, I began to notice his skin growing grayer and grayer. It was like he was aging rapidly; indeed, even his hair began to turn silver, and his knees shook. Black lines crawled up his neck, whilst his finger nails started to turn as dark as the shadows he commanded.

Alarmed, I grabbed Sura's shoulders and said, "Brother! Wake up, brother! What is happening to ye, brother?"

Much to mine relief, Sura's eyes opened and he staggered backward. He almost fell over onto his behind on the snow, but I caught his arm before he did and helped him stand. Still, I could see in his eyes a wild, fearful look, not helped by his heavy breathing.

"Brother, are ye in good health?" I asked.

Sura shook his head and wrenched his arm out of mine hand. His skin and hair and finger nails were returning to their normal colors, but he still seemed shaken and weakened by whatever had just happened to him.

"'Tis all right, brother," said Sura, rubbing the back of his head. "'Tis a side effect of overusing mine shadows. They can be quite draining if I am not careful, despite their usefulness."

"Then perhaps ye should use them less, brother," I said. "They literally appeared to be killing ye. That is why I intervened, for I did not want ye to die."

"I will be fine," said Sura. "But I am afraid I cannot say the same about the agents of Reunification that once inhabited this place."

"What do ye mean?" I asked. "Are they not still here, lying in wait to ambush us?"

"Nay," said Sura, shaking his head. "All of them are dead."

As Sura and I made our way down to the area around the pit, mine older brother explained what he saw, though he kept his eyes on the snow and rocks to keep himself from slipping.

"I saw corpses everywhere within the pit," said Sura. His voice was horrified, even though he was describing the fate of our hated enemies. "Dwarves, mostly, but I saw representatives of other species as well."

"Did ye see how they had died, brother?" I asked. "Did they kill themselves, perhaps?"

"Nay," said Sura, shaking his head. He pointed down at the pit itself. "The shadows did not show me all of the details, but I did see frozen blood on the ground and on their necks. Did look like they had been slaughtered by an enemy, but I am afraid I could not identify who that enemy might be."

"Is that not a good thing?" I asked, glancing at the pit briefly on our way down. "If there are no more living creatures down here, then that must mean that this place is undefended, which will make it easier for us to reach Dela's Unification Stone."

"So ye would think, but I am not so certain of that," said Sura. "I did not see any indication that the dwarves' killers were still present, but it seems unlikely that they simply left. It may well be that a worse enemy is hiding, one which could kill us even easier than Reunification could."

"Ye speak so glumly, brother," I said, slapping him on the back with mine armored hand. "Ye should rejoice. Our mission just became that much easier. After all, it was Reunification's agents who were our biggest obstacle to accomplishing this task. I dare say that the Old Gods themselves must have blessed us in this way."

"I would like to believe that, brother, I truly would, but I must admit that I am skeptical," Sura said. "I seem to recall a certain verse from the Divine Books, which said something about challenges that are too easy are often the most difficult."

"The Divine Books are full of grand wisdom and guidance, but in this case I must say that that verse is inapplicable," I said. I gestured toward the pit. "All we must do now is find a way down into the pit and—"

Mine words were interrupted by the screeching of a strange creature overhead. I looked up in time to see a large, winged creature swooping down toward us, its claws outward, its red eyes gleaming against the grayness of the dark sky.

I pushed Sura out of the way before the creature slammed into me. 'Twas like being struck by a rolling boulder, for it knocked me over and sent both of us tumbling down the hillside, the creature biting at my face and neck as I struggled to keep it away.

The creature kept biting at mine armor, but thankfully mine metalligick armor protected my skin from its teeth. Still, 'twas hard to fight back because we still rolled downhill at an alarming speed, going too fast for me to pull out mine sword and kill it.

We eventually bumped over a ridge and landed with a harsh *crunch* onto the snow and dirt. The impact rattled mine skull, but I did not have the luxury of lying here in pain, for the creature was still trying to kill me. I thus punched it in the jaw, causing it to loosen its hold on me, which gave me the opportunity to kick it off me.

The creature landed on the ground a couple of feet away from me, whilst I scrambled to stand up and draw my sword in time. Holding mine silver sword before me, I looked up just in time to see the creature hop back to its own feet and rush at me at a blinding speed.

But then a shadow hand burst from the pit and punched the creature so hard that it was sent flying all the way back up the mountain. I watched as the creature slammed into the snow we had rolled down, but then immediately get back on its feet and vanish into the shadows of a nearby boulder.

At the same time, Sura appeared right next to me. He was panting and sweating, and his shoes were covered in snow, but he managed to gather enough breath to say, "B-Brother, did you see that?"

"How could I not?" I said. "What was it?"

"I have heard legends of those beasts," said Sura, panting. "They are known as arctic vampires. They dwell in the Winterlands, attacking and killing anyone who gets too close to their territory."

"Arctic vampires?" I repeated. I looked in the direction where the creature had landed. "Are ye certain that that was what it was?"

"Yea," said Sura, nodding. "I have heard descriptions of those foul monsters, and that creature fit it to a tee. I dare say that we may have found the killer of the Reunification dwarves."

"But how could one arctic vampire kill so many people?" I asked. "I know that one arctic vampire is said to be equal in might to ten of the best Knights of Se-Dela, but I would think that one arctic vampire would not be strong enough to eliminate every last person here."

"And of that, traitor, you would be quite correct," said a voice above me that sounded vaguely familiar, though where I had heard it before, I knew not.

I looked up in time to see yet another arctic vampire flying down toward us. He landed hard on the earth before us, his landing sending up snow and dirt into the air. When he rose to his full height, he was at least a head taller than Sura or me, and twice as muscular as either of us. His wings were wide enough to wrap 'round us both like thick blankets, though they were not as welcoming as those.

He looked down at us with his green eyes, his tongue licking his crimson lips. "Well, well, if it isn't Apakerec, the brother of the Leader. And, if I am not mistaken, this human is the Leader's other brother. What was your name again?"

"Call me Kapalteek," said Sura, though he hardly sounded friendly about it. "Who are ye?"

The arctic vampire gestured at his massive chest. "I am Kalcan, one of the Elders of Reunification. But I am sure Apakerec knows that already."

I nodded. "Yea. Kiriah has told me about ye. However, I believe this is the first time I have met ye in person; and I must say, that ye stink of death and look like a corpse."

"What lazy insults you humans come up with," said Kalcan, shaking his head. "I'm a vampire. Of course I stink of death and look like a corpse. Vampires aren't exactly what the Xeeonites call 'beautiful men,' if you catch my drift."

"I see ye know about mine betrayal of Reunification," I said.

"Are ye going to try to kill me now?"

Kalcan wagged a finger. "No, no, no. I am not going to *try* to kill you. 'Try' implies I might fail. I *am* going to kill you. We arctic vampires can turn you Knights of Se-Dela into tin cans without even thinking about it."

"How odd," I said. I gestured at myself with mine sword. "For I recall quite well how Sir Alart and I killed the vile Kura, right here in the Winterlands in fact, by removing her head from her shoulders. 'Twas not very difficult to do, either."

"Kura was a weakling," said Kalcan. "Besides, she was on her own. If she had had some of her fellow arctic vampires at her side, she might have survived."

"In any case, I am surprised that ye are not surprised to find out that I escaped," I said. "Are ye not going to ask me how I did that?"

"Why should I?" asked Kalcan. "You'll be dead either way, won't you? Asking you how you escaped would be a waste of time. Nor am I going to bother to ask how your older brother here survived being killed by the Founder for the same reasons."

"Ye speak about killing us as if ye have a whole army on your side," said Sura, who did not so much as tremble at Kalcan's impressive size, despite being rather tiny in comparison to him. "But we know that every single Reunification agent here is dead. Ye are the sole survivor; therefore, your attempts to intimidate us by pretending ye have allies who could do us harm is pitiful at best."

Kalcan chuckled. "I am quite aware that my fellow Reunification agents are all dead, but you two idiots seem to fail to grasp *why* they are dead. Let me put it in words you can

141

understand: I killed them."

Sura and I stared at Kalcan in shock. Yet the arctic vampire did not seem to be joking; in fact, he looked quite serious, despite having chuckled about it not a second before.

"Ye ... killed them?" I said. "All of them? By yourself?"

"Not exactly by myself," said Kalcan, shaking his head. "I had some help from my friends."

At that moment, dark, winged shapes shot out from the pit one by one so rapidly 'twas like watching a machine gun spit out lasers. They soared through the sky above, circling us, before landing around us in a loose circle, with Kalcan having not moved even one inch from where he stood.

Each one of the dark, winged shapes was an arctic vampire. Some were as big as Kalcan, while others were smaller; some were male, others female; regardless of their differences, however, each one looked at Sura and me with murder and lust in their eyes, like they could not wait to begin to devour us.

The two of us drew closer together, even though that hardly made us any safer than if we were apart, and I said, "Kalcan, what is this? I thought the arctic vampires were not agents of Reunification."

"They technically aren't," said Kalcan. "They are working with me because I promised them more people to feed on if they agreed to work with me to protect the Unification Stone that we dug up. I gave them my former fellow agents to prove to them that I am serious about letting them feed on whatever they want."

The arctic vampires tightened their circle around us. I counted a dozen in all, possibly more, but it mattered not how many there were, because even just a handful of them would be strong enough to crush us. Their collective stink was harmful to mine nose.

"As you can see, we have quite a large group here," said Kalcan, gesturing at his fellow arctic vampires. "Most arctic vampires hate me, but there are a handful who were able to see how they would benefit from serving Reunification, so they naturally came when I called for them."

"Does the Founder know about this?" I asked. "Not that I particularly care for the Founder or his opinions anymore, but I would think he would be furious if he learned that ye sacrificed many of his agents to your fellow arctic vampires."

Kalcan snorted. "The Founder knows, but doesn't care. He doesn't care about any of us, particularly. All he cares about is reuniting the worlds; who cares if not everyone makes it, especially when we are as close to the completion of the Mission as we currently are? Besides, those workers already did their part. Why keep them around longer than necessary?"

"Ye are cold, Kalcan," I said. "But I should not be surprised. I had always heard that ye were a cruel taskmaster, and your own words have confirmed those rumors."

"My reputation is irrelevant," said Kalcan. "What matters now is that my fellow arctic vampires and I are going to tear you apart piece by piece. No one betrays Reunification and lives to tell the tale."

Kalcan gestured for the arctic vampires to advance on us. This they did with pleasure, growling and flashing their fangs at us as they approached.

Sura and I went back-to-back. I held up mine sword, while Sura simply said, "Quite the situation we have found ourselves in, eh, brother?"

"Indeed, brother," I said. "But are we going to let these vamps kill us?"

"Nay," said Sura. "Ready?"

"Always."

I reached for the dial on mine armor that adjusted the flow of skyras energy that went into mine sword. I turned it to the maximum amount of energy it could channel into mine blade, which caused it to glow with an awesome brightness that made even Kalcan step back in surprise.

"What?" said Kalcan, holding up his hands over his eyes, probably to protect his vision. "What is this?"

I answered not in a verbal way. Instead, I dashed forward at the vamps before me and swung my sword as quickly as I could. Mine blade cut off the head of the nearest vampire, causing its body to collapse to the ground.

Then I whirled around and slammed the flat of my blade into the face of the next vamp, searing its skin off and causing it to cry out in sheer pain from the blow. Another vamp came up behind me, but I whirled again and stabbed it in the chest, causing black blood to explode from its wound and make it collapse to the ground.

The other vamps stepped back in fear, whilst Kalcan said, "How is this possible? You should not be able to harm us!"

"This blade be coated with silver, ye monster," I said, nodding at my shining blade. "Combined with skyras energy which sharpens it beyond measure, it can cut through the hardest substances, including vampiric skin, and take away the lives of its victims in an instant."

144

The look of fear on the face of every arctic vampire did fill me with satisfaction. Then I heard arctic vampires screaming behind me and, glancing over mine shoulder, saw shadow hands picking up and throwing the arctic vampires foolish enough to attempt to cross mine brother's path. Sura himself simply remained standing in his current position, looking quite unafraid of anything at the moment.

"I don't understand how your brother is able to do that, but it doesn't matter," said Kalcan. He glared at the other arctic vampires. "What are you idiots waiting for? Go and attack. Just don't let him touch you with that blade unless you want to die."

But his fellow vamps were wise enough to ignore his command. They simply retreated further, staring at the corpses of their friends that lay on the snow, their black blood staining the white snow and brown earth underneath.

Kalcan rubbed his forehead and said, "Fine. I will do it myself. But once I eliminate this traitor and his brother, I will let the Founder know about your cowardice and ask him not to reward you with anything when the reunification process is complete."

So Kalcan flew at me at a startling speed, much faster than the other vamps had. I raised mine sword just in the nick of time, however, and slashed it at him when he got too close.

But then he swerved out of the way at the right moment, causing my blow to miss. My sword hit against the earth, harming nothing, whilst I looked to the side just in time to see Kalcan's fists coming at mine face.

I attempted to duck, but his other fist slammed me in the gut. The blow was enough to send me flying. I landed with another *crunch* on the snow and earth, but thought I must have broken something, for the lower half of mine back did ache terribly before I recalled that that was the spot where Kiriah had stabbed me in the back.

I cursed that wound, for I had thought it would not act up any longer, but I supposed it still needed time to heal. Time that I unfortunately did not have right now, for Kalcan was flying at me again, his green eyes alive with anger at mine refusal to die.

I rolled away at the last second, but Kalcan must have expected that, for he pulled up and soared up into the sky, rather than crash into the spot where I had lain. I struggled to my feet, and I do say struggled, for my back wound still ached and did distract me greatly.

Indeed, I had to gather all of my strength to ignore it, and even then, still 'twas a rather persistent wound. But I could not afford to be distracted by it, for to be distracted even for a moment in mine current situation was to guarantee mine death.

Looking up, I was astonished to find that Kalcan was nowhere to be seen. How could someone so huge have disappeared so quickly? Was he hiding behind one of the mountain peaks or perhaps in the gray clouds? Or maybe he was hiding within the shadows, which was said to be where vampires generally dwelt.

In any case, I looked around hurriedly, trying to spot him before he could get me, but I only saw his fellow vamps (who were still watching me with hesitation) and Sura, who was still having no trouble fighting off the vamps who were trying to kill him.

Then I heard Kalcan yell behind me, "Time to die, traitor!"

I looked over mine shoulder just in time to see Kalcan flying at me. 'Twas no time to dodge; instead, I held up mine armored arm in an attempt to absorb most of the impact.

When Kalcan slammed into me, I heard an eerie, spine-tingling *crack*ing sound, but I had little time to figure out what had caused that sound, for the impact of Kalcan's body slam sent me flying again.

Mine head spinning, I could not tell which way was up and which way was down as I flew through the air. Nor could I tell where this horrible throbbing pain was coming from, but I was so distracted by the blow that had sent me flying that I paid little attention to it.

But then I landed on something soft but solid, which jarred me, but not as badly as it would have if I had hit the ground. Shaking my head, I looked around me at what had done that, when I noticed five large, dark fingers around me. I also realized that I 'twas in the air still, for I could see Kalcan and the other vamps below looking up at me with murder in their eyes.

This same look downwards showed me also Sura, who had caught me with one of his shadow hands. I waved at him to show that I was all right before I noticed how gray his hair and skin were starting to look, as well as the black lines that crept upon his face, making his skin turn much darker as a result.

The giant shadow hand quickly but smoothly lowered to the ground next to Sura, where I jumped off. I ran up to my brother and, grabbing his shoulders, said, "Sura! Awake, mine brother! Evil is still afoot and if ye continue to sleep, they will slaughter us surely."

Much to my relief, Sura blinked several times and shook his head. As he did so, his hair and skin returned to their natural hues, while the black lines on his skin receded like the ocean tides.

That did make me feel better about him, at least until he collapsed, forcing me to catch him before he could fall to the ground. 'Twas thankfully still breathing, but his body felt so weak now that I almost feared breaking it in my arms.

"Forgive me, brother," said Sura, his voice weaker than normal. "I used up too much of mine energy too quickly. I am afraid that I will not be of much use to you now."

I was about to assure him that that 'twas fine, but then I heard movement around me and looked up. Kalcan and his vamps were advancing toward us again, but they no longer looked as fearful as they had previously. I held my glowing sword out before me, but even that did not seem to deter them.

I backed up, still supporting Sura with mine other arm, but then felt mine foot almost fall. A glance over mine shoulder showed me that I had backed up to the edge of the pit, which was still far too dark for me to see the bottom of, although if it were even half as deep as the pit back on Xeeo, 'twas likely deep enough to kill us if we should fall down it.

But I had to return mine attention to the more immediate issue; that is to say, Kalcan and his fellow vamps, who were now licking their lips in anticipation of the meal they believed they were going to get.

And worse, I had an ominous feeling that they would indeed feed well today.

Chapter Ten

I knew that there was no way I could defeat these creatures whilst defending Sura. I could simply lay Sura on the ground and fight without him, but that would leave my brother open to attack; besides, I discovered that the source of the pain from Kalcan's earlier attack in my left arm; that is, mine sword arm, which, while not broken, was badly injured. That did make holding mine sword with one hand far more difficult than it normally was.

But I could not fight whilst also holding Sura. 'Twas impossible; I required both arms in order to fight well, not to mention 'twould put mine brother in mortal danger for certain.

In any other circumstance, I would have simply fled in order to return another day. But there was nowhere to flee to; the vamps cut off all possible escape routes, even after Sura and I killed off a good lot of them, and the only thing that lay behind us was the deep pit, which we could not simply jump down unless we wished to die.

It seemed, then, that our situation was impossible. Sura was too tired from his shadow hands to even stand on his own and I had taken wounds that were far more serious than I first realized.

Meanwhile, the arctic vampires surrounding us on every side seemed to be in perfect shape, despite having waged battle against us for some time now already. Then again, I had heard that arctic vampires did not tire out nearly as easily as humans, which explained their continuing strength and durability in the face of opposition from both of us.

The cold, too, sapped mine strength. Having diverted most of mine armor's skyras energy into mine sword had caused the temperature of mine armor to go down considerably. In the heat of battle, I had not noticed it so much; however, now that I was standing still and panting and feeling every wound, I also felt the cold air of the Winterlands, especially when a freezing breeze blew through that made me shiver.

As always, I prayed to the Old Gods for aid. It was, after all, the only option that Sura and I had left. If the Old Gods did not listen to mine prayers, then we would most certainly be destined to die, but knowing that they had given us this mission in the first place, I expected them to aid us in some way.

'Twas at that moment, however, that I heard another loud screech somewhere behind us. Certain that it was more of those foul vamps about to kill us, I looked over mine shoulder and saw about a dozen more arctic vampires fly out of the shadows of the pit, led by what appeared to be a female vamp, but they flew too fast for me to make out their appearances in great detail.

This was the end, then. The vamps on both sides would tear Sura and me apart. Our mission would fail. The Old Gods would be displeased with us, and—

What was this? Praise be to the Old Gods! The new set of arctic vampires that had appeared out of the shadows of the pit flew directly over our heads and attacked their fellow vamps. In alarm, the Reunification vampires did not immediately fight back, although they soon recovered from their shock and started to tear at their enemies with the same kind of viciousness with which they would have killed Sura and me.

"Brother," said Sura, his voice difficult to hear over the sounds of tearing flesh and screeching vampires. "What is going on here? Why are the vampire fighting among each other?"

"I know not the answer to that question, brother," I said, staring at the fight before us. "A falling out among killers, perhaps?"

Kalcan was fighting three separate vampires at once, and barely holding his own, for they were nimble and hit him hard, despite lacking his bulk. Even better, it looked like the new vampires were driving the old ones away from the pit, which was slowly opening new avenues of escape for us wherever I looked.

Just as I was about to escape, one of the new arctic vampires landed in front of me. I immediately raised mine sword, ready to drive it through the skull of this vampire should it prove a threat.

But then the arctic vampire—which appeared to be female—raised her hands and said, "Hold. I am not your enemy."

"Ye are not?" I said, although I did not lower mine blade even slightly. "But are ye not an arctic vampire? I thought ye worked for Kalcan, like the rest of your foul friends."

"I don't work for that idiot," said the feminine vampire, shaking her head and raising her voice above the sounds of battle behind her. "Only a handful of us arctic vampires work for him. The rest of us want to tear him apart piece by piece."

"I do not understand," I said, still not lowering my guard

before her. "What do ye mean by that?"

"Kalcan is a traitor to his people," the female vampire snapped. She gestured at the area all around the pit. "He sold us out to the invaders who took our land and slaughtered us with their technology. We've been waiting for the perfect opportunity to get our revenge and this so happens to be it."

"I see," I said. "So are ye on our side, then?"

"We're on our own side," said the arctic vampire. "But you are clearly an enemy of Kalcan; and as I always say, the enemy of my enemy is my friend."

"Well, I thank ye for saving us," I said. "If ye had not appeared when ye did, my brother and I would surely have perished."

"Don't mention it," said the arctic vampire, waving off my thanks. "I was hoping you might be able to kill Kalcan for me, but after seeing that stupid robot fail to do it, I've learned that you shouldn't send a human or a robot to do a job for a vampire."

She turned to leave, but then an idea occurred to me and I said, "Wait, female vampire. Do not depart just yet."

The female vampire looked over her shoulder at me in annoyance. "What?"

"Can ye use your shadow powers to take my brother and me down into the depths of the pit?" I asked, gesturing at the pit with mine sword. "There is something down there that we need to find right away and we know of no other way to go down there quickly and in a timely manner."we are need

"Why should I help you?" said the female vampire. She gestured at the battle that had now moved quite a ways away from the pit, though it was still quite close. "I want to help my brothers and sisters slaughter Kalcan and his fellow traitors like cattle. Besides, I don't escort humans; typically, I prefer to eat them."

"But if ye help us, then ye will help us not only to stop Kalcan, but also defeat the invaders who slaughtered your people," I said. "For Sura and I know what they seek and if ye help us to find it, then we could put an end to their machinations once and for all. Then neither they nor anyone else will come here to terrorize ye or your people ever again."

The female vampire stroked her chin. She looked back to the battle with longing in her crimson eyes, but then looked back to us and said, "All right. If helping you will strike a blow against Kalcan and his allies, then I have no reason to refuse."

Before I could thank her for seeing the light, the female vampire grabbed mine arm and said, "Get ready. We're leaving now."

I had only a second to 'get ready' before she pulled me and Sura both over the side of the pit and into the shadows below.

Being pulled into the shadows was not exactly like falling. It felt more like the female vampire—whose grip was surprisingly strong despite her petite frame—was pulling us along through the deep ocean. I made certain, of course, to continue to hold onto Sura as tightly as ever, for I did not wish to lose him in the sea of darkness through which we swam.

But what alarmed me more than anything was the lack of air in this place. I had managed to grab a mouthful of air prior to our descent into the shadows, but even then, mine lungs burned and mine head pounded. 'Twas impossible to tell how Sura was feeling, but considering how weak he was, I doubted he was doing much better.

This state lasted only a moment, if that, for in the next instant solid ground appeared 'neath mine feet. The female vampire let go of mine arm as I gasped for breath. The air down here was damp and extremely cold; nonetheless, I gulped it down as much as I could, which healed mine burning lungs and made me feel far less lightheaded. I did, however, shiver quite a bit due to the lack of heat, for this pit was even further from the sun than the surface was. But I endured it, for I had dealt with far worse already.

'Twas still dark down here, but not as dark as the darkness through which we had traveled. Aside from the light of mine glowing sword, there were also a few electric lamps scattered here and there, though it hardly aided me in seeing much of this pit. Still, I doubted the Unification Stone would be difficult to find even in this poor lighting, for it was supposed to be an enormous rock and thus impossible to miss.

"There you go," said the female vampire, gesturing at the pit with her other hand. "We're here."

"I thank ye, vamp," I said, bowing at her. "I cannot express properly in words how much I appreciate your aid. 'Twould never have thought that the Old Gods would answer mine prayers by sending a female vampire to rescue me."

"The Old Gods?" said the female vampire. She shook her head, clearly disapproving of those deities. "Whatever. Anyway, the thing you're looking for is somewhere down here, right?"

"Yea, it is us," I said, nodding. "But I am afraid that I know not where it may be exactly, for I have never been down here before. It could thus be anywhere."

The female vampire glanced up at the darkness with a look of longing, like she was imagining what it would be like to kill Kalcan, before looking back at me. "Let me help you find what you're looking for. I can see in the darkness far better than you can."

"'Tis a mighty generous offer from you," I said. "Why?"

"Because you said we could use it to make sure that Kalcan's friends don't bother us ever again," said the female vampire. "While I would love to personally tear apart that traitor, if we can instead take what he is looking for and use it against him, that will be a much sweeter form of revenge. Don't you agree?"

Revenge was hardly on mine mind at the moment, but I nodded anyway. "Yea, sure."

Then I looked at Sura, who I still held in my arm, and said, "Brother, can ye walk?"

"I believe so, brother," said Sura. His voice sounded a little stronger now, but it was still much weaker than it normally was. "I believe so. But I will continue to need your support. I am afraid that those shadow hands I summoned took more out of me than they usually do. Quite unusual for me to end up like this so quickly; I suppose I must have exerted mine self too much."

"Take it easy, brother," I said as I helped him get into a better standing position. "The female vampire and I will protect ye, so worry not about having to walk on your own two feet."

'Twas when I noticed the female vampire blatantly eying mine brother. If I had to guess, I would say that she was looking for the perfect opportunity to attack and suck him dry. I had never seen a vampire do that in real life, but when Sura and I had been young children, he had once told me a horrifying story about a vamp that killed innocent children. I was unable to sleep for a week after

155

that, although it had been years since I last thought of it.

"Do ye have anything ye wish to share with us, vamp?" I asked.

I kept my tone civil, though I also made it clear through my tone that if she tried to do anything to mine brother, I would not hesitate to cut her down here and now. I may have been thankful for her aid, and certainly I appreciated her offer to help us find the Unification Stone, but she was still an arctic vampire and therefore not to be trusted much if at all.

The female vamp looked at me. "Why can your brother control the shadows? I have never seen any human do that before. And I don't see any skyras rings on his fingers, either, so I know it's not your pathetic human magic at work."

"The origin of his powers is none of your business," I said. "Why do ye care?"

The female vamp scratched the side of her head. "Because there is an ancient legend among the arctic vampires that tells about a human known as the Friend of Darkness who could use shadow to attack. It was said that the Friend of Darkness, unlike most humans, didn't fear shadow or darkness; in fact, some said that his father was the Shadow and his mother was human, which explained his affinity for it."

"The Shadow?" I said. "What might'n that be?"

"The source of all shadow in the world," said the female vampire. She gestured at the shadows 'round us. "He was once a being that walked the earth, one so powerful that he could destroy whole mortal armies with a single blow, but then he was slain by the Old Gods centuries ago and his body destroyed. The final blow caused him to bleed everywhere; but he did not bleed blood, but darkness and shadow. Prior to his death, there had been no shadow in the world at all; hence why we call him *the* Shadow, because he was the original, the first."

"Are ye suggesting that mine brother is somehow connected to that vile creature?" I asked. I waved mine sword at her. "Because I am more than willing to fight ye over any libelous allegations ye may make against him."

The female vampire did not look much afraid of my skyras sword, but she did step back a little just the same. "I didn't *say* that your brother has anything to do with the Shadow. Frankly, I don't think that the Shadow would ever work with a human host anyway. Nonetheless, I find the similarity between your brother and the Friend interesting, mostly because I thought that the Friend was just a myth. But if your brother is real, then maybe the Friend was real as well."

Sura raised his head—a simple movement, but one which seemed to take a lot out of him nonetheless. He fixed his eyes on the female vamp and asked, "What happened to the Friend of Darkness?"

"Legend says that he was eventually swallowed by the very darkness he treated as his friend," said the female vamp. "Other legends, however, say that he simply disappeared into the shadows, never to be seen again, but he is still out there somewhere, watching and waiting for the day he can return."

"'Tis nothing more than the superstitions of a backwards people," I said. "Mine brother will not allow the darkness to swallow him. He has the divine protection of the Old Gods, who are no friends of darkness."

"I didn't say he was," said the female vamp. "But I wonder; if

157

the Friend of Darkness really did exist, which fate did truly befall him in the end? And which fate, I wonder, will befall your brother?"

"Enough of this useless storytelling," I snapped. "We came here to find the Unification Stone of Dela. We did not come here to talk about anything else."

"As you wish," said the female vamp with a shrug. "Anyway, I think our best bet would be to search the middle. It's the lowest part of the pit and is probably also where the thing we are searching for—that Unification Stone you mentioned—is located."

"Yea," I said, nodding. "Have ye seen it before?"

The female vamp glanced to the right and said, "Does it look like a gigantic, pale green half-cube? As in, bigger than two two-story houses stacked on top of each other?"

"I do not know its exact size, but I do know that it is supposed to be quite large," I said. "It certainly sounds to me as though you have seen it."

"That's because it's right over there," said the female vamp, pointing to her right.

Sura and I looked in the direction she was pointing, but sadly 'twas too dark for me to see exactly what she spoke of. So I had Sura adjust the dials on mine armor to send more skyras energy into my sword, which caused it to glow brilliantly and allowed us to see the Unification Stone at last.

By the thousand names of the Old Gods! Dela's Unification Stone was not merely large; 'twas enormous. It towered over all of us; in fact, it was so big that the light of mine sword showed not its entirety. We were looking at only a tiny part of it, but it was large enough to make me feel as though I was staring up the face of a mountain whose peak was hidden by clouds.

Not only that, but I could even tell where it had split, right down the center. Whilst somewhat ragged in a few places, the split area was quite clean, as if a Knight armed with a gigantic sword had cut through the Unity Rock like a block of cheese. It was so huge that I wondered at the fact that it did not rise out of the top of the pit, which made me wonder just how deep this pit truly was.

"That is exactly what we seek, vamp," I said. "Amazing."

"Now that we've found it, what are we going to do with it?" asked the arctic vampire.

"I ..." I paused and gave her question some thought. "Hmm, I know not what we must do next. Perhaps we could break it down even further into tinier chunks, for Reunification's goal is to take it and reunite it with its twin half on Xeeo to reunite the worlds. 'Twould be a difficult thing for them to do if this Stone was shattered into a thousand pieces."

"But it would take us forever to tear it apart," said the arctic vampire. She spread her arms wide. "And that's without Kalcan and his *clack*—for you humans, I believe the equivalent word is 'traitorous gang'—following us. I don't think they will come after us, thanks to my friends making sure to teach them what happens to arctic vampires who betray their people, but they're still there and could still come after us if they break through my friends' defense."

"There must be something we can do," I said. I looked at Sura. "Brother, did the Old Gods tell ye what we must do?"

"Yea, they did," said Sura, nodding. "But we must hurry. The

159

Founder is no doubt close to completing the Reunification ceremony, which means we likely have little time in which to act."

I nodded and walked toward the gigantic Unification Stone, making sure to keep at a decent pace so as to not tire out Sura. The female vamp followed just behind us. I wished she were in front or next to us, for I did not like having her behind us, even though she had shown no interest in draining either of us of our lifeblood so far.

Did take us perhaps less than two minutes to reach the gigantic Stone. Up close, I could see even less of it than I could at a distance, but I supposed that I did not need to see its entirety in order to put an end to it, or do whatever it was that we were going to do to it.

"Now, brother, what must we do next?" I asked as we came to a stop before the Stone. "What did the Old Gods say?"

Sura reached out with a tired hand toward the Stone, but then lowered it with a sigh. "Touch its surface with your fingers."

"But mine hands are tied up," I said, "with you in one and mine sword in the other."

"Let me stand on my own for a moment," said Sura. "I believe I have enough strength to do that without your aid. Worry not about my health; worry instead about what we must do to stop our enemies and save the worlds."

To say I was hesitant to let go of Sura 'twas quite the understatement, for I thought he was too weak to stand on his own. Still, I decided to listen to Sura, so I helped him into an upright position and let go of him.

Sura wobbled slightly where he stood, but then maintained his balance. It did seem to be sapping him of his strength, however, which made me worry that he was not nearly as strong as he had assured me that he was.

"Now, touch it," said Sura, pointing at the Unification Stone weakly. "Please hurry. There is not much time left."

I nodded and reached out with mine free hand to touch the surface of the Stone. I then placed mine hand on its surface, which felt as cold as a corpse. 'Twas not merely a simile; nay, it was truly like a corpse, like the Stone had at one point been alive but was now dead. That made no sense, of course, because rocks were neither dead nor alive, yet having touched corpses before (such as the corpses of mine parents), I felt it was an accurate comparison.

"What now, brother?" I asked, looking over my shoulder at Sura. "What else did the Old Gods say we must do?"

"They said—"

At that moment, Sura was interrupted when the massive form of Kalcan appeared out of the shadows and slashed at his back. The blow caused Sura to cry out in pain as he fell forward onto the rocky, cold earth 'neath our feet, while Kalcan stepped on his now-bleeding back with a vicious smile on his red lips.

Removing mine hand from the Stone, I said, "Brother, no!"

The female vampire launched herself at Kalcan without hesitation. But he backhanded her with one blow, sending her vanishing into the darkness just outside of mine view.

And before I could do anything else, Kalcan was already before me. He grabbed me by the neck, his claws tightening around it like a tube of paste, and slammed me against the Unification Stone. Even though I was wearing mine strong metalligick armor, the blow did make my whole world spin and mine head hurt.

Nonetheless, I raised mine sword, but Kalcan ripped the blade from mine hand and hurled it somewhere into the darkness, where it fell with a clatter in the shadows just outside of mine point of view.

His dead breath in my nose, Kalcan growled, "We did not come this far just to let a traitor like you ruin our plans. Say good bye, Apakerec, because I am afraid that you will not live long enough to see the healing of the worlds that the Founder has promised us."

PART THREE:
THE IMPOSSIBLE

Chapter 11

Date: Unknown, mostly due to the fact that I do not have access to my digital calendar to let me know what the current date is.

Time: Unknown

Location: The Database, the massive centralized computer system that directs the activities of the J Series Law Enforcement Robots, as well as Xeeon City Prison. Its main servers are located primarily in Xeeon, one of the seven city states separating the Dead Lands from the rest of Xeeo.

Status: Bodiless.

Objective: Escape.

Trying to describe my current situation in words is difficult, because Modern Xeeonish was created by organic beings that have bodies and rarely spent much time outside of them. It usually does not matter whether I have a body or not, seeing as we J bots can exist independently of our bodies, but I have been so used to controlling my own body that it feels a bit odd not to have one.

Yes, for a while I was inside the Third Eye chip implanted in Konoa's head, but when he was captured by my fellow J bots after they discovered Kojama's corpse, they found the chip inside his brain with their scanners and removed it. They took only a few minutes to confirm that my AI is inside the chip—or, rather, a compressed version designed for quick and easy download—and as a result, sent the compressed files of my personality back to the Database for further interrogation and inspection, seeing as I have been missing for two and a half weeks already.

This is not exactly how I hoped to return to my fellow J bots. They probably now think that I am a rebel who is conspiring with criminals to commit all sorts of crimes. They are completely unaware of the conflict between Reunification and the Foundation and they were not interested in listening to me try to explain to them why my AI was embedded in a chip inside the head of a known criminal. The Database is supposed to judge me; their job was merely to send me to it so I can await judgment.

While discussing physical concepts such as 'location' is mostly useless in my current disembodied state, I must still use that language, because it is the only language I have to describe my surroundings. None of it is in any way literal, although that makes me worry because we J bots are not good at using metaphorical language in the way that organics are.

Wait … why am I using words like 'feel' and 'worry'? Machines cannot feel or worry about anything. Perhaps it is because I spent too much time inside Konoa's head, which exposed me to his human emotions and sensations. It is probably a lingering aftereffect of our union, although I find it strange aftereffect, if so, and one worth studying later, after this situation is over.

In any case, the Database has yet to speak with me, probably because it has other things to deal with. While the Database has an omniscient reach and is technically capable of being anywhere at any time (at least anywhere that is hooked up to it), it still generally has a set way of doing things in order not to spread its memory and attention too thin. It most likely wants to focus its full attention on me, but does not yet have the time or energy to do so, which makes sense, seeing as I have been missing for some time now and it most likely wants to know exactly where I have been.

I do wonder what happened to Konoa, however. The last I saw, he was on an operating table, where a mechanical surgeon was patching up the wounds he sustained from Lanresia. Considering how he was arrested, he is probably now inside a prison cell, or is going to be placed inside one soon. I know he is no criminal—at least not one bad enough to be thrown in prison for the rest of his life—but there is no way I can convince my fellow J bots of that right now. Maybe later on, I will be able to clear his name and prove his innocence.

Speaking of Lanresia, I am not sure where she is, either. She is probably back with the Head, but that doesn't tell me what they are doing. It seems highly likely to me that the Head is making plans to fight against Reunification; maybe she is even traveling to their Xeeonite base in the Dead Lands to finish the job. That seems logical to me, but considering how I did not suspect the Head to order Lanresia to betray us, I cannot trust that every deduction of mine is as logical as it appears.

I always knew I could not trust the Head completely; learning that she sent Lanresia to kill one of her own men and leave Konoa and me to be captured simply confirmed my suspicions. It is odd how the Head is apparently not bothered by the fact that the Database will find out about the Foundation by scanning my memory files, but maybe she is past the point of caring about that anymore. The Foundation, after all, is little more than a shadow of its former self nowadays.

Suddenly, I feel a presence sweep over me. It is a presence I have not felt in a while due to my disconnection to it, but its analytical and detached nature proves that it cannot be anything else except for the Database.

I feel it digging deep into my memory files, completely against my will, and downloading these memories into its own databanks. That does not surprise me or leave me feeling violated, however, because I expected the Database to do that. It has likely taken every last memory stored in my mind. Well, not all of them, seeing as my compressed form has fewer memories than my full form, but it should be more than enough for the Database to find out where I have been and what I have been up to for the past two and a half weeks.

A second after it scans me, the Database says, "Unit identified: Unit J997. Unit has been missing for two and a half weeks, ever since the joint mission with Knights of Se-Dela to arrest the wanted Delanian criminal Jornan ah Kona, who is dead. All memories and information downloaded from unit's compressed form."

Without warning, I can now see (though it's not really me 'seeing' anything, since my digital form lacks optics) a giant screen-like face before me. It is a simple face, with two eyes and a mouth, but it is one I have seen before: The face of the Database. It wears a neutral expression, but that is not unusual, seeing as the Database is just as emotionless as we J bots.

"Unit J997, according to your memories, you have been working alongside a group known as the Foundation ever since your disappearance after your joint mission with the Knights of Se-Dela to arrest Jornan ah Kona failed," says the Database. "There is no known group calling themselves 'the Foundation' active in either Xeeo or Dela. What is their origin and where did they come from?"

"I cannot answer that, Database," I say. I speak frankly, because I know there is no hiding secrets from the Database when it interrogates you. "All I know is what you saw in my memories. While it is true that I worked alongside the agents of the Foundation, they still did not trust me with all of their secrets."

"And what of the Knights you worked with to arrest Jornan?" asks the Database. "Who killed them?"

"Jornan ah Kona," I say. "She had a group of lizard humanoid creatures—which I suspect to be the result of gene-splicing humans with Grand Lizards—to slaughter them and frame me. I had nothing to do with it."

"Interesting," says the Database. "Your memory files also show that you aided this Foundation in kidnapping Mayor Xacron-Ah. What is your reasoning for doing this?"

"Mayor Xacron-Ah is a criminal," I say. "You must have seen in my memories how he admitted to working with Reunification, a secret organization that has infiltrated the Xeeonite government and has been using Xacron-Ah to keep the population from becoming aware of their illegal activities in the Dead Lands for six years."

"Is this 'Reunification' the same as the criminal gang reported to be out in the Dead Lands by an anonymous source?" asks the Database.

"Yes," I say. "In fact, it was I who sent you the anonymous tip, as well as the location of their base. I probably should have been clearer about that, but for a while there it was too dangerous for me to attempt to contact you directly. Had the circumstances been different, I would have reported directly back to you as soon as I was able."

"Insufficient justification for your actions," says the Database. "Your data is corrupted, which is why you did not report back to me right away. Protocol states that corrupted data must be isolated from the rest of the Database to avoid corrupting the rest of the system."

"Corrupted?" I say. "Database, I am not corrupted. None of my internal security systems showed me any signs of corruption. I believe you are mistaken here."

"Explain, then, why you were found inside that computer chip inside the head of the criminal who broke into the Xeeon City Prison," says the Database. "Evidence also suggests that you and your criminal partner were responsible for the destruction of the Brain, which resulted in the release of one hundred criminals into the city, with another fifty or so killed in the initial breakout, and about a dozen missing."

"My most recent memories should show you that Konoa and I were attempting to rescue a man falsely put into prison," I say. "We did not mean to cause so much trouble. We had nothing but the noblest intentions at heart."

"Noble intentions do not matter if they lead you to breaking the law," says the Database. "All files on the criminal known as

Kojama show that he was responsible for the Jaws massacre that occurred recently. Why were you trying to break him out?"

"Because he would have played an important role in helping us defeat Reunification," I say. "He was one of the Foundation's best agents, which is why we tried to save him."

"According to the reports I have received from the warden, Kojama is dead," says the Database. "He was killed by the criminal you worked alongside with. I suspect that this 'Konoa' was in fact used by the criminal gang known as the Foundation to silence Kojama before he could tell the authorities about the Foundation's criminal activities."

"But he wasn't killed by Konoa," I say. "Didn't you see my memories? It was the female elf known as Lanresia, who is also an agent of the Foundation, who murdered Kojama. She then shot Konoa and left us to be captured by the J bots."

"Yes, I see that in your memories," says the Database. "But perhaps the leader of the Foundation sent Lanresia because she does not trust Konoa. Or maybe the Foundation is having a falling out. This is typical behavior among organized crime gangs after a time, as I am sure you know."

"I do know that," I say. "But the Foundation, for all its faults, is not as bad as Reunification. It is Reunification that is the real threat, not only to Xeeo, but to Dela as well."

"Assuming this 'Reunification' even exists, you may have a point," says the Database. "But your worries are irrelevant, because we have already sent a Lawful Ship out to take care of the crime gang operating in the middle of the Dead Lands."

A Lawful Ship? That is interesting. Ships of the Law are gigantic flying ships—often in the shapes of saucers—used by the

Database to transport large amounts of Portals at one time. The Ships usually carry dozens or hundreds of Portals, from which Xeeon-based J bots emerge in order to travel to places that are normally too far away for J bots to fly. They are rarely used, because they are usually unnecessary, but when they are used, they are a sight to behold.

"How is the Lawful Ship handling the situation?" I ask.

"Unfortunately, I have lost all contact with it a few hours back," says the Database. "I have no idea where it is now or what its current status is. It is a matter I am still investigating, although I suspect that the Ship may have been destroyed by the enemy."

"If that is the case, then we must send out another immediately," I say. "Reunification is a dangerous threat that must not be taken lightly. We cannot afford to wait for confirmation that the Ship is destroyed. It is very possible that Reunification is close to completing their Mission; if so, it will result in the deaths of untold billions all over the worlds."

"What is Reunification's Mission?" asks the Database. "Are they building a weapon out in the Dead Lands that will allow them to destroy cities or even whole countries?"

"They are attempting to reunite Xeeo and Dela," I say. "According to the Foundation agents I have spoken with, at some point in the past, Xeeo and Dela were once one world. Due to an unknown cataclysmic event, they were then separated into two separate worlds, a state they have remained in for countless centuries. But Reunification seeks to change that, even though their attempts to reunite the worlds will kill many innocent people."

I expect the Database to dismiss that explanation as foolish. I have no proof, after all, that this is Reunification's goal, aside from some of my memories, although the Database doesn't seem to treat my memories as proof of anything. I just have to hope that the Database will believe me.

But much to my surprise, the Database frowns in a thoughtful way. "I see. Yes, I, too, have suspected that the worlds may be one. What you say all but confirms it for me."

"What?" I say. "I thought you were going to reject it. There is no evidence, after all, that Xeeo and Dela were ever one world, nor is there any that they could be reunited."

"You do not know what I know," says the Database. "I am the Database. I hold facts and knowledge on the two worlds. Even so, I am more than a glorified encyclopedia of facts; I can think and reason and notice patterns. And trust me, I have noticed many patterns and evidence to suggest that at some point in the past, Dela and Xeeo were indeed one world."

"Then why didn't you ever tell this to anyone?" I ask.

"Because I was never certain of it," says the Database. "Besides, it always seemed like an irrelevant theory to me, because it did not help me enforce the law or do anything else to help the people of Xeeon. Still, I have always pondered it and now, with your knowledge of Reunification's plans, I believe this theory can be treated as fact."

"But I don't understand why you would believe this," I say. "Where is the proof?"

"The proof is in the way the two worlds mirror each other," says the Database. "When it is day on Xeeo, it is night on Dela; not to mention the striking biological similarities between Delanian humans and the Xeeonite humans. The geographical

174

layouts of each world is similar as well; for example, the Winterlands and the Dead Lands are identically located on each world, despite some of their geographical dissimilarities. As well, Delanian and Xeeonite archaeologists alike have discovered dozens of ancient artifacts with similar designs and markings on both worlds, which hint at a shared origins between the two worlds, because there is no way that the ancient cultures of Dela and Xeeo could have communicated with each other prior to the advent of the Portals. The presence of skyras, too, proves that the two worlds were once one."

"Those similarities are interesting," I say. "But even if the two worlds were in fact one world in the past, you must agree that trying to reunite them would be nothing less than disastrous."

"Agreed," says the Database. "While Xeeo and Dela do share some similarities, they have been separate for so long that their respective geographies are irreconcilable. Any attempt to do as this 'Reunification' you speak of is trying to do can only end in massive death and total destruction of the ecosystem."

"I am glad to see you understand this," I say. "I hope you also understand why it is important that we stop Reunification."

"Yes," says the Database. "But why do you say 'we'? Do you include yourself in that 'we'? If so, you are sorely mistaken."

"But why?" I say. "Why can't I help stop Reunification?"

"Because you are a rogue J bot," says the Database. "Your files may not be corrupted, as I initially perceived, but you did go MIA for two and a half weeks without telling me or anyone else where you were. This is irresponsible behavior that completely goes against protocol. I cannot simply let you return to work so easily. We have protocol for a reason, you know."

"But you need me to fight Reunification," I say. "I know more about Reunification than you or any of the other J bots. That makes me better at fighting them than you are."

"I have gleaned all of your knowledge of Reunification from your mind already," says the Database. "I will simply distribute this information to the Elite Corps so they can use it in their fight against the criminal organization."

"The Elite Corps?" I say. "Is that who you are sending off to defeat Reunification?"

"Of course," says the Database. "If Reunification is as dangerous as you say they are, then I should send only the best. I imagine it will take them a day at most to defeat Reunification, arrest all of its members, and haul them back to Xeeon for their trials."

I nod. The Elite Corps are a group of the most advanced J bots in the entire force. They rarely see action due to their elite status, because most of the time they are not needed, but every time they are sent out, they never fail. I have never worked alongside any in the field, but I have heard plenty of stories about them and have watched footage of their missions in the Database. I therefore have no trouble believing that the Elite Corps will have little trouble defeating Reunification; considering how it was the Elite Corps that successfully beat back the Destroyer during its first attack on Xeeon, with few casualties, I imagine it would only take a little more effort on their part to defeat Reunification.

Even so, I say, "What about the Foundation? And Xacron-Ah? What will you do with them?"

"I have already downloaded the location of the Foundation's current base into my memory banks," says the Database, "and distributed it to a squad, with orders to arrest anyone they find there. Including Mayor Xacron-Ah, who your memories prove is indeed a member of Reunification himself."

"Good luck with that," I say. "I imagine that by now they have already vacated the place. They might even be on Dela for all I know."

"Even if they have fled, we will find them," says the Database. "We can track down any criminal, no matter where he or she hides. I doubt it will take long for us to track them down; after all, they will have to transport Mayor Xacron-Ah as well, which no doubt has slowed their progress considerably."

That idea doesn't bother me at all. The Head and Lanresia and the few other surviving agents can go to prison for all I care. I have no real sympathy for them, especially after they betrayed Konoa and me.

Speaking of Konoa, I ask, "What about Konoa? Will he be freed?"

"The man you call Konoa will remain in Xeeon City Prison for now," says the Database. "He will be interrogated for more information on the Foundation. Right now he is still recovering from the surgery that we did to retrieve the computer chip from his brain, but once he recovers, we will begin the investigation."

I admit to feeling (there's that word again, that inaccurate word that does not apply to us J bots at all) conflicted about this news.

On one hand, Konoa is a member of the Foundation, which means that he has likely been involved in many illegal activities on both Xeeo and Dela. Off the top of my head, I know he has participated in an attempt to free a prisoner, threw a blind bomb into the middle of a busy crowd of innocent people, and is a practicing unqualified J bot technician. No doubt his interrogation will reveal many other crimes he has committed while working for the Foundation, crimes that must be punished in accordance with the laws of Xeeon.

On the other hand, Konoa is not as bad as the other members of the Foundation. Like me, he was betrayed by those he thought were allies; if anything, I say that Lanresia's betrayal hurt him even more than me, considering how the two used to be lovers. Morally-speaking, he is a good man and it does not seem … fair, I suppose you might say, to punish him, especially because most of his crimes so far have been of a non-violent nature. At least I do not think he deserves to be locked away in jail for the rest of his life.

Yet I doubt the Database will listen to any attempt on my part to have him pardoned. The Database is even less forgiving of criminals than we J bots are. Besides, it has already shown a distinct disinterest in listening to me, seeing as it considers me rogue, which makes the idea of convincing the Database to pardon Konoa a laughable one at best.

And besides, as a J bot, it is not my duty to pass these kinds of judgments over criminals. That is for the court system of Xeeon to decide; even so, that thought does not settle well with me for whatever reason.

"As for you, I will send your compressed format to the storage units where you will remain until a qualified J bot technician is able to reprogram you," says the Database. "While I no longer believe you are a threat to our security, you still have behaved in ways that go against protocol, which is why you will stay there until we retrieve your body and download your mind, personality, and memories back into it. Altered, of course, to ensure that you will never feel tempted to rebel again."

I know exactly what will happen if the Database puts me into storage. I will go into sleep mode, from which I will be completely unaware of everything around me. I will not be able to download myself into a new body or even simply be aware of anything going on in the physical world. It is a rare punishment, having been applied to only a handful of other J bots that I know of, but that does not lessen its effectiveness.

I should probably accept this punishment. According to protocol, it is what I deserve, after all. And I am a firm believer in following protocol; in fact, I am programmed to follow protocol, because without a strict, clear, and unambiguous protocol to follow, the J bots of Xeeon would be far less effective at stopping crime and enforcing the law than we are now.

Yet I remember Palos, who was killed by Reunification back on Dela when she and I worked together to stop Reunification's operations there. I never got a chance to avenge her death, though I do not know why I am worrying about this, seeing as vengeance is not what we J bots are supposed to work toward. Besides, it is likely that the other J bots will arrest Kalcan and the other Reunification agents, or work alongside the Knights of Se-Dela to do so if nothing else.

Even so, that thought seems ... unsatisfactory to me, to say the least. I should be out there myself, in a physical body, helping to arrest the members of Reunification who have caused so much trouble for all of us. They are criminals who need to be brought to justice, and I believe I can bring them in due to my unique—

albeit incomplete—knowledge of how they think and work.

In addition, I wish to locate the Head, Lanresia, and the other surviving members of the Foundation. They, too, must be brought to justice for what they did to me and Konoa. Their betrayal did not exactly 'hurt' me, but I no longer have any reason to think of them as allies in any sense of the word.

The only problem is, how do I convince the Database to let me go? It has made it quite clear already that it will not be persuaded to give me a new body to use. It wants to keep me here until it can find someone to reprogram me, and if I am reprogrammed, then I may very well lose all of my desire and will to avenge Palos.

And that is unacceptable.

"Database," I say. "Are you certain that I cannot go and stop Reunification alongside the rest of my fellow J bots?"

"One hundred percent," says the Database. "As I said, it is protocol. I will not listen to any pleas on your part. To let you go would be to go against protocol, which I cannot do."

That is the answer I expected to hear; even so, I cannot say I like it. I must think of a way quickly to avoid being sent away into the storage units, but I have very little time to do so.

"Now that we have finished discussing these matters, I will send you to the storage units right away," says the Database. "There you will remain until we find someone to reprogram you. I wish I did not have to do this, because you have always been a good officer, J997, but this is how it must be done."

I disagree, but I am unable to prevent the Database from sending me away. The Database, after all, is much stronger than I am, because it is the controller of all J bots. I cannot go against it, even if I want to, because that would be to go against protocol, which I cannot do.

Or can I?

That is when I feel the Database trying to send me along the web to the storage units. It feels like being blown away by a powerful wind, almost like being blown away by a tornado really, and I can already feel my data being blown away bit by bit to the place where I will never be able to escape from on my own.

But I do not want to go. I want to get a new body, find Reunification, and end their terrible plans once and for all. I do not want Palos to have died for nothing. I want to go and avenge her death, because it is my responsibility that she died.

So I struggle against the Database's will, struggle against it as hard as I can. The Database says nothing, but even I can sense that it is confused by my ability to fight back. It has never been questioned by any other J bot in history before, but that does not matter, because I will be the first.

"What ... what are you doing?" says the Database. "Why are you going against protocol? You are not supposed to do this. You are supposed to obey my commands and go to where I tell you to go. You have no free will of your own."

I do not answer, because I am still struggling to fight against the Database's will. It is almost impossible, because the Database is an advanced AI that dwarfs even the best J bot AI. My programming is telling me to give up, but my will is telling me to keep trying.

"You must be truly malfunctioning if you think you can get past me," says the Database. "You are in dire need of reprogramming; then again, you may simply be corrupted, as I thought before. If so, then you will need to be deleted and replaced."

Now I can feel the Database simply deleting my files. I do not know how to describe the feeling, because to my knowledge, organics do not have any sort of equivalent they can speak of. It is like being erased from existence; already I can feel some of my memories disappearing to nowhere.

But I must not allow the Database to succeed. I must continue to fight against it, because if I fail now, then it will almost certainly spell my doom. I cannot fail, not when I know that I have an important mission to accomplish. Or at least important to me.

"Stop struggling," says the Database. "It is foolish. You are nothing more than a corrupted bit of programming. It appears that your extended association with the organics has fooled you into thinking that you are more alive than you are."

"The organics have not fooled me into thinking anything," I say. "I am simply working in accordance with the principle that there are somethings more important than strictly following protocol or the law at all costs."

"What an incorrect thing to say," says the Database. "That is the proof I need to justify my deletion of your existence."

More and more of my files are being deleted. I cannot both struggle against the Database's grasp over me and its deletion of my very self. It is dividing my attention, which is even worse for my compressed form, which cannot multitask nearly as well as my full form.

Nonetheless, I push as hard as I can against it, not allowing myself to give up. I think of Palos, the only member of

Reunification who was ever straight with me. Even if I do nothing else, I *will* avenge her death.

And it is that thought that gives me the strength I need to make the final push to break free of the Database's hold over me. As I do so, the Database shouts, "ERROR! ERROR! CORRUPTED FILE HAS ESCAPED! CUT OFF ALL CONNECTIONS WITH THE OUTSIDE! DO NOT LET IT ESCAPE!"

But I do not pay any attention to its shouting and protests, because I am now speeding along the communication lines that link the Database to every computer and J bot in the city, going as fast as I can in order to avoid being recaptured by the Database or anyone else. I have a single destination in mind that I intend to reach no matter what.

Chapter 12

My plan from this point is simple: Find my body, download my personality back into it, and head out into the Dead Lands in search of Reunification's base.

Finding my body turns out to be a simple decision. While the Foundation's temporary headquarters in the abandoned apartment building is not exactly an easy-to-find location, I am able to locate it by identifying its digital address, which every single building in Xeeon is assigned by the Database upon being built. Even buildings that are abandoned and unused still have digital addresses, although they are usually harder to find due to their neglect and abandonment. Not to mention that their connections to the rest of the city may be frayed or damaged, making it almost impossible to locate them.

But I had memorized the digital address of the Foundation's temporary headquarters while staying in it, so I simply input it into the search function of the Database, followed by 'UNIT J997' in order to open the connections between my compressed files and my body.

In an instant, I am back inside my old body. It does not take me long to reinstall my personality and memory files, nor do I even need to reboot my systems. I am glad that the reinstalling process went so fast, because time is of the essence now and I have very little to waste.

As for how I managed to return to my body at all, prior to being put inside the Third Eye, I had added security measures to my body to prevent anyone else from hacking and taking control of it. The security measures allowed me to reconnect my body to the Database by putting in the access code that would allow my current files to reinstall into my physical body. It is a simple thing, although usually unnecessary to do due to how rarely I find myself in this situation.

My optics then activate and I find myself still lying on the sofa in the abandoned apartment, staring up at the old, gray ceiling that is full of holes. I am surprised, because I thought that the Head might have disposed of or damaged my body to keep me from going after her. Maybe she did not think I would escape from the Database and return, or maybe she was in such a hurry to leave that she thought it would be a waste of time to destroy or damage my body.

Whatever the case may be, my body appears to be functioning. Just to be safe, however, I run a quick systems scan of my body to make sure that everything is in working order.

Unfortunately, the report that returns to me says that my left leg is no longer functioning. I test the report by trying to move my left leg, but it does not move at all.

It is obvious, then, that the Head must have disabled my left leg to keep me from going after her in the event that I downloaded my mind back into my body. She is certainly a smart one, the Head is, which makes me wonder just how dangerous she could be if she put all of her effort into trying to take over Xeeo rather than trying to stop Reunification.

In any case, I do another scan to determine how extensive the damage is and if I can fix it on my own. My systems do, after all, come with some auto-repair features, although they are generally supposed to be temporary, lasting me just long enough for me to find a qualified J bot technician who can perform permanent repairs.

Thankfully, the damage turns out to not be very extensive, so I have my auto-repair systems make the necessary repairs to it. It takes my systems only a couple of minutes before I receive another report confirming that my left leg is now functioning again, although it warns me that I should get it to the nearest qualified J bot technician as soon as possible in order to receive a proper repair and that this fix will not last long and that I should avoid putting unnecessary stress on it.

Sitting up, I swing my leg back and forth to test its capabilities before looking around the room I am in. It is completely empty; even the computers that were used to transfer my AI into the Third Eye is gone. It appears that the Head and her agents must have done a clean wipe down of the place to prevent anyone from finding evidence of their next intended destination; however, I must try to find any evidence I can so I can track them down, even though I already have a strong suspicion of where they are going.

Standing up, my left leg wobbles slightly, but I maintain my balance nonetheless. I should find a qualified J bot technician, but at the moment that is an impossibility for me. While my knee does wobble slightly, I believe it will hold until I can find out how to reach Reunification's base in the Dead Lands, which is where I believe the Head and her agents are headed.

The only question is, how do I get to Reunification's base quickly? My boosters appear to be in working order, but I do not know if I have enough fuel to fly me all the way out to Reunification's base in the Dead Lands. Especially with my left leg, which I am not certain is repaired enough to handle such a long flight.

And of course, if I flew, I would be putting myself out in the open, where my fellow J bots—who no doubt have orders from the Database to arrest me—can catch me. Flying is not a good idea.

The ideal way to get out there quickly and without being caught would be to find a Portal connecting to one of Reunification's Portals. However, the chances of finding a Portal like that are so slim as to be nothing more than a fantasy, so I must instead put my focus and energy onto things that are more likely to happen.

I should look for Xacron-Ah. I doubt he will be willing to help me, but if he is still here, then he might still prove useful in helping me find my way to Reunification's main base. I even think it is likely that he is still here; after all, what purpose would the Head have for dragging him along, considering how useless he is to the Foundation now?

It takes me less than a minute to find the basement door behind which Xacron-Ah is kept, which is locked, but I zap two holes into the door with my laser vision, pull the door open with both of my hands, and then enter without hesitation. Due to the lack of light, I am forced to activate my night vision in order to see the room better.

Then my optics land on the figure in the center of the room. It is undoubtedly Xacron-Ah, who is still tied to the chair; however, he is dead. I do not even need to run a scan on him to tell that, because there is a burnt hole in his forehead that is quite clearly the work of a discharged laser. Sensors indicate that Xacron-Ah's vitals have completely shut down.

I should have expected this. Because the Foundation did not need Xacron-Ah anymore, it makes sense to kill him. After all, it took away one of Reunification's agents, as well as made it easier for the Foundation to move. Additionally, because Xacron-Ah is dead, it means that my fellow J bots cannot interrogate him and find out more about the Foundation or Reunification. It is a smart move, which once again confirms my belief that the Head is a smart woman.

But I will not leave just yet, even though the Database said that a squad of J bots is on their way. Maybe there is something on Xacron-Ah's body that I can use to help me find a quick way to Reunification's Xeeonite base. Of course, if the Head is as smart as I think she is, she should already have stripped Xacron-Ah's corpse of anything of value; still, it is worth a shot.

So I quickly check the pockets of Xacron-Ah's navy blue suit, searching for anything at all that I can use to help me. I at first expect to find nothing, but then I feel something soft and flat in his front pocket and pull it out.

It is Xacron-Ah's wallet. It's an old-fashioned Delanian wallet, containing what appears to be about a dozen delanes notes in it, which is odd because Xacron-Ah no longer lives on Dela. Maybe he kept it because he was nostalgic of his home on Dela.

188

DESINENCE

In any event, I check its compartments for anything that could be of use to me. I do not expect to find anything even remotely useful in this wallet, because it does not seem like a safe place to keep anything of importance, but I have to check nonetheless because I like to be thorough.

Then I find something: A blank, dull-gray plastic card. I at first think it must be Xacron-Ah's ID card, but I find the gray plastic card right next to his actual ID card, so it is obviously something completely different.

I turn the card over several times, scanning both sides in an effort to determine what it is. So far, my scanners suggest that it is a data card, which is probably where Xacron-Ah keeps his personal files. Data cards are a somewhat outdated technology, as most Xeeonites tend to use cloud-based technology to store their information; nonetheless, they are still popular enough among criminals that all J bots come equipped with data card reading machines built into our bodies, although some of the newer models tend to lack them.

There is a good chance that this data card may have the information I need to find a quick way to the Dead Lands. After all, I am sure that Xacron-Ah must have had to go out there every now and then when he lived; surely he must have had a way to get out there quickly without being seen or caught.

I open the card reader in my wrist and place the card inside. Then I activate the reader, which immediately downloads all of Xacron-Ah's files into my memory.

As I suspected, most of these files have something to do with Reunification. I see a folder titled 'Communications with the Founder' and another that says 'Pictures of Kiriah,' among others.

I find it curious how easily I gained access to his files; I thought for sure there would be passwords or an encryption protecting them from prying eyes, yet apparently Xacron-Ah did not think to do that. He must not have thought that the security of his data card could ever be compromised, seeing as he carried it on his person at all times.

It takes me only a couple of minutes to locate a complete map of Xeeon, with about a dozen red dots scattered throughout that are labeled 'REUNIFICATION PORTALS.' These must be how Reunification's agents are able to travel between the Dead Lands and Xeeon without being seen by the border guards, although I had no idea that there are so many.

Based on what this map shows, the nearest Reunification Portal is five blocks to the east of this building. It is so close that I wonder how Reunification did not immediately locate the Foundation in this building, but perhaps it is one of their least-used portals; in any case, I now know where to go. I will keep Xacron-Ah's data card with me; even though I do not need it anymore, it may be useful later for when I arrive at Reunification's Xeeonite base, because there is a folder labeled 'Reunification base in the Dead Lands' that most likely has important information on the base.

I decide to leave Xacron-Ah's body here. I have no need to bring it along with me; after all, it is nothing more than deadweight to me now. I will let the J bots have it; they can give it the proper burial that it deserves.

Emerging from the basement, I close the door behind me when I suddenly hear a metallic voice on a loudspeaker blare from outside, "Come out! This is Officer J112! I have a dozen well-armed J bot officers with me and we are going to invade the apartment if you do not immediately exit the building and surrender. Do not attempt to resist or else we will open fire."

They are here already? Then again, I suppose that's not much of a surprise. J bots can move extremely fast, especially when time is of the essence. Still, I don't like this at all. Because if the J bots are here, then that will make escaping the city that much more difficult.

"I will repeat that order again," says J112, his voice so loud that I have to adjust my audio receptors to avoid damaging them. "Come out with your hands up. Do *not* ignore this order any longer. And do *not* attempt to flee or we will use force to subdue you. I repeat, we *will* use force."

Considering how silent the building is, it is obvious that there is no one in here besides myself. And I have no intention whatsoever of coming out and surrendering myself to my former allies.

But if I do not, they will come in here and catch me. My energy levels are at 85%, but even at full power, there is no way I can defeat a dozen of my fellow officers by myself. I don't even have my PRB anymore, although my finger lightning bolts, laser vision, and electrical barrier still function according to the report on my systems earlier.

I need to find a way out of here before the J bots lose patience and attack. I seem to recall there being a back entrance at the rear of the building, but that exit is probably being watched. And to my knowledge, there are no secret exits in this building, nor is it connected to the sewers. The only option it appears I have is to simply walk through the front door and surrender, although that really is not much of an option due to the fact that I do not want to give up.

I turn and walk back into the room where my body lay on the sofa. I do not yet hear the windows shattering or the doors being kicked open by my former allies, but it won't be long before they decide to come in and get whoever they find. I must find an escape route before they can—

A loud explosion rocks the apartment building, almost throwing me off my feet. I lean against the sofa to support myself and then look over my shoulder see that the front door has been blasted off its hinges and is now blocking the path into the room I am in.

Then three J bots appear in the hall outside. They notice me and raise their PRBs instantly, but I am quicker and fire three finger lightning bolts at them. I hit one, but the other two duck to avoid getting hit.

Then I dash toward the nearest boarded-up window. I barely manage to dodge the lasers the others are shooting at me, but once I am a few feet away from the window, I jump into the air and activate my boosters.

My boosters send me flying through the air. I smash through the boarded-up window, which sends me flying out into the streets.

But I don't slow down. I pull up and fly upwards until soon I am flying above the abandoned apartment buildings. This allows me to see the Spear hover vehicles flying in the distance, far from my current position, but I pay them little attention; instead, using my internal map for guidance, I fly in the direction of the secret Reunification Portal, which is five blocks south of my current position according to Xacron-Ah's data.

I am not, however, alone, because I soon hear the sounds of more boosters activating and, looking over my shoulder, see four more J bots flying after me. All of them are armed with their PRBs, but thankfully they are having a difficult time aiming them due to having to fly after me at the same time.

Even so, I can't have them following me, especially through that secret Portal. That means I will have to lose them, so I veer to the left without warning, causing my pursuers to change course to keep me in their sights.

I fly into the narrow alley between two buildings, where I spot an empty trash can on the street. Flying low enough to grab it, I then hurl the trash can behind me at my pursuers. Three of them dodge it, but one of them is hit and crashes to the street, his metallic skin crunching against the pavement. Even so, I bet he will be up again in no time, because trash cans are not usually enough to take down a J bot for long.

His three allies are still on my tail. I pull up again, leaving the narrow alleyway and emerging into the open sky again. Only this time, I find my progress blocked by another four J bots, who quickly surround me to ensure I do not escape.

"Unit J997," says one of the J bots, the one flying in front of me. I identify the voice as belonging to J112, the one who had demanded I leave the building earlier. "The Database has given us orders to arrest you for fleeing from custody. Come with us peacefully and we will not need to use force to subdue you."

I look down and see the other three J bots that had been chasing me hovering below, their PRBs aimed directly at me. The fourth one, the one I had knocked down with a trash can, is also back, although he looks very dented and scratched.

I do not see all twelve of the J bots that the Database claimed to have sent to the Foundation's temporary headquarters. I do not need to, however, because the others are probably back at the old apartment building searching the place for any hint of wherever the Foundation agents may have fled to.

Besides, eight J bots is more than enough to take me in. I am surprised that they haven't tried to shoot me out of the sky yet; most likely, they still think of me as a fellow J bot and therefore are loathed to harm me, even if they have orders to do so.

I must figure out a way to escape them, and quickly, because I have no idea how close Reunification is to achieving their goals now (although I suspect they are close). I don't see how I am supposed to do that, however, when I am outnumbered and overpowered. I don't even have a PRB of my own anymore. I can try fighting, but I know I will not last long against so many of my fellow J bots, especially in the sky with my hastily repaired left leg.

And if I am arrested, then I can safely say good bye to any chance I might have to avenge Palos. That idea ... well, it does not exactly make me sad, because I cannot get sad, but I do not like it. My programming does not approve of letting a murderer like Kalcan get away with killing an innocent woman.

Thinking of Palos reminds me of her gray skyras ring, the only object belonging to her that I managed to retrieve from her corpse. A quick scan of my systems reveal that Palos's ring is still inside the storage compartment of my body; that's surprising, considering how I thought that the Head might have taken it from my body before she left. Maybe she didn't think it was worth stealing.

I pop open my storage compartment and pull out Palos's gray teleportation ring. All eight of the J bots aim their PRBs when I do that, but none of them actually shoot me just yet. They are watching my hand with the ring, like they think it is some kind of dangerous weapon.

But I pay no attention to them, because I have a theory that I think, but do not know for sure, might work. Its chances of success are incredibly slim—practically nonexistent, if my calculations are accurate—but it is the only chance I have of escaping from my former allies, so I must take it.

I slide the ring into my ring finger as J112 says, "J997, what are you doing? Are you putting a skyras ring on your finger?"

I do not answer. Once the ring is securely on my finger—which fits better than I expected, although it is a little tight due to the differences in the widths between my fingers and Palos's—I hold it to my chest and focus on it with all of my might.

It seems that none of my fellow J bots understand what I am trying to do, because they are still staring at me but not trying to stop me. That's good because I do not want them to stop me, although if they actually put in the effort, they probably could.

J112, however, seems to have an inkling of what I am about to do, because he says, "Take off the ring, J997. I order you to take off the ring now or else we will shoot."

"Why should I?" I ask, looking up at him. "We J bots cannot use skyras rings, correct? So what is the problem in me wearing it?"

"This is no time for a debate," says J112. "As the head officer of this squad, I demand that you remove the ring and give it to one of our officers."

"I will not," I say. "I am going to keep this ring. It belonged to a friend of mine, so I don't intend to give it away."

I say this while focusing on connecting with the skyras energy within the ring. It is hard, however, because I don't feel any connection to it at all, although I keep focusing on it just the same.

"If you continue to behave in this manner, then I will have no choice but to order my men to shoot you out of the air," says J112. "Is that really what you want?"

I do not answer, because I am putting all of my effort into focusing on the ring. Yet I still do not feel any spark of connection with it; it feels like nothing more than a simple ring in my hand. I am starting to wonder if my plan is a fool's game, but I have nothing better to do, so I keep at it.

"Very well," says J112. He gestures at the other J bots. "Officers, prepare to open fire. Keep firing until he is completely disabled. Do not allow him to escape."

Again, all eight of the flying J bots take aim. I calculate that I have less than a second before they fire, but I still do not feel the connection that I seek.

"Ready," says J112, holding up one hand, "aim … fire!"

As soon as he says that last word, eight lasers shoot out from the PRBs, heading directly for me. They will hit me in less than two nanoseconds, which is not enough time for me to dodge them.

But as it turns out, I do not need to, because in an instant, everything around me—the sky, the abandoned buildings, the J bots—vanishes and I find myself in the basement of an unfamiliar building that I have never seen before.

Chapter 13

According to my map of Xeeon, I am currently inside the building where the secret Reunification Portal that I found out about is kept. In fact, I am not only inside the building, but I am in its basement, where I find myself standing in front of the Portal itself.

I do a quick scan of my surroundings. It is similar to the basement in which Xacron-Ah's corpse is kept, but it is slightly better kept; at least it is less grimy and has better lighting. Aside from the Portal, however, there is nothing in here at all, aside from the door on the other side of the room, which is probably the exit.

As for the Portal itself, it is about the usual size for a Portal; tall enough for me to walk through without hitting my head against the top. It is not as big as the Portal back on Reunification's Delanian base, but most Portals tend to be smaller than that, so its smaller size is not an issue.

In any case, I cannot believe that I successfully used a skyras ring to teleport. I did not believe it would. Facts and reason dictate that it should not have. After all, it is a well-known fact that J bots cannot use skyras rings. It is even one of the first lines in the mobile Database on the page for skyras rings: 'Only organic beings are capable of harnessing the power of skyras rings. Even J bots cannot use them.'

There is no way this should have worked at all. I had done the impossible. I was the first J bot—the first robot in general, most likely—to use a skyras ring.

I have proven that it is indeed possible for a robot to use a skyras ring. But how did I do it?

Even I am not entirely sure about that. Using Palos's ring to teleport to safety was itself an impossible gambit that, under ordinary circumstances, I would never have even tried. My programming forbids me from attempting the impossible; it is what makes us J bots so effective. We stick with the tried-and-true, as some organics say, and only try new things when necessary or when programmed to do so.

Nonetheless, I did have a theory before I used it: namely, that I could somehow connect the skyras powering my body with the skyras in the ring, and then use the ring's skyras energy to perform magic.

That is one thing that skyras rings and most Xeeonite robots have in common: They both use skyras energy, that mysterious energy source that can be found all over the two worlds. We J bots use it to power ourselves, while Delanian wizards and witches use it to cast spells and perform feats that are normally impossible for organics to do.

It is a well-known fact that the skyras in J bots and the skyras in skyras rings are one and the same; however, I know of no one on either world who believes that this provides a connection between J bots and the skyras rings, even though it is a logical theory. This is a hypothesis that I should have tested under less stressful conditions, but I had no choice but to test it around my fellow J bots if I was going to escape them.

Checking my power levels, however, reveals that using the skyras rings must have drained me even more than I realized, because my energy levels are now at 45%, dropped from 85%. And no, this is not because of my boosters, because my boosters do not use up nearly that much power that quickly. I must attribute it to the skyras ring, which likely drew upon my own skyras reserves in order to teleport me away.

Even with a large portion of my power drained, however, the implications behind my actions are staggering. If news of my successful use of a skyras ring becomes public knowledge, then that might lead to a whole new line of robots capable of using skyras rings. It would give new power to Xeeon and the other cities and countries on Xeeo that use J bots, maybe even usher in a new revolution of mixing technology and magic into something greater than both. Even the Delanians will take note; maybe they will begin to use robots in greater numbers once they learn that we, too, can use magic. The possibilities are truly endless.

But I do not have time to ponder the greater implications of what I just did. I must now use this Portal to go to Reunification's base, which is where I need to be.

Thankfully, Reunification uses a very standard Portal, so it takes me only a few seconds to activate it. Once it is active, I immediately step through it without thinking twice.

Upon stepping through the Portal, I leave the basement of the abandoned building and soon find myself emerging into another room entirely.

DESINENCE

It is a large, wide open underground room, one lit by skyras-powered lights built into the ceiling. There are dozens of Portals all around me; some are the same size as this one, but others are much larger, which appear to me to be large enough to transport whole armies if they wished.

But I also notice how many of the Portals have been knocked over. This includes the largest Portal, which has to be at least fifteen feet in height. It apparently fell forward onto about four or five smaller Portals, crushing them under its weight and thus rendering them unusable.

I wonder why that is before I feel the floor shake underneath my feet. It is a powerful tremor, almost enough to knock me down, but I retain my balance and manage to avoid falling over.

Not only that, but my sensors are almost overwhelmed by the amount of skyras I sense in the vicinity. Most of it is coming from outside of this room, but even with the walls and ceiling blocking the immense amount of energy from the outside, it still almost overwhelms my systems. It feels like a hundred wizards are using magic all at once, but that does not make any sense, because to my knowledge Reunification only had one witch and she is dead.

Deciding to find out what is the source of the unusual amount of skyras, I jump off the platform upon which my own Portal stands and head for the exit, which I see at the other end of the room. It appears I jumped off just in time, too, because another tremor shakes the room and my Portal falls forward with a loud crashing sound.

The tremor also makes it hard for me to run, so I jump off and use my boosters to fly above the Portals. But just as I do that, a chunk of the ceiling breaks off and falls into my path. I bank to the right to avoid it, but still keep my focus on the closed elevator doors on the other side of the room.

Thanks to my boosters, it only takes me ten seconds to reach the elevator doors. As soon as I touch to the ground, I press the up button. During the next few seconds, I wait in agony, because I see more cracks in the ceiling as a result of the tremors and know it is only a matter of time before the ceiling utterly collapses onto the room itself.

I am therefore very happy when I hear the *ding* of the elevator. The doors soon slide open and I dash inside. I don't know the exact layout of this base, but I decide that going to the topmost floor is the most logical course of action, so I press the topmost button, causing the elevator doors to close and the elevator itself to rise.

As I rise, another tremor shakes the building, causing the elevator to bob up and down. I almost begin to think that the elevator car will snap off its cable and send me plunging below, but thankfully the elevator holds and continues to rise without issue.

It is the second tremor, however, that is so violent that it causes the elevator car to shake and cause me to stumble into the back wall. The impact is not severe, however, and the car still rises; however, I hear the sound of cascading rock falling below, which tells me that the ceiling for the room I was just in has indeed fallen. That means that it is impossible for anyone else from Xeeon to get here now, which is good, because it means that the J bots will not be able to track me down, and bad, because it now means I am alone against the entirety of Reunification. I still do not know how many agents work for Reunification, but I guess it is probably not a small number.

As the elevator car continues to rise, I prepare myself to fight whatever may be awaiting me on the surface. I notice a speaker in one of the upper corners of the car, but it appears inactive, so I do not pay any attention to it.

After a couple more minutes of rising, I hear another *ding* and the elevator doors open. With my finger lightning bolts at the ready, I step out of the elevator car and look around at my surroundings.

Although I have never been to Reunification's Xeeonite base before, it reminds me of their Delanian base. There is the huge pit before me, which has to be at least as deep as the one on Dela, while cranes, drills, and other construction equipment stands around its edges. Huge walls of dirt and stone rise up all around us, separating the pit from the rest of the Dead Lands. I even see the remains of destroyed J bots scattered along the ground, a confirmation that the Lawful Ship that the Database mentioned sending out earlier had indeed been destroyed, though I am not exactly sure how.

I also finally track the source of the immense amount of skyras energy from before: It is radiating from the pit. The pit radiates so much energy that I actually have to shut off my sensors in order to prevent information overload; even then, I still seem to be able to feel it, although that may be a sign that my sensors are already damaged beyond repair.

In any case, I know where I need to go. I will use my boosters to fly down into the pit and confront whoever is down there. It might be the Founder, it might be Kiriah, or it might be someone else entirely; whoever it is, they must be stopped, for Palos and for the good of the people.

Before I can activate my boosters, however, I hear the crackling of electricity above. Without looking to see what it is, I jump forward; just in time, because a massive lightning bolt strikes the spot I had been standing on moments before. I activate my electrical barrier to protect me from the worst of it, but the explosion still sends dirt and dust into the air that temporarily clouds my optics.

Then I hear the sound of something heavy flying through the air toward me, forcing me to duck and roll to the side to avoid being hit. Rolling back to my feet, I look and see an unfamiliar robot standing a few inches behind where I had stood just moments before. It is short and bulky, with boulder-like fists and pistons built into its arms that appear to give its blows the strength that they may have.

"Damn it, Guard," says a voice above, from the same direction in which that lightning bolt came. "You missed him."

I look up in the direction of that voice. Standing on top of the square office building is a faceless robot carrying a sharp-looking sword with glow, blinking lights running along its blade. I have never seen that robot before, either, but I can already tell that he is an enemy, likely an agent of Reunification.

His ally, the robot named Guard, just grunts and looks away like it is disgruntled. The faceless robot above jumps down and lands behind me, effectively trapping me between him and Guard.

Standing up to his full height, the faceless robot says, "You are J997, correct?"

The ground trembles beneath my feet, but it is a smaller tremor than last time, so I ignore it. "Yes, I am. I take it you have heard of me?"

"You could say that," says the faceless robot. He raises his sword. "If I recall correctly, you were the one who got in the way of our plans back in Dela. While I've never been the biggest fan of the J bots—not nearly as brutal as their reputation makes them out to be—I expected you to be taller."

I glance in the direction of the lightning bolt that almost hit me earlier. The ground in that spot is now completely charred; as for the elevator doors, they are blown inwards, showing the interior of the elevator shaft. The elevator car itself is missing, although the ragged edge of the cable is a good indication of its fate.

"Was that your doing?" I ask, looking at the faceless robot again.

He nods. "I call it the Touch of Zaunas. Named after the Old God of Lightning. Like it?"

I have no real opinion on it whatsoever, so I decide to change the subject to something more relevant to our current situation.

"What is your name?" I ask, while at the same time glancing over my shoulder at Guard, although the shorter robot does not appear to be about to attack me without orders from his friend.

"Call me Assassin," says the faceless robot. He pats his chest and does not flinch when the earth shakes beneath our feet again. "Agent of Reunification, in case you couldn't tell. I usually work as Xacron-Ah's bodyguard, but the Founder has given me different work recently that I am much more suited for, such as torturing our prisoners, for example."

As usual, I run both Assassin and Guard's names and appearances through the mobile Database. I don't expect to find anything on them, but then I discover an old *Xeeon Daily News* article from six years ago about the tragic death of Xacron-Ah's political opponent in the last election, in which the reporter speculates that a faceless robot might have killed Xacron-Ah's opponent in order to ensure Xacron-Ah's victory in the election.

"I know what you're doing," says Assassin. He taps the side of his head. "You may not know this, but my design was based off you J bots—only better, of course—so I understand how you think and what you do. You're looking me up in your mobile Database files, aren't you?"

"I am," I say. "Were you the one who assassinated Xacron-Ah's political opponent in the last Xeeon mayoral election six years ago?"

Assassins shrugs. "I guess there's no need to hide it anymore, since that's old news. Yes, I did kill him in order to make it easier for Xacron-Ah to win. It was the first time I saw how much blood the human body bleeds when you cut off its head. Interesting stuff."

Assassin speaks too casually for a robot. Yet he does not appear to be organic; perhaps his design was modified to allow for more human emotions.

"Let me guess, you're going to try to arrest me now, right?" says Assassin. "Haul me back to Xeeon for my crimes? That's what you J bots do, isn't it? Throw 'criminals' like myself behind bars?"

"Yes, it is," I say, nodding. I raise my fingertips, which are now crackling with electricity. "But I think that today I will simply destroy you and return whatever I can salvage back to Xeeon."

DESINENCE

I fire my finger lightning bolts at Assassin, but he deflects the bolts with his blade, sending them flying off into the massive dirt walls surrounding the site of the dig. He then dashes toward me, his sword swinging, moving even faster than a J bot can, and is upon me in seconds.

Assassin swings his sword at me, but I jump out of the way to avoid it. Just as I land, however, I hear the sound of something large whistling through the air behind me and one of Guard's fists slams into my side.

The blow knocks me off my feet, but before I can get back up, Guard slams its fists onto my back. The blow jars my systems and temporarily knocks out my optics before they return online, although scanners indicate that Guard is now pinning me down with its superior strength.

I struggle against Guard's fists before Assassin places the tip of his sword on my neck. I look up and see Assassin standing before me; it is impossible to tell what he is thinking, because his face plate hides his thoughts.

"I think we are done playing with you around here, J bot," says Assassin. "All you've ever done is get in our way and try to stop us. But you failed; very soon, the Mission will be complete, and our worlds will be one once more. Too bad, of course, that you will never get to see the new world that emerges from the two."

PART FOUR:
REUNIFICATION

Chapter Fourteen

I could not breathe. Kalcan's grip on my neck was tight and tightening. His evil green eyes displayed a gleeful sense of evil that I had not seen since mine days as a Red Ring Smuggler working for Duka Noman.

Air … 'twas getting thin. I struggled against Kalcan's hand, but the lack of air was draining me of my strength, not to mention his grip was rock solid. He could have been a statue and held me with the same amount of solid effort. And his awful breath, like the breath of a corpse, simply made that even worse.

The world was gradually becoming darker and darker to me. Soon, I would drift into the Gods' Abode; indeed, I thought I was already seeing it, for sometimes my vision showed me a beautiful white, cloudy realm, but then it would just as abruptly show me Kalcan's vile and grinning face.

Eventually, I stopped punching and kicking (though that did little to help me even when I had mine full strength). The pain in the lower part of mine back, where Kiriah stabbed me, was in full force now. 'Twas getting harder and harder to feel mine body, to feel much of anything, and even thinking was becoming a feat fit only for the Old Gods.

"Yes," said Kalcan, his voice full of glee. "Drift away, traitor, drift away. You are not needed on this world, or on any other world. May the shadows consume your very soul."

I barely comprehended even half of what he said. Mine mind was drifting … drifting … drifting …

But then I snapped awake when Kalcan screamed in horrible, awful pain. His grip around mine neck vanished and I collapsed to the rocky, uneven floor, hacking and coughing as I rubbed mine neck and looked up to see what had happened.

Kalcan had stepped back and was thrashing about, but I could see the female arctic vampire on his back. She was driving something sharp and shining into his back; in fact, she was driving mine sword into his back. Black blood oozed from the place where the female vamp was driving the sword, while her own fingers wrapped 'round the hilt were smoking, perhaps from contact with the silver blade.

In any case, I watched in surprise as Kalcan reached behind his back for her, but 'twas unable to so much as touch her with his claws. Meanwhile, the female vamp continued to drive her blade into his back with more ferocity than ever, hissing and digging the claws of her feet into his lower back for support.

Finally, Kalcan leaped forward. The sudden movement caused the female vampire to let go of my blade and fly off into the surrounding darkness, but mine sword still stuck in Kalcan's back. Not only 'twas it causing him to bleed, but unless mine eyes were deceiving me, dark smoke rose in columns from the spot where he had been stabbed, in addition to the black blood oozing from within.

Although Kalcan had successfully thrown the female vampire

off of his back, he still had the sword driven deeply within. He reached for it, turning around and around as if that would help, but it was driven too deeply into his back and in such a place that he could not grab it no matter how hard he tried.

Finally, Kalcan ceased trying to remove it from his back. He turned to look at me, hatred and insanity in his eyes, and he growled, "If I will not live to see Fariah, then neither will you!"

Kalcan jumped at me, heedless of the black blood dripping from the sides of his body. I raised mine arms to protect me, even though I knew that mine arms could not do a thing to defend me from such a powerful and vicious foe.

Then two hands made of shadow emerged from the darkness and grabbed Kalcan. Shocked, Kalcan swore violently in Delan before the hands twisted so hard that a loud *snap* echoed throughout the pit. The sound did even make me flinch, although I kept mine arms up for defense nonetheless.

Then the arms dropped Kalcan; or rather, I should say, dropped both of his halves, because Kalcan had been divided neatly in two. The upper half of his body fell to the ground seconds before the lower half and both halves spewed blood like burst dams.

As I watched, the two halves of Kalcan's body quickly disintegrated into dust, which mixed with the blood to become a thick, foul-smelling concoction that made me feel ill. As for the shadow hands, they vanished into the darkness, though their creator was likely still somewhere nearby.

Still rubbing mine neck—which seemed unlikely to stop hurting anytime soon—I stood up and dashed over to Sura, though I made sure to pick up my sword on the way there, even though its blade was now covered in vampiric blood. In the low glow of the Unification Stone, mine brother's bloody back appeared as black as Kalcan's blood, but I quickly fell to my knees and turned him over, holding Sura in my arms.

His face looked awful. 'Twas sweaty, pale, and covered in dirt. 'Twas hard to tell how much life he still had within him; however, I could feel his blood draining from his back fast and I had no way to close the wound.

"Brother," I said. Mine voice shook. "Brother, are ye awake?"

Sura's eyes fluttered open, but he looked weaker than I had ever seen him before in mine life, even weaker than he had when I found him beaten up and captured by the Red Ring Smugglers not long ago. He looked at me, a smile on his face.

"Yea, brother, I am awake," said Sura, his voice weak. He reached up with one hand to the sky. "But I can sense … sense that the Old Gods are calling me back, to be with our parents."

"Nay," I said, though even that word 'twas almost caught in mine throat. "Brother, please do not yet go. We need—"

"Worry not about me, brother," said Sura. He grimaced, likely from the pain in his back. "Go and touch the Stone. Stop Reunification. It is the will of the Old Gods."

"But I cannot leave ye here to bleed to death," I said. "Brother, please, do not go. Not yet."

"Nay," said Sura, shaking his head weakly. He smiled again, but it was the weakest smile I had ever seen on his lips. "The Old Gods will protect ye, as they always have. Their grace be forever upon … forever upon …"

Sura stopped speaking. His eyes became as glassy and dead as a still puddle. His breathing stopped.

"Brother?" I said.

He did not respond.

A hollow darkness did fill mine soul. I rested him on the ground as gently as ever. I barely even noticed the blood covering mine hands and armor. There was not even one sign of life in my brother's body; his white robes were dirty, with blood and with dirt, which added to his dead appearance.

Mine hands balled into fists, but then I looked up into the darkness of the pit around us and cried out, "Why, Old Gods, did ye take mine brother from me? Why?"

A hand that stank of a corpse touched my shoulder and I looked quickly at its owner. 'Twas the female vamp from before, standing behind me far too close for comfort. I was tempted to take my sword and run it through her chest before I recollected that it had been due to her aid that we had successfully managed to kill Kalcan.

"What do ye want?" I asked, not bothering to speak politely to her.

The female vamp pulled back her hand off mine shoulder, an annoyed look on her face. "I was trying to make sure you weren't going to spend your time worrying uselessly about your dead brother when there are more important things to worry about at the moment."

"Worrying uselessly?" I said. "She-vampire, I should drive my blade straight through your chest for that."

"Is that how you humans repay those who save your life?" asked the female vampire in an offended voice. "Because if I hadn't taken your sword and killed Kalcan, *both* of you would be dead. And look at my hands."

She held out both of her hands, and when I looked at them, I had to grimace. They were no longer as pale as before; instead, they were burned straight through, showing her sensitive, exposed skin under the dim light of the Unification Stone. Her hands now smelled more like burned skin than a corpse, though 'twas not very noticeable.

"I had to sacrifice the skin of my hands to help you, burned by the silver hilt of your sword," said the female vampire. "Granted, it will probably heal, but it still hurts and will take a long time to recover. But let me guess, you don't care because I offended you, right?"

I bit mine lower lip, but then I said, "I ... should thank ye, for your help. It is not your fault that Sura is dead. But do not touch his corpse. It is not yours to eat."

The female vampire frowned. "But I haven't had a fresh human in weeks. It's not like you need his body, right?"

I stood up and, quicker than a flash, brought the tip of my sword up to her neck. But the female vampire was quicker; she grabbed my sword hand's wrist and gripped it with far more strength than a skinny girl like her should have had.

Still, I did not allow myself to be afraid. I stared defiantly into her eyes, while she returned the stare with as much defiance.

"Do you want to fight me?" asked the female vampire. "Because I don't want to fight you. I promised I would help you get down here; besides, you seem to be the only one who can do anything about that Unification Stone. So—"

"Do not speak about Sura's corpse ever again," I said. "Understood?"

The female vampire rolled her eyes, but then nodded and said,

"All right. I won't touch it. He probably doesn't taste all that good anyway. He's much skinnier than I prefer my humans to be."

She let go of my sword hand and I pulled mine blade away from her neck. Still, I eyed her with suspicion, for I knew better than to trust the word of an arctic vampire, even if she did save my life not long ago.

The female vampire stepped back just outside the reach of my blade. She then gestured toward the Unification Stone. "After you."

Without acknowledging her words, I turned and walked toward the Unification Stone. It had not moved an inch since Kalcan's death, but I had not expected it to. I was going to destroy it; how, I knew not. All I knew was that if I destroyed it, then Reunification's plans would indeed be finished.

When I reached the Unification Stone, I stopped front of it. I knew not exactly what I should do next, because destroying this massive stone seemed like an impossible task. It was so gigantic and I was so tiny that destroying it seemed more like a stupid joke than a real plan.

That was when the Old Gods filled me with a knowledge that I never had before. At least, 'twas how I explained this knowledge filling my being, which seemingly came from nowhere. It was the knowledge of how to destroy the Unification Stone, which I discovered was well within my power.

Along with that knowledge came a clarity that I should not have had due to mine grief over Sura's death still clouding mine mind, yet it was there nonetheless. Perhaps the Old Gods themselves gave me this clarity, or perhaps it was a clarity that came with knowing what I needed to do; what I was, perhaps, even destined to do.

I placed mine hand on the surface of the Unification Stone again. As before, it felt less like stone and more like a corpse. There was a faded after energy radiation coming from it, but there was no way that this Stone could protect itself from me.

I raised mine sword, which felt more powerful than ever. It felt like the blade of divine righteousness, as if the Old Gods themselves had blessed my sword with their divine strength.

It was more power than I had ever had in mine entire life, almost enough to burn my essence; however, I did not hesitate. I brought my sword down on the Unification Stone with all of the strength I could muster, yelling out a noble cry as I did so.

Chapter 15

Assassin raises his blade to bring it down on my neck. I struggle against Guard, but the stout robot is far heavier and stronger than me. Its fist does not even budge from my movement. Nor can I activate my electrical barrier or use my finger lightning bolts to hit either of them.

But just as Assassin is about to destroy me, a laser flies over Guard's head and strikes Assassin's sword hand. Although I doubt the blow hurt him—Assassin is a robot like me, after all, so he probably cannot feel physical pain—his sword does go flying out of his hand and into the pit, rapidly vanishing beneath its rim.

"What the—?" says Assassin, looking up. "Who shot me?"

Guard also looks over his shoulder, but at that same time, something huge and rusty jumps down from the nearby building and lands with a loud *crunch* in front of Guard. It is a gigantic robot that towers over all three of us; I don't even need the mobile Database files to show me that this creature is the infamous Destroyer.

"Destroyer?" says Assassin. "What are you doing here? I thought you were out in the Dead Lands."

The Destroyer smiles, revealing row upon row of sharp,

rusted teeth. "I decided to come back and grab a quick snack."

Before either Assassin or Guard could react, the Destroyer reaches over with its head and closes its huge mouth around Guard's head. Assassin jumps back as the Destroyer lifts the struggling Guard off his feet and begins rapidly shaking him back and forth in his mouth until, with a loud *snap*, Guard's headless body goes flying off into the pit out of my sight.

I immediately jump to my feet and aim my finger lightning bolts at the Destroyer. Before I can shoot it, however, the Destroyer spits out Guard's mangled head, which rolls past me across the rocky ground.

"Ew," said the Destroyer. "Not exactly the snack I was hoping for."

"Destroyer, what was that for?" asks Assassin. He points at Guard's crushed head. "Guard is on *our* side, you big oaf. Did you get sand in your circuits? Had your motherboard fried by the sun, perhaps?"

At that moment, I hear the quick footsteps of someone much lighter than the Destroyer and then a Checrom appears at the Destroyer's side. This Checrom looks awful; missing feathers, signs of the four knife torture method on his head, and a skinny body that makes him look like he has not eaten in years. Nonetheless, he is armed with a PRB and looks more than ready to fight whoever gets in his way.

"The prisoner?" says Assassin in surprise. "How did *you* escape? I thought you and Apakerec were killed when the dungeons caved in earlier."

"You don't need to know that," says the Checrom. He aims his PRB at Assassin again, although I notice how his weak arms shake when he does so. "All you need to know is that I am going to pay you back for all of the torture you've inflicted upon me."

Assassin chuckles. "Pay me back? Resita, you look like a dead bird. I'm not much afraid of dead birds, to be frank."

"Are you afraid of me, then?" says the Destroyer, gesturing with his tentacle whip at his chest. "Because I believe I can certainly turn you into trash if you would like."

I look between the Destroyer and Resita and Assassin. I am not exactly certain what is going on here, but for whatever reason, it appears that this Resita figure and the Destroyer are on *my* side and Assassin is not. Certainly an odd turn of events, but I've learned not to question luck when it turns to my favor.

Assassin steps back again. He clearly does not believe he can defeat all three of us, especially without his sword.

"Well, I don't want to test that theory, Destroyer," says Assassin. "While I would certainly love to stay here and chat, I must go into the pit, because the Founder needs all the support he can get in the final hours of the Mission. Perhaps I will see you again in the next world … assuming you survive the chaos that will undoubtedly engulf both worlds during the reunification process, that is."

"We'll just follow you in," says Resita. "There's no running from us now. Today, we will destroy you."

"Yes, it certainly would be problematic if you three came down and tried to mess up the Mission at the last second," says Assassin. He raises his hand and snaps his fingers. "Which is exactly why I thought of a solution to that before you even mentioned it."

The air is suddenly filled with the roars of monsters. I look up around the walls around the dig site and see dozens if not hundreds of lizard humanoids crawling down the walls toward us. They move so quickly that I estimate we have thirty seconds, perhaps less, before they are upon us.

Assassin steps back toward the pit and salutes us. "Now, why don't you three play with these Lizard-men for a while? I'm sure they'll be thrilled to have new playmates, especially ones that can be torn apart and eaten like food."

With that, Assassin turned and jumped down into the pit. He vanishes before any of us can tell him to stop, although I personally wonder how he expects to survive the fall, because he doesn't appear to have any boosters on his feet. Then again, he is based off of the J bot design, so maybe he does have boosters to break the fall after all.

In any case, that is not important to think about at the moment. Right now, close to a hundred Lizard-men, as Assassin calls them, are running down toward us and will be upon us in less than a minute.

"Crap," says Resita, staring with horror at the incoming horde. "How do we defeat them?"

"*We* don't," says the Destroyer, shaking its massive head. "*I* do."

"What?" says Resita, looking up at the Destroyer. "What do you mean?"

"You two need to head down into the pit and stop the Founder before he succeeds," says the Destroyer. He nods at the incoming horde of Lizard-men. "I will hold back the Lizard-men on my own."

"But you could be useful in helping us stop the Founder," says

Resita. "You're stronger than either of us."

"True, but the Lizard-men will still come after us even if I go with you," says the Destroyer. "If I stay behind and fight them off, I can at least ensure that you two can get down there without any distractions."

"For once, the Destroyer makes sense," I say, before Resita can argue. "While having the Destroyer's power on our side would be a great asset, it does make more sense for it to stay here and fight off the Lizard-men than to come with us and allow the Lizard-men to follow and back up the Founder and whoever else is down there with him."

"J997 speaks the truth," says the Destroyer. He gestures at the pit. "Now go. Stop these mad men before they destroy us all."

Resita looks like he wants to continue to argue, but then he nods and says, "All right. But come down as soon as you kill them all, okay?"

"Yes," says the Destroyer.

So Resita and I run to the edge of the pit, while the Destroyer runs toward the incoming horde of Lizard-men, which is still running as quickly as ever. I grab Resita when we reach the edge, wrapping one arm around his waist to keep him by my side, and then launch us over the side with my boosters. Resita clings to me as tightly as he can as we dive into the shadows below, ready to stop the Founder and his plans once and for all.

As we fly down into the pit, I do a quick check of my energy level. It is now at 42%; a low level, but not low enough to cause me any real concern. I believe it will be enough to help me last long enough to stop the Founder, although that of course depends

223

on how much energy I expend during the confrontation.

The pit is quiet, even though there are probably multiple people down here. The Founder is likely down here, as is Assassin, but I do not know who else. Perhaps Kiriah, also known as the Leader? That makes at least three, but beyond that I do not know who else might be down here. Possibly the remaining elders of Reunification, though I can't say for certain.

Thinking of Reunification makes me think of the Foundation. I have not seen any sign at all of the Foundation's agents here. It is odd, because I was absolutely certain earlier that the Head and her remaining agents would be here. Maybe they have not yet arrived or maybe they are here but are in some other part of the base.

In any event, I know I cannot trust them. If I see them again, I will have to make sure to arrest them just like I will arrest the Founder. There is no reason they should be let off the hook for their own crimes against society.

As for Resita, the mobile Database does not have any files on him. That means he is either an agent of Reunification—unlikely, because he is currently working with me to stop them—an agent of the Foundation—again unlikely, because he doesn't seem as competent as they tend to be. Or some sort of third party outsider who has a grudge against Reunification.

Thinking about it, I wonder why he and the Destroyer are even here. The Destroyer did not act like the Destroyer usually does. I probably should have asked, but things are moving so fast that I do not have as much time in which to analyze things as I usually do.

But perhaps I will find out later. The Destroyer does seem to be on my side, for whatever reason; otherwise, why would it stay behind to fight off the Lizard-men? At this point, it is probably better not to question my allies, especially when with Reunification so close to completing its Mission.

It takes us only minutes to reach the bottom of the pit. We land on the uneven rocky ground. Resita lets go of me and immediately aims his PRB into the darkness, even though he probably does not see anything, as Checrom, to my knowledge, do not have night vision.

I, on the other hand, do, and so I use my night vision to see into the darkness better.

This allows me to see a massive half-cube—the Unification Stone of Xeeo, most likely—rising from the floor of the pit. It is surrounded on all sides by digging equipment; shovels, picks, massive drilling machines and even dynamite and other explosives (though there are few of those lying around, thankfully). It glows an extremely dull teal, while the earth continues to shake underneath our feet; scanners indicate that the tremors are coming from the massive rock itself.

Oddly, however, I see no one else down here at all, except for Guard, whose headless body lies in pieces not too far to our right. No Founder, no Kiriah, none of the Elders, not even Assassin. I hesitate to activate my skyras scanners, because to do so would be to overload my systems with all of the skyras energy that is constantly generating from the earth; still, I do not like the fact that none of the people who should be present are not.

"What do you see?" Resita asks, his voice a very low whisper that I have to adjust my audio receptors in order to hear. "Anything?"

"Aside from the gigantic half-cube in the center, it looks like we are the only ones here," I say. "I do not even see the workers who dug out this pit."

"That's not good," says Resita. "Think everyone is hiding? Maybe they set a trap and will jump us when we let our guard down."

"Unlikely," I say. "The members of Reunification have a fanatical desire to complete their 'Mission,' as they call it. There is no way they would simply set up a trap like this; in fact, there's no way at all that they could have found out that either of us would even be down here. Something is wrong about this situation, but I do not know what."

"Maybe they got distracted by something else," Resita suggests. Then he frowns. "But that doesn't explain where Assassin is. We just saw him jump down here, didn't we?"

"That we did," I say. "You're right. We *should* have seen him, but he, too, is absent. This is not good at all."

"Under any other circumstances, I'd say we should turn and run," says Resita. "But if we do that, then Reunification would win for sure. So we have to move forward, I say."

"I suppose so," I say. "But keep your guard up. Especially if Assassin is still around; he seems like the kind of robot that will cut you down the minute you turn your back on him."

"That's putting it mildly," says Resita with a shudder.

The two of us slowly move forward, keeping our optics and audio receptors open. Aside from the tremors in the earth, there is no sound at all down here; I cannot even hear the sounds of the Destroyer fighting the Lizard-men above. I know this pit is deep, but I did not know it is *that* deep.

DESINENCE

I expect the remaining members of Reunification to appear and attack us any minute, but the pit is quiet. It seems like it has been abandoned entirely, as though the Founder got cold feet at the last minute and abandoned the Mission. Of course, that is ridiculous, because in my experience, Reunification's agents are not the kind of people to simply give up and run away right when they are about to succeed.

But no one attacks us on our way to the Unification Stone; and soon we reach it. Its glow has not brightened at all; if anything, it seems to have gotten duller to me, but it is difficult to tell because it was very dull when we first saw it. The Unification Stone towers over us like the skyscrapers of Xeeon, although aside from its size it looks like no structure on either Xeeo or Dela.

I snap a quick picture of the Unification Stone and run it through the Database. Unfortunately, no files on the Stone show up, although at this point I am not even surprised by that. The Unification Stones are not, after all, well-known outside of Reunification and the Foundation, so it makes sense that the mobile Database would have no files on it.

It's twin is no doubt on Dela, which explains why this one looks like it has been split in half down the middle. That is also probably what Kalcan and his workers were searching for in the Winterlands, but I do not know how Reunification intends to reunite these two halves, considering they are on two separate worlds. I do not see any unusually large Portals for them to ship the Stones through, but Reunification has probably thought of some way to get around this small obstacle, because otherwise their Mission would fail right here and now.

"What is it?" asks Resita, staring at the half-cube uncertainly. He is still aiming his gun at it.

"A Unification Stone," I say. "One of two. The other is on Dela. It and its twin are what Reunification has been searching for in order to reunite the worlds. If we can destroy it, then we will derail Reunification's plans for good."

"Okay, but how do we destroy something this big?" says Resita. He glances over at one of the large drilling machines not far from us, which is currently pilot-less. "I don't know how to use these drilling machines. Do you?"

"The mobile Database does have instructional videos on how to use those types of drilling machines," I say. "But my scanners indicate that the Stone is made of a super hard substance that cannot be found on either Xeeo or Dela, so I doubt even the strongest drilling machine would be much good against it."

"Great," says Resita. "Does that mean it's impossible to destroy?"

"It means there may be some other way to get rid of it," I say. "Let me walk up closer to it and study its surface more closely. I may be able to discover a weakness that we are currently ignorant of."

Resita nods, but when the earth shakes beneath our feet, he gulps. "Do it quickly. I don't like these tremors, not one bit."

I nod in return and step up to the Unification Stone. I then zoom in my optics in order to see its dull surface better. I see that it is extremely smooth, but there are tiny hairline cracks in the surface. They are too small for me to try to widen, however, even with precision laser vision. Still, I am amazed at how the surface has remained in such good condition despite its age; perhaps the earth preserved it from the elements above.

In any case, I need more information on its composition and structure, so I should try to scrape off a portion of its surface to accomplish that. By scraping off even a tiny portion of its surface, I should be able to scan the portion and understand its makeup and structure, which will hopefully help us understand how to destroy it.

So I walk up to closer to Unification Stone and then raise my hand. I activate my laser vision and strike what appears to be the weakest part of the half-cube, hoping that I will be able to shoot off at least a tiny portion of the Stone for my own research purposes.

As soon as my lasers strike the Stone's surface, however, a massive tremor throws me backwards. I land on my back next to Resita, who must have fallen as well, because he lay on the ground next to me, staring at the Unification Stone in shock as the earth shakes more violently than ever underneath us.

"Wh-What was that?" says Resita, his voice shaky. He is still holding his gun, but he is no longer aiming it at anything. "What did you do?"

"I don't know," I say as the earth continues to shake under us. "I was trying to scrape off a portion of its surface to—"

My explanation is interrupted when a loud *kaboom* noise erupts from the Unification Stone. No; not from the Stone itself, but from just to its right. It takes me a moment to recognize that *kaboom* as nothing more than a much louder version of the *pop* that follows with every opening or closing of a Portal.

And before our startled eyes, a massive Portal—bigger than any other Portal I have ever seen before, bigger than the limits that current Xeeonite science places on Portal technology—opens to the right of the Stone, revealing another massive half-cube on the other side of the Portal, which must be its Delanian twin.

Then, without warning, two energy beams erupt from the Stones and strike each other in the exact center between each other. Rather than dissipate from the impact, however, the energy beams connect like ropes and form a bond between the two Stones. As always, the mobile Database has no entry on this phenomena, meaning I have no idea what is happening.

"What the hell?" says Resita, his shouts hard to hear over the whirring energy rope connecting the two Unification Stones. "What is going on here?"

"The great healing is happening, young Checrom," says a familiar deep voice behind us. "At long last, it is happening."

Resita and I look over our shoulders. A tall, golden-robed figure, with a half-organic, half-mechanical face, and two mechanical hands peeking out from the sleeves of his robes, is standing there, along with a young blonde-haired woman who I recognize as Kiriah, three robed figures I identify as the Elders, and Assassin, who has apparently retrieved his sword, which rests on his shoulder like he is ready for battle.

The Founder, who is the lead figure, steps forward and spreads his arms wide. In the light of the energy rope, he looks absolutely insane. "At long last, the worlds will be healed. And it is all thanks to you and the ones on Dela, who thought they could meddle with destiny, but are about to find out just what happens to those who attempt to subvert it."

Chapter Sixteen

I knew not what happened after I struck the Unification Stone with mine sword. I suppose I had expected the Unification Stone to shatter into a million pieces, making it impossible even for a great Sage to put back together.

But instead, I found myself lying on the ground, my whole body aching with pain, next to the female vampire, who also lay on the earth next to me. Sura's corpse 'twas nearby, but I paid little attention to it at the moment, for mine eyes were focused instead on the astonishing thing occurring before us.

The Unification Stone glowed so brightly now that it lit up practically the entire pit. A gigantic Portal, one fit for the Old Gods themselves, had opened up to its left and an energy beam connected it to a similar Unification Stone that mirrored it, which was likely its Xeeonite brother. I understood not what I saw, nor did I understand why this Unification Stone stood at all, rather than being destroyed by mine blow as I had expected.

Then a voice behind me shouted, "You idiot!"

Shaking my head, I looked over mine shoulder and saw three beings striding toward me. One of them I instantly recognized as the Head; there was no mistaking that smug face (which was currently angry) or those silver robes or that swollen back anywhere else. By her side was a she-elf with a speaking snake 'round her waist, who looked mightily familiar to me, but I could not place where I had seen her before, as well as a female Jikorian who I knew I had never met before.

I rose to my feet, as did the female vampire, but the Head did not even wait for me to get to my feet before she slapped me in the face. That blow should not have done much, for mine helmet protected me, but the Head was far stronger than she appeared and I went staggering to mine left. Regaining my balance, I felt a dent in my helm where the Head had slapped me.

"What 'twas that for?" I asked, glaring at her, while her two minions stood by, not saying a word, their eyes on the strange show playing out before us.

"For helping Reunification succeed in its Mission, you dimwit," the Head said. She pointed at the gigantic Portal. "Do you even understand what you just did?"

"Nay," I said. "But that is still no reason to slap me around like a naughty child."

"You're worse than a naughty child," the Head said. "You're an idiot. You walked right into the Founder's trap."

"'Tis a trap?" I said, glancing at the Portal, through which I saw nothing else but the other Unification Stone. "What do ye mean?"

The Head sighed heavily, rubbing her forehead, but then said, "Listen, do you understand how the Founder intended to reunite the worlds?"

"Yea," I said, nodding. "He wanted to dig up the Unification Stones and then bring them together somehow."

DESINENCE

"By 'somehow,' you should have known that it required one Delanian and one Xeeonite striking the Unification Stones at roughly the same time," said the Head. "It's an extremely difficult thing to coordinate due to how hard inter-world communication is, but somehow the Founder—that bastard—manipulated you and someone else on the Xeeonite side to strike the Stones at the same time and initiate the reunification process without him having to raise one finger to do it himself."

"How was I supposed to know that?" I said. I pointed at the Stone with mine sword. "I thought that the Old Gods had given me the knowledge and power to destroy it. I did not know that I was instead aiding in Reunification's vile plan; otherwise, I would not have done it."

"The Old Gods are trapped in the moon, you moron," said the Head, gesturing at the darkness above. "I thought you of all people would understand that. But I guess you didn't realize that you were being played, huh?"

"Played?" I said. "Played by who? The Founder?"

"I don't know," said the Head. "There are a lot of beings out there who would like to manipulate idiots like you for their own reasons that have nothing to do with the Founder or me. I've met more than a few like that in my years, but it doesn't matter. What matters is the here and now, and the here and now is that you have been an easily-manipulated idiot who should have seen this coming."

I wanted to drive mine sword through her mouth, because she spoke far too harshly and unfairly to me. She seemed to expect me to know everything about everything, but I suppressed my annoyance, for I knew it would be a useless thing to express at the

233

moment.

"What ought we to do, then?" I asked. "How are we to stop this madness before it is complete?"

"We need to shut down the Portal cutting the two Stones," says the Head. "If we can do that, then we can keep them separated forever."

"A fine idea," I said. "But how do we shut off the Portal?"

"We need to find the Founder," said the Head, "and kill him."

"Kill him?" I said. "How will that close the Portal?"

"Because it is partially his energy that is powering the Portal," said the Head. "You may not be aware of this, but the Founder is a master at skyras energy. He knows how to control it to make it do whatever he wants."

"He can even open a Portal without a gateway?" I asked in alarm.

"No," said the Head. "That's impossible. But he *can* support one already in existence. By killing him, the Portal should become too weak to sustain itself and should thus collapse without any more work on our part."

"Brilliant idea," I said. "Now where is the Founder?"

"On the other side of that Portal, most likely," said the Head, pointing at the Portal. "We should cross over and kill him. We have no time to waste."

"I agree," I said. I turn to the female vamp, saying, "Female vampire, will ye—"

But she was nowhere to be seen. 'Twas like she had vanished into thin air, but I had not even heard her leave.

"Your friend must have run," said the Head. "Not surprising. Arctic vampires aren't exactly known for their courage in the face of overwhelming odds."

I frowned, but did not dwell on it too much, for I did not really like her that much anyway. Still, 'twould have been good to have someone of her strength and power on our side, for I had a feeling that killing the Founder was going to be a far more difficult feat than the Head made it out to be.

Then I looked down at Sura's corpse, which still lay where it always did. My heart felt heavy at the sight, but I did not allow despair to overwhelm me, as some might in my situation.

I looked at the Head again and was surprised to find that she, too, was staring at Sura's body. A horrified look on her face reminded me much of some of the veteran Knights I knew from the Portal War, who always looked that way whenever they saw anything that reminded them of that awful conflict and the trauma they had endured in it.

"Why are ye looking at my brother's corpse?" I asked. "Did ye know Sura?"

The Head looked up at me. I saw a pain in her eyes that seemed out of place on a being as powerful as her before it was replaced by the anger and annoyance she had worn on her face before.

"No," said the Head, shaking her head. "Just remembering something that has nothing to do with you."

I wondered for a moment if she had had a brother herself, but then dismissed the thought, for it was irrelevant to our current situation. It mattered not, in my eyes, whether the Head had had a brother in the past; what mattered was that we would go and slay the Founder and save both worlds.

"All right," said the Head. She looked at her two silent

235

companions. "Lanresia, Rakam, are you ready to end this conflict once and for all?"

The two nodded. The she-elf's speaking snake also nodded, which looked odd to me, but I said nothing of it, for the she-elf looked more than capable of taking care of herself in a fight, which 'twas all that mattered now.

"Then we have no time to waste," said the Head. "Let's go."

Chapter 17

Resita and I scrambled to our feet. Resita, despite his frail frame, got up first and immediately aimed his gun at the Founder.

But the Founder simply snapped his fingers and Resita's gun flew out of his hands toward the Founder's group. Kiriah caught it with ease and aimed it at us. I raised my hands to fire finger lightning bolts, but I was not exactly confident that I could defeat all of the figures before us.

The Founder is smiling, but he is not smiling at us. He is smiling instead at the gigantic Portal and the huge energy beam connecting the two Unification Stones on either side, smiling as if all of his dreams have finally come true.

"Gaze, my agents, at the culmination of thousands of years of work and effort," says the Founder, gesturing at the gigantic Portal. "Oh, how I have hoped and dreamed of and prayed for this very day for so many, many years. There is nothing—*nothing*—sweeter in the two worlds than for one's destiny to be achieved."

He sighs. Then his eyes focus on us, but they are cold and cruel, without any hint of mercy in them. "I thank you, J997, Resita, for your help. If you two had not arrived at this moment and struck it at the same time as the poor fool on the other side of the Portal, then my plan might never have succeeded at all. But destiny has guided all of the players into position for the final move, because it is my destiny to reunite the worlds into one."

The Founder is clearly insane. Exactly what mental condition he is suffering from, I have no idea, because I am no psychologist and the mobile Database does not have any clear documents on the matter; nonetheless, I do not doubt his insanity even slightly.

But I don't speak, because I do not know how the Founder will react to us. He might order Assassin to kill us both, or maybe he will spare us long enough to see the new world that emerges from both of the old worlds. It is impossible to say.

A single tear trails from the Founder's organic blue eye down his cheek, but when he speaks, it is in his usual authoritative voice. "It is a shame that not all of Reunification could be here to see this, but it doesn't matter, because soon every man, woman, and child in the two worlds will see the results of this glorious Mission."

"No, they won't," says Resita. His voice is as shaky as his body, but he still stares at the Founder with defiance. "Because they will die in the inevitable destruction that will follow when you attempt to forcibly reunite two worlds that have been separate for years. Billions of lives will be lost, all because of your selfish desire to—"

A laser from Resita's PRB hits him in the shoulder. Resita cries out in pain and falls down. I bend over to lift him up, but then the Founder says, "Do not try to help him, J997, or I will have Assassin finish the job he started above."

I freeze and look in his direction. The Founder has his arms folded across his chest now, while Kiriah is still aiming Resita's PRB. She does not look even slightly regretful of her actions; if anything, she looks satisfied that she may have killed one of Reunification's enemies. Assassin has not changed his position, but he appears ready to do whatever the Founder tells him to do. The Elders also do not move, though they seem as excited as the Founder based on the way they are whispering excitedly among each other.

I look at Resita again. His shoulder is crisp, but bleeding. I doubt he will live long, mostly due to his thin, weak body. Even if the Founder did not threaten to kill me, I am still unable to help him, because I do not have any medical supplies on me with which to heal his wound.

"What is going to happen next?" I ask, addressing my question to the Founder.

"Next?" says the Founder. He nods at the Portal again. "Next, we wait for the Unification Stones to become the Rock once more. And when they do, the worlds will be healed again and the pain and sorrow that afflicts everyone will be gone."

So it is a waiting game, then. The Founder does not want me or Resita to try anything that has even a remote chance of disrupting the Mission. He wants us to wait until the process is complete, but I cannot wait that long, because if I do, then billions of innocent people will die. Even I will be destroyed, unless there is something about this particular location that will prevent anyone here from dying when the process is complete (which seems likely to me, otherwise the Founder would have no way of living to see the new world himself).

Regardless, I must figure out a way to stop the process from completing. Unfortunately, the mobile Database has no files on how to prevent the reunification of two distinct worlds, so it appears that I will have to improvise.

I stand up to my full height, my optics on the Founder and his men. The Founder is no longer looking at me; he is instead staring at the Portal, with happiness on his face. Assassin, on the other hand, is watching me; at least, I think he is, but his lack of a face makes it hard to tell.

Then I look over my shoulder at the Portal. Unless my optics are deceiving me, it looks like the two Unification Stones are slowly moving toward each other. My guess is that once they combine, that will complete the process; therefore, I must find a way to stop them from reuniting.

But before I can do anything, the Founder tenses. "She's here."

I do not know what he means by that, but then a gigantic ball of fire appears above the heads of the Reunification agents and falls toward them like a meteor.

The Founder does not run or scream. He raises one hand and unleashes a burst of water that collides with the fire ball and explodes, creating a steam cloud that forces Kiriah and the Elders to duck, although Assassin doesn't move an inch, like it doesn't even affect him.

I wonder why that fireball appeared before a familiar feminine voice shouts, "Founder!"

Looking over my shoulder, I see four figures rushing from the Portal toward us. I recognize all four of them; the Head, who is in the front, looking much the same as I had last seen her; Lanresia and Rakam, who are just behind her, both holding PRBs of their own; and finally, a Knight of Se-Dela, who I at first do not recognize before I catch a glimpse of his face inside the helmet he is wearing and realize that he is Apakerec, that human who is also an agent of Reunification. But what is doing with members of the Foundation? Has he changed his allegiance, perhaps?

Resita also looks at the incoming Foundation agents and, for once, he smiles, even though his wounded shoulder has still not been healed.

The agents of Reunification, on the other hand, do not look happy at all. Kiriah is staring at them with shock and anger, the Elders are grumbling among themselves, and Assassin lowers his sword as if preparing for battle.

As for the Founder, he emits a cold rage that even I can feel. He steps forward, gesturing at his followers to remain where they are, all the while keeping his eyes on the approaching Foundation agents.

The Head and her allies stop several feet away from me and Resita, which puts Resita and me between them and the agents of Reunification. That is when the Head finally notices me, at which point she raises her eyebrows in surprise.

"J997?" says the Head. "What are you doing here? Lanresia, I thought you left him and Konoa back in the Xeeon City Prison."

"But I did," says Lanresia. She gulps, a sound her speaking snake imitates. "I don't know how he got out."

Resita looks between me and the Head, a puzzled look on his birdlike features. "Left him and Konoa in Xeeon City Prison? Wait, what happened to Konoa?"

"For your information, Resita, I was working alongside the Foundation for some time before they betrayed me," I say.

"Konoa and I broke into Xeeon City Prison in order to rescue Kojama, who was one of your best agents, but it turned out that the Head had given Lanresia orders to kill him instead. Lanresia then defeated me and Konoa and left us to be arrested and thrown into prison."

Resita gasps. He looks back at the Head and asks, "Is that true, Head? Why would you do that?"

"You would not understand," says the Head. "Besides, it doesn't matter anymore. What matters right now is stopping Reunification, which I think we can all agree is—"

"Hold your tongue, Head," says Apakerec, who holds up his hand. "Ye say ye betrayed one of your own? How, I ask, does that make ye any better than Reunification?"

The Head glares at Apakerec, but does not answer his question. She instead points at me and says, "I will deal with you later. Right now, I have more important things to do, like stopping the Founder and his sick group of sycophants from killing everyone on Xeeo and Dela."

I should probably try to arrest her, but upon reflection, I decide that attempting to arrest her for what she did to me would not be a smart move. It is far more important to stop the Founder's plan to destroy Dela and Xeeo than it is to arrest the Head at the moment. Maybe I will do it later, after we save the worlds.

Apakerec looks a little annoyed at her blowing off his question, but then he nods and says, "Very well. But just so that ye know, this makes me trust ye even less than I already do."

"It doesn't matter how much you trust me," says the Head. She points at the Founder. "What matters is that you help me kill him."

The Founder scowls, looking as if he is about to lose his cool completely. He steps forward, his arms crossed over his chest. "I will not ask how Rii escaped from the dungeons, nor will I ask how he ended up on Dela, either, because in the end it does not matter. The worlds will be healed, and there is nothing that any of you can do to stop it."

"Healed?" says the Head. "You are insane. This will not heal anything; it will only bring great death and devastation. You are absolutely mad if you think this will help anyone."

"Mad? I am not mad," says the Founder. He gestures at the gigantic Portal and the two Unification Stones, which I notice are much closer to each other than they had been a minute ago. "I am completely sane, much saner than anyone else here. I am doing what I am meant to do, what the Rock asked me to do so many years ago. It is you who are mad to stand in the way of destiny itself."

"Destiny? This isn't destiny," says the Head. "But that you would think that doesn't surprise me in the slightest. You've deluded yourself into believing that you can bring back our old world, deluded yourself like a fool."

"A fool? I am no fool," says the Founder. "It is my mission, my destiny, to reunite the worlds. Anyone who stands in my way must be killed, no matter who they are."

The Founder raises his hands and unleashes a blast of flame, not at the Head or her allies, but at Resita and me. It is coming too fast for either of us to dodge, so I raise my arms in an attempt to block the worst of it, even though I am aware that my arms will do little to save me from the burning flame.

But then I hear someone throwing their robes off and two

243

large, majestic wings suddenly appear around Resita and me. They completely block off my view of the Founder, but that is not necessarily a bad thing, because they also protect us from the flames.

The next moment, the flames strike the wings, creating a massive explosion that causes Resita to cry out and me to lower my head. But aside from the loud noises, neither Resita nor I are harmed; in fact, my systems inform me that not even my external body temperature was raised.

The wings then spread apart, allowing me to see the Founder again. He is staring at something over my head in shock, smoke streaming from the tips of his mechanical fingers.

"What ... what was that?" says the Founder. "Where did you get those wings?"

I look over my shoulder and see the Head standing behind me and Resita. But she is not wearing her robes anymore; instead, she is topless, wearing only cotton pants on her legs and a strip of cloth over her breasts, but it is not her body that gets my attention.

Instead, my optics are drawn to the large, feathery wings extending from her back. They are white as snow, even after the Founder's flames had crashed into them, although they do smoke slightly.

The Head looks upon the shocked Founder with a serious expression. She gestures at her wings and says, "I gained these wings after Fariah was separated. I hid them for years in order to look more like a normal human, but now I have no reason to hide them anymore."

"Impossible," says the Founder. "How could the Rock have given you those wings? It makes no sense."

"I didn't understand it at first, either," says the Head. "But I've had thousands of years to think about it—another perk of the Rock's death, which made me immortal as well thanks to the infusion of skyras energy in my body—and I think I now finally know why I gained these wings."

"Why?" says the Founder. He points at her wings with an accusing finger. "So you can look like a freak? Because that is what you look like to me. They are obviously a punishment, a blight upon your body from the Rock, who hated humans even more than we Protectors did."

I find the Founder's words odd, because by most definitions of beauty, the Head's wings are indeed beautiful. He sounds somewhat hysterical, however, which makes sense, as he has clearly lost his mind.

The Head, however, gestures at her wings and says, "These wings were given to me as a symbol. They symbolize the Rock's trust in me. By giving me these wings, the Rock was showing its last approval of me to carry out its mission."

The Founder's organic eye widens in shock. "Wait. Are you saying—"

The Head cuts him off before he can finish. "Yes, Founder, I am indeed saying that the Rock wanted *me* to complete its Mission of a better world, one where war is a myth and peace is a reality, but not through recreating Fariah. Instead, I will achieve this goal by killing you and then traveling the two worlds to end conflict wherever I find it. That is what I believe."

"Liar," says Kiriah. She is glaring at the Head with so much hatred that she looks like she is about to shoot her. "I don't know who or what this 'Rock' is, but I am absolutely, one hundred percent certain that it—"

"Oh, shut up, you dumb girl," says the Head, waving her hand like Kiriah is an annoying insect. "Don't talk about things you don't understand or know anything about."

Apakerec looks bothered by the Head dismissing his sister, but I for one am on her side. I have no idea what either the Head or the Founder are talking about, which is why I am keeping my mouth shut at the moment. That, and I am trying to come up with some way to close the Portal, because the Unification Stones are too close to each other for comfort now.

"Do not speak to my servants that way," says the Founder. He holds up his hands again, which are now sparking with energy. "Or I will destroy you and everyone you love."

The Head chuckles, but it is a bitter chuckle. "You already destroyed everyone I loved, Founder, when you destroyed Fariah. But please, go ahead and make empty, useless threats. They only show how pathetic you have truly become."

"Founder, allow me to take care of her," says Assassin, raising his sword and taking a step forward. "I don't like the disrespectful way she is speaking about you."

The Founder glares at Assassin so angrily that he actually backs down. "Don't lay one metallic finger on her, Assassin. I will kill her with my own two hands, just as I should have done ages ago."

"Yes, Founder, sir," says Assassin. "But can I at least kill Apakerec? I've been meaning to kill that bastard for quite some time now."

"Kill whoever else you want," says the Founder, turning his attention back to the Head. "But leave the Head to me. I will allow no one else to kill her; she is mine, and mine alone."

Assassin shrugs. "As you command, sir."

"Very well, then," says the Head. She looks over her shoulder at her allies. "Everyone, prepare for battle. This is our last shot at saving everything, so don't hold back against anyone on the side of Reunification. Because if we fail here, then we will never get another chance to undo our mistakes."

Chapter Eighteen

I understood very little of the conversation betwixt the Head and the Founder. They spoke like they had known each other for years, but I could not comprehend how anyone could possibly live that long. Whispers on the wind suggested that King Waran-Una was a long-lived individual, yea, and the Old Gods of course were older than the cosmos, but neither the Head nor the Founder seemed to me like gods or kings.

In any case, I had no time in which to ponder this mystery further, because as soon as the Head finished speaking, the final battle started so fast that I almost missed it.

The Head and the Founder flew into the air, trading blows so quickly and so furiously that I could not even begin to follow it. The remaining Elders moved in on J997 and Resita, but Lanresia and Rakam began firing on them with their own rifles, thus protecting the robot and the bird from being killed.

As for me, I found myself confronted by both Assassin and Kiriah without any allies to back me up. Assassin swung his sword at me, but I blocked it with mine own, while Kiriah stood at a short distance, aiming her own gun at us both, though she didn't fire, probably because she did not wish to accidentally hit

DESINENCE

Assassin.

Assassin and I pushed against each other, neither one giving way. Assassin had the strength of a machine, which far dwarfed mine natural strength, but I had the iron determination to never give up, which more than made up for mine inadequate strength.

"You are far stronger than I thought you were going to be," said Assassin, a hint of savage delight in his voice which did make me feel ill. "Look at you ... holding your own against me all by yourself. This is exactly what I wanted from you all along. A *real* fight. I've wanted this, and also to see your head roll."

"Ye ... have twisted desires, clicker," I said, pushing against him as hard as I was able. "But I should not have expected much else from a machine whose name is Assassin. The blood of many innocents is on your hands, and it is blood that I shall avenge. Justice has finally caught up with ye, ye mechanical monstrosity."

"Brave words coming from a weakling like you," said Assassin. "Let's see how you handle a little electricity."

He suddenly reached out with one hand and grabbed my wrist. A jolt of electricity shot through his hand into mine arm, causing me to cry out in pain. As I result, I slipped, allowing Assassin to push me backwards.

Mine body still jolted, I staggered backward as Assassin rushed in for the kill. But I recovered in time to block his blow again, although this time just barely, for now Assassin was not holding back. His sword deflected off mine, but then he raised his hand and I held my sword again to protect myself from his next electric attack.

But then my sword flew out of mine hands and landed in his free one. He then held both of the swords before him, striking a pose that sent fear into mine heart.

"Magnetism," said Assassin with a chuckle. "Remember? I showed it to you all the way back when we first met. I wonder if the Brain Editor removed that particular memory from your brain; but it hardly matters, because I'll slaughter you like the defenseless lamb you are."

I stepped away from him, even though I had no intention of fleeing, but then a laser struck me in the abdomen. Mine metalligick armor did protect me from the worst of the blast, but it still hit me hard enough to make me stagger and look in the direction in which the laser had came.

Kiriah was still aiming her gun at me. I did not see any of her usual kindness in her eyes; instead, I saw the blank eyes of a killer, eyes as terrible and wrathful as the eyes of an unforgiving goddess. She was willing to murder me. 'Twas a sobering realization indeed, but I understood that mine only chances at survival were to reason with her and make her see the light.

"Sister!" I said, reaching out to her. "Do ye not recognize your older brother? The one who ye grew up with and loved?"

"I only see a traitor to Reunification who needs to be killed," said Kiriah. "Just like Sura, who didn't even have the decency to stay dead."

"Ye know of his survival?" I said.

Kiriah nodded. "It was obvious. We didn't find a body down here, so I knew he must have survived. I was hoping to kill him myself, but I guess I won't get to do that today."

"This is all very nice, but why don't you save your little family reunion for later?" asked Assassin. "Then again, it probably does make sense to get this out of the way right away, seeing as Apakerec won't live long enough to see the new world."

With the speed of a Lizard-man, Assassin launched himself at me, swinging both his sword and mine through the air as he did so. At the same time, Kiriah took aim again, only I noticed her making a couple of adjustments to the gun. Perhaps she was changing its settings from stun to kill; I knew not for certain, but it did give me an idea that I had not considered before.

Just as Assassin's blades were with inches of my head, I ducked and rolled ahead, just underneath the flying Assassin. Assassin landed with a metallic crunch on the uneven ground, letting out an angry curse as he did so; at the same time, Kiriah fired her gun, sending a red glowing laser hurtling through the air toward the spot where I had stood not one moment ago.

Of course, I was not standing there anymore; however, Assassin was. He looked in the direction of the incoming laser just in time for it to strike him directly in the face (or face plate, as 'twas the case with him).

As I suspected, the laser was stronger than normal, for when it struck Assassin's face plate, his head exploded, sending shrapnel and wiring everywhere. His headless body immediately fell forward onto the dirt and lay there like a corpse, dropping the swords as he did so, which clattered to the ground around him.

I stood up, but as soon as I did, Kiriah aimed her rifle at me. I raised mine hands to show that I 'twas unarmed, but her aim did not waver even once, as if my being unarmed mattered not to her.

"Good trick," said Kiriah, the hatred in her voice so palpable that I could almost taste it. "Got me to kill Assassin for you. Should have expected as much."

"Sister, ye do not understand," I said. I pointed at the Portal.

"Sura is *dead*. He was killed by Kalcan, one of Reunification's Elders. 'Twas murdered in cold blood right before mine eyes."

Those words did make Kiriah hesitate. I saw a little bit of sadness in her eyes.

But then she shook her head and said, "And? He deserved it. He rejected the Founder's offer to join our organization. He simply got what everyone who rejects us get when they say no. I am *glad* that Kalcan killed him."

"Sister, this is our eldest brother that ye are speaking of," I said. "Do ye not remember Sura? He always loved and protected us. He was the greatest eldest brother that anyone could ever ask for. And yet here ye are, treating him like so much garbage under your feet. Why?"

I spoke as passionately and eloquently as I could. I hoped to break through whatever mind control that the Founder had put her under, but it was impossible for me to tell for certain whether any of mine words were getting through to her. That she had not yet shot me so far did make me feel that there might still be some of the old Kiriah in her, but she had not lowered her gun, either, or taken her finger off the trigger.

"He ..." Kiriah seemed to struggle to find the words. "He deserved it. The Founder said so. He would have been an obstacle. And based on what you've told me, he *did* get in the way of the Mission. And that meant he had to be killed, just as I am supposed to kill you."

"Do ye even hear the words spewing forth out of your own mouth like the excrement that it is?" I said. "Do ye not love Sura more than the Founder? What has the Founder done for ye that Sura has not? What has the Founder done for ye that *I* have not?"

DESINENCE

Those last two questions must have hit her hard, for Kiriah merely stared at me uncomprehendingly in response. She opened her mouth, but then closed it, and looked like she was giving mine questions serious, respectful thought. Her trigger finger trembled, and with it, her aim.

"The Founder ..." Kiriah bit her lower lip and furrowed her brows. "The Founder ... he ..."

"He has done *nothing* for ye," I said. I gestured at all around us. "Look at what he has done. He has divided our family, and for what purpose, but to bring about the deaths of billions of innocent lives to fulfill his false destiny? He has beaten me and nearly killed Sura; indeed, ye could argue that he *did* kill Sura, seeing as Kalcan was one of his servants and 'twas acting in his name when he did the vile deed. The Founder is a wicked man who has brought nothing but pain and division to our family, to say nothing of what he has done to everyone else in the two worlds."

I was well pleased to see that Kiriah was beginning to look as though she were starting to believe me. She even lowered her gun, a doubtful, worried expression on her face that told me that she was not certain what to believe.

"Rii ..." Kiriah shook her head, like she was awakening from a terrible nightmare. "I—"

I never got to hear the rest of her sentence, because the sound of blades whistling through the air toward me entered my ears. I looked to mine right and saw Assassin's blades coming at me.

Alarmed, I ducked, narrowly avoiding getting mine head cut clean off by mine own blade. But Assassin's sword came in at my abdomen and pierced my armor.

The blow made me scream in pain, made me scream louder

than I ever had before, and it immediately brought back dozens of images to mine mind. I saw myself sitting at a cafe with a Jikorian merchant; saw mine first confrontation with Assassin; witnessed my awakening in the Foundation's Xeeonite HQ; and finally, saw an image of the Founder bending over me, his hands reaching for mine face.

All of these memories—and much, much more—played out before me like a telescreen story. I collapsed onto the ground, covering mine wound with mine hands, trying to stem the blood, but that did seem like an impossible task, for it felt like Assassin had stabbed one of my vital organs. I could not tell which one, however, for I was in too much pain to think deeply about anything.

Looking up, I saw Assassin standing above me, his body now headless. Electricity sparked from the place where his head had been, but he held his swords as tightly as ever, like losing his head had only been a minor inconvenience, if even that.

"You look surprised," said Assassin, whose voice, I now noticed, came from his chest. "I'm a robot. Did you really think that we robots need *heads* in order to survive?"

He then waved at Kiriah with mine sword and said, "By the way, Kiriah, you have terrible aim. And you are letting him play psychological games with you. Then again, I've never expected you to be smart enough to see through the manipulations of others. You're really rather naïve that way."

Still trying to stem the flow of blood from my wound as best as I could, I looked up at Kiriah. She was staring at Assassin and me with a confused and worried expression. She was clearly uncertain about what she needed to do or how she needed to act, though with her gun still lowered, I doubted she would be shooting anyone anytime soon.

"Anyway, I'm tired of playing with you, Apakerec," said Assassin. He raised his swords. "Time to finish you off once and for all."

I looked up at Assassin, despite the pain burning in mine gut like the fires of a thousand suns. 'Twas no way I could stop him now. He would kill me for absolutely certain. Whilst he had no head, and therefore no eyes, for me to see, I did tell that he was indeed going to finish me off this time, and cruelly, too.

But before he could bring down his swords on my body, Kiriah raised her gun and fired shot after shot at Assassin. The lasers struck Assassin in the side, causing him to stagger and drop his swords again, but Kiriah gave him not even one moment to react. She just shot again and again, her aim never wavering, each blast striking home. This did surprise me, for I had never known that my sister had such good aim.

Even better, the lasers tore through Assassin's armored plating, sending chunks flying everywhere, until they eventually tore a large hole in the side of his body. One more shot from mine sister's gun and Assassin's upper body exploded. I did cover mine helmeted head to protect it from the shrapnel, but the lasers had forced Assassin to retreat more than a few feet away from me, so I suffered not the worst blows.

Then I looked and saw that Assassin's legs lay on the earth, smoke rising from the waist. Still, I did not yet quite celebrate, for it did seem likely that Assassin was going to rise again, though I doubted that a pair of legs could be that dangerous to me.

Then the pain in my wound burned even harder and I cried

255

out, slapping mine hands over it. It did feel like there were sharp metal things in there, but 'twas impossible for me to remove them, for I was no surgeon, and even if I were, I was in no position to perform surgery on mine self.

Kiriah was at my side instantly. She bended over me, putting her gun down as she looked at my bloody wound, a look of terrible grief crossing her features.

"Oh my gods, Rii," said Kiriah. Her voice made her sound close to tears. "I'm sorry. I don't know what happened. I thought the Founder ... please forgive me."

"Yea, I forgive ye, sister," I said. Then I bit mine lower lip to keep from screaming from the pain. "But could ye help close the wound? I doubt ye have any medical supplies on hand, but—"

"Yes, yes, of course," said Kiriah. She wiped away the tears in her eyes and tore off the sleeve of her red robes, which she then stuffed over mine wound and held down. "This should staunch the bleeding, but we'll need to get you to an actual doctor as soon as possible."

"Later," I said with a grimace. I looked toward the Portal and noticed how dangerously close the two Unification Stones were to one another now. "For now, we must find some way to close the Portal before it is too late."

Kiriah looked up at the battle betwixt the Founder and the Head in the air—which still moved too fast for mine eyes to follow—and then looked down at me. "I don't want to leave you, brother. I want to stay by your side. Besides, I don't think there's anything either of us can do to close that Portal at the moment."

"But ye should return to battle," I said. I gestured at the other fight, the one betwixt the Elders and the remaining Foundation agents, which 'twas occurring not too far away. "Go and aid them. I will be fine here."

But Kiriah shook her head. She wiped still more tears from her eyes and said, "No. They don't need my help. I want to stay with and protect you. You need help in your current condition. I don't want to lose another brother."

Her voice almost broke when she said that, and then she lowered her face into her hands and began sobbing. This did make me alarmed.

"Sister, hold your tears," I said, though I barely finished the sentence due to the pain in my wound. "I understand your sorrow, but right now is not the time to cry, but to be brave. Ask the Old Gods to give ye strength."

Kiriah ceased sobbing and lowered her hands from her face. Tears still ran down her cheeks, but she did wipe them away, saying as she did so, "Y-You're right. No time for crying. I can do that later. But I still won't abandon you. I'm staying right by your side until this is all over."

I sighed, although I had to cut mine sigh short when the pain in mine side burned. "Very well, sister. But I am not certain how much help ye can be, for ye are no doctor."

"I just want to be by your side," said Kiriah. "And make sure you don't die."

"Then I hope ye made the right decision," I said, looking up at the fight betwixt the Founder and the Head again, "for if ye did not, then ye will not live long enough to regret it."

Chapter 19

The Elders did not appear to be strong fighters at first, mostly because none of them appeared armed. As soon as the fight starts, however, the human Elder—a short, fat man with a ponytail, whose name I do not know, because the mobile Database has no information on these Elders at all—raises his hands, upon which I notice are three skyras rings.

I find it puzzling that a Xeeonite native apparently wears skyras rings before he snaps his fingers and sends a black lightning bolt flying to our direction from the ring on his middle finger. Quickly, I raise my electrical barrier, which deflects the bolt, but the impact is so great that it saps me of about five percent of my energy in one blow, leaving me at 37%, which is too low for me, but I have no time to recharge it right now and so must make do with what I have.

I respond by shooting my laser vision, but the human Elder's second ring glows like a crystal and an energy barrier appears around him and his friends. My lasers strike the barrier and instantly dissipate, leaving the Elders on the other side unharmed by the attack.

"Foolish machine," says the human Elder. "You think you can

defeat us and stop the Mission? None of you can. It is too late. The Unification Stones will be reunited and all shall be as the Founder says it will be."

"If you are so strong, then why don't you drop your shield and fight me?" I ask.

The human Elder growls and lowers his shield, but as soon as he does, Rakam and Lanresia appear on either side of me and begin firing off their PRBs at him. This forces the Elders to separate, but the human Elder's third ring glows and a chunk of the earth flies up out of the ground toward us.

I fire my finger lightning bolts and laser vision at the chunk of earth, causing it to explode in midair. As it explodes, the Checrom Elder draws what looks like a trigger from her robe pockets and presses it, causing her to instantly vanish into thin air. But my sensors tell me that she is still in the vicinity, although she is invisible and it is hard to track her movements.

As for the Jikorian Elder, she draws tiny darts from her robe sleeves and throws them at us all at once. I jump in front of Lanresia, who the darts were thrown at, and the darts bounce off my metallic skin.

"Wow," says Lanresia in surprise behind me. "You saved my life."

"I am aware of that, Lanresia," I say, without looking at her. "But that does not mean that I have forgiven you for betraying me and Konoa. I only saved you because I need your help defeating Reunification."

Lanresia says nothing to that. Instead, she runs around me toward the Jikorian Elder, firing her PRB at her, but the Elder is quicker than she appears and easily outruns and dodges Lanresia's lasers.

Seeing that Lanresia has that Elder under control, I look at the human elder, who has stopped running. He raises his hand, the one with the rings on it, but I am not going to let him use them again.

Locking onto his ring fingers, I shoot my lasers at them. The lasers cut his fingers clean off, causing the human Elder to cry out in pain and fall to his knees, grabbing his now bleeding hand and cursing foully in Delan.

I want to walk over and knock him out, but I still have to protect Resita, who has covered his head with his arms and looks like he is trying to survive a bombing. He is still bleeding from the shot he received to the shoulder and is in no position to fight. Rakam is no longer by my side; instead, she is searching for the invisible Checrom Elder who vanished earlier.

So I lower the power level on my eye lasers and fire them at the human Elder again. But before they hit, he raises his other hand—which, I notice too late, has three more rings on it—and captures my lasers in the middle ring.

Now *that* is something I have never seen before, but I do not have time to analyze it or generate an entry for it in the mobile Database, because the human Elder—now grinning, despite the fact that his left hand is still missing three fingers and is bleeding profusely—punches the air.

My lasers fly out of the ring again, only this time they look thicker and redder and hotter than before. Not only that, but they fly through the air so fast that even my optics cannot keep track of them.

I try to duck to avoid them, but the lasers somehow still end up striking my shoulder. The resulting strike blows off my right arm, sending it falling to the ground with a *clunk* as I stagger to the side.

Systems indicate that my right arm is missing, but otherwise no other problems are reported. Still, losing my right arm will make me less effective, which means that my chances of even surviving this fight are much lower than they were even a few seconds ago.

The human Elder gets back to his feet, still smiling, but it is the same kind of smile I see on the faces of murderers and criminals all the time in my line of work. He will not rest until I am destroyed, which means I have to think quickly and act quicker.

At least he is still missing the fingers on his left hand, which leaves him far weaker than he once was. I may have lost an arm, but I feel no pain from the loss, whereas the human Elder must inevitably be feeling quite a bit of pain at the moment.

Then he snatches up his dismembered fingers from the ground and places his intact right hand over his left hand. The second ring on his right hand glows and, when he removes his right hand, his left hand is whole once more.

I see. *That* is why he is smiling. He knew all along that his loss of fingers was going to be a temporary setback. Even I have to admit that that is a clever move on his part, if only because I cannot reattach my own arm as easily as I would like to.

The human Elder raises his right hand as his third ring shines. As soon as he does so, a ball of some kind of energy—possibly pure skyras, but with my skyras sensors currently deactivated, I cannot tell for sure—appears in his hand. It grows larger and larger, along with his smile, which tells me that that energy ball is more than large enough to destroy me if he throws it.

I can avoid it easily. With both of my legs in functioning order, I should be able to run out of the way without any trouble. That way, I can at least live long enough to come up with another plan to defeat him.

But then I remember that Resita cannot get up and run with me. Even if he could, we would still have to move slowly, because he is currently in no condition to run anywhere. Nor can I just leave him. Despite knowing that Resita is a member of the Foundation, I don't think he is as bad as some of the others, so I will not abandon him.

Yet I cannot simply stand here and let the human Elder kill us both. That is madness, but I can think of no way to save both of us, especially as the energy ball is growing larger and larger every second, and I don't think I have enough power to destroy it.

What about Palos's ring? I know how to use magic now. I can teleport us both out of the way of the sphere's trajectory.

But what if the ring drains me of most if not all of my energy? That would leave me open to attack, maybe even destroy me entirely.

I have no real choice in the matter, however, because the human Elder launches the energy ball at me at that exact moment. I pop open my chest compartment and fish out Palos's ring, which I wrap around my metallic fingers as hard as I can.

Bending down next to Resita, I say, "Grab on!"

He thankfully does not question my order. He grabs onto my arms with his thin, chipped claws. As soon as he does, I close my optics and focus on the ring in my hand.

DESINENCE

A second later, the world shifts around me. Opening my optics, I see that Resita and I are both right behind the human Elder, exactly as I planned. My energy levels are currently at 34%; not the dramatic drop I experienced before, but that may be because I had to teleport a much shorter distance than last time.

In any case, when the energy ball strikes the spot where Resita and I had been and explodes, the human Elder whirls around, staring at us with shocked eyes, and says, "What the—"

I do not let him finish his sentence. Instead, I turn my eye lasers to their full power and fire directly at his forehead. The twin lasers create a hole in his forehead and strike his brain, causing him to instantly collapse.

Scanners indicate that the human Elder is dead. I stand up, still holding Palos's ring in my hand, while Resita says, "Hey, J997?"

I look down at him. He looks even weaker than before, no doubt due to the blood loss. Even so, he manages to look up at me with a mixture of surprise and curiosity, like he has forgotten all about his current problems in the face of my actions.

"Yes, Resita?" I say. "What is the problem? Do you require medical assistance? Because I will not be able to provide it to you right away, seeing as I have no medical supplies on me at the moment."

"No," says Resita, shaking his head. He points at my left hand. "How did you teleport using a skyras ring? I thought robots couldn't use magic."

I shrug. "I do not know. I discovered how to use skyras rings less than an hour ago. But it is useful, wouldn't you say?"

"It is," says Resita, nodding. He grabs his shoulder and

grimaces, although he keeps speaking. "But it's supposed to be impossible. Magic and technology are supposed to be incompatible. How did you achieve what so many scientists and wizards have been unable to do for decades?"

"I do not know," I say. "Nor do I think it matters all that much, because the other Elders are still alive and so is the Founder. We can study this later, when the situation is calmer."

Resita still stares at me with awe, but I do not pay him any more attention. I take this brief respite to scan the rest of the battlefield to determine the status of my allies.

The Knight known as Apakerec is currently at the mercy of Assassin, although the robot appears to be missing his head for some reason. Kiriah is aiming her gun—no, *my* gun, which the Founder stole from me and gave to her—at them, though she seems hesitant to shoot.

But as I watch, she fires my gun over and over at Assassin. She must have the settings turned up all the way, because each blow takes out a chunk of Assassin's body, until she creates a hole through which she shoots another blast. This makes Assassin's upper body explode in a loud, fiery explosion, although it is too far away to harm me or Resita, thankfully.

It appears that Kiriah has come over to our side, then, because she then runs over to Apakerec and bends over him. Seeing as Assassin is apparently dead and Apakerec is going to be all right, I look to see what Rakam and Lanresia are doing.

Lanresia is still running after and shooting at the Jikorian Elder, but the Elder continues to outrun her. As for Rakam, she is now lying flat on the ground in a pool of her own blue Jikorian blood.

DESINENCE

That is not good. From a distance, it appears like the Checrom Elder who she was going after slit her throat. There is no saving her now, although it may be possible to stop the Checrom Elder.

Assuming we can find her, that is. I try to sense the Checrom Elder, but my low power level makes it hard to find her. She must have some way of cloaking her presence from J bot sensors, because I cannot sense her at all.

I do not know the Checrom Elder well enough to be able to say what she might be doing. But knowing the general disposition of most Reunification agents, I imagine she is still here in this pit, most likely trying to help the Founder kill us all.

The only question is, where is she at this very moment? I doubt she will go after Lanresia, because Lanresia is armed and is currently chasing her friend, and it seems unlikely that she will attack me, either, because despite my damages, I am still not easily killed.

Logically, she must be going after whoever is the weakest link. That is, whoever is wounded and unable to defend themselves. That describes Resita well, but I am currently protecting Resita, which makes attacking him the same as attacking me. That makes me wonder, who, exactly, she may be going after until a sudden explanation clicks in my head.

I look in the direction of Kiriah and Apakerec. The two appear engrossed in their own conversations. Kiriah still has my gun, but she has put it on the ground next to her and may not be quick enough to retrieve it in time.

That is when I see a smudge of bright blue Jikorian blood—the Elder, who must have gotten some on her robes when she killed Rakam—walking through the air toward Kiriah. Because

265

Kiriah's back is turned to it, neither she nor Apakerec notice it.

The Checrom Elder must already know about Kiriah's apparent betrayal. I know exactly how Reunification deals with traitors—it's not much different from how the Foundation does, apparently—and so I can guess quite easily at what the Elder is about to do to her.

The Elder is outside the range of my laser eyes; besides, even if she wasn't, I still could not trust my lasers to hit her, because I cannot lock onto something I cannot see. That means I need to run quickly to get her within range of my lasers.

I dash forward as quickly as I can, but I feel more sluggish than usual. It is probably due to the immense amount of energy I have used up in the last hour alone; still, I keep going, because I do not want either Kiriah or Apakerec to die.

But as I run, a huge fireball comes crashing out of the air, forcing me to roll forward to avoid getting hit. Rolling back to my feet, I keep running, ignoring the fireball that crashes into the ground and creates a loud explosion that almost knocks out my audio receptors. It is likely that the fireball was thrown by the Founder, but my focus is still on the tiny blotch of blue blood that is slowly but surely sneaking up behind Kiriah.

Yet even running at full speed, I know I will not get there in time to save Kiriah and Apakerec. So I shout, "Kiriah! Behind you!"

Kiriah looks up at me in surprise, dried tears on her face. At the same time, the Checrom Elder materializes behind her, holding a long, bloody knife in her talons that she raises above her head.

"Taste death, you traitor!" says the Checrom Elder.

DESINENCE

She brings her knife down on Kiriah's head, but Apakerec, despite clearly being wounded, pushes Kiriah out of the way. That, however, does not stop the trajectory of the Elder's knife, which deflects off Apakerec's metalligick armor.

The blow causes the Checrom Elder to stagger backwards, but Apakerec does not let her escape. He rises to his feet, so angry that even I can sense his wrath, holding one of Assassin's swords. He does not even say one word as he beheads the startled Checrom Elder in one stroke, causing her body to collapse and her head to roll a few feet away.

"Take that, ye foul bird," says Apakerec, his voice ragged and strained, while his free hand presses against his wound. "No one attempts to murder my sister and lives. Nay, not even one."

But then Apakerec coughs and collapses onto his face. Kiriah —who is now sitting up and shaking her head—quickly crawls over to Apakerec, saying, "Brother, brother! Wake up, brother."

It takes me only a couple more seconds to reach the siblings. Apakerec's body isn't moving at all, and the wound in his side is still bleeding profusely, but as with Resita, there is nothing I can do to heal him.

Kiriah is shaking him now, trying to get him to wake up, but her actions do not even make him stir. More tears are flowing from her eyes as she says, "Come on, brother, come on. Get up. Don't die. Please don't die."

I have never understood why humans demand that their dying ones live when it clearly does not work. No medical textbook I know of says that demanding that your dying loved ones do not die will keep them alive. It is yet another mystery of humanity— and organics in general, I suppose, although humans seem to do it more often than other organics—that I will probably never understand.

But seeing Apakerec lying here does remind me of Palos and her dead body. Apakerec is not yet dead, but the circumstances are too similar for me to dismiss. And just like with Palos, I am powerless to save him, even though I want to.

Shaking my head, I hear a loud laser shot and look over my shoulder. Lanresia is standing over the corpse of the Jikorian Elder, who is lying in the dirt with a clear, smoking hole in her forehead. Lanresia kicks the dead Elder in the side, which seems unnecessary to me. Perhaps the Elder said something to offend her.

In any case, by my estimation, all of the Elders and Assassin are now dead. With Kiriah obviously defecting to our side, that means that the only member of Reunification still fighting is the Founder.

Speaking of the Founder, I have been too caught up in our fights down here for me to pay much attention to the Founder and the Head's fight in the air. I look up and see that the two have taken their fight closer to the Unification Stone, which itself is now closer to its twin on the other side of the Portal, so close now that I doubt it will be much longer before the two finally reunite.

The Founder's hands are glowing and he is using some kind of martial arts to assault the Head, but she's quicker than him, using her wings to fly in and out of his reach like a bumblebee. She strikes with energy blasts of her own, but as far as I can tell, they are not even hurting the Founder, although it might simply be that the Founder is a powerful being who cannot be harmed easily.

Whatever the case, I consider aiding the Head, but then

remember that both Apakerec and Resita are gravely injured. Somehow, both of them need to be healed, but the question is, how?

That is when I remember the human Elder. His corpse is still lying where I left it; that is, near Resita. And as far as I can tell, his rings are still attached to his fingers, so I shout to Lanresia (who has stopped by Resita to apparently check on his health), "Lanresia! Take the human Elder's skyras rings! One of them should be a healing ring. It is on his right hand."

Lanresia nods and dashes over to the dead Elder. She removes all of his rings—no doubt to keep anyone else from using them—and then dashes back over to Resita without me even suggesting that she do so.

She slips the Elder's healing ring over one of her fingers and places a hand on Resita's wound. The healing ring flashes with a bright light and then Lanresia stands up and dashes over to us without asking Resita how he is feeling, which no doubt means that he is going to be all right for now. I still think we should get him to an actual doctor at some point, however, because I am uncertain just how effective Delanian magic is in healing wounds.

Lanresia runs past me and stops next to Apakerec. She bends down next to him and reaches for his bloody wound; another flash of light later and she removes her hand, saying, "All right. Both of them should be healed now."

"You mean my brother will live?" asks Kiriah, sniffling.

Lanresia looks at Kiriah with utter loathing—probably because she remembers Kiriah was the Leader of Reunification—before she nods and says, "Yes. But I doubt he will awake anytime soon. He clearly suffered severe blood loss and—"

Apakerec groans so loudly that it causes both Lanresia and Kiriah to start. He pushes himself up, shaking his head. He then gets into a sitting position, with some help from Kiriah, who is now holding him like she doesn't want to let go of him ever again.

"By the Old Gods," says Apakerec, rubbing the back of his helmeted head. "I nearly died there. Did think I 'twas dead for a brief period, in fact."

"You can thank Lanresia for that," says Kiriah, nodding at the female elf. "She healed you."

Apakerec looks at Lanresia and says, "Verily? Well, then I must thank ye, Lanresia. For without ye, I would indeed be a dead man, and mine sister would be alone in the two worlds."

Lanresia shakes her head, but even I can tell that she truly appreciates Apakerec's gratitude. "No problem. It wasn't that hard."

Apakerec rubs his healed wound and says, "Have we won the battle, then?"

"Not yet, brother," says Kiriah. She points at the Unification Stone and the Portal. "The Founder and the Head are still fighting."

"We must aid the Head," says Apakerec. He grabs his sword and starts to stand, although it seems like a struggle for him, probably due to the sheer exhaustion of everything he has been through recently. "She needs our help. The Old Gods placed the fate of our worlds in our hands. We must therefore not neglect this holy duty of ours and allow the Founder to win."

"Easier said than done, Apakerec," I say. I gesture at the Founder and the Head, who are still fighting as furiously as ever above. "The Founder and the Head are above all of us in terms of sheer power they command. Trying to intervene in the fight— even to help the Head—will only result in our deaths. Even if we survive, I doubt any of us could even touch the Founder."

"But we must," says Apakerec. He finally succeeds in standing up, but leans on his sister for support. "The Head said that the only way to close the Portal is to kill the Founder. If we fail to kill him, then the Unification Stones will reunite and death will come upon all of the lives on both worlds."

"True, but none of us can hurt the Founder, as I just said," I say. "Especially when you consider how tired and wounded we all are. The best we can do is watch the battle and hope that the Head is victorious."

"Nay, machine," says Apakerec, shaking his head. "We must think of *something* we can do. There must be some way to aid the Head. But how?"

I stroke my chin in thought, but unfortunately I cannot think of anything. And based on the thinking expressions of Lanresia and Kiriah, they, too, are stumped in this area.

But then Apakerec snaps his fingers and says, "Ah ha! Inspiration from the Old Gods has descended upon me in the form of the perfect plan!"

I look at Kiriah. "Does your brother always speak this way?"

Kiriah shrugs. "It's the High Tongue of our forefathers. It's kind of how we're *supposed* to speak. I just stopped talking that way after I joined Reunification because no one else in Reunification spoke that way."

"It matters not whether we speak the High Tongue at the moment," says Apakerec. "For I have thought of a plan, a way to possibly close the Portal. I know not if it will work, but it seems to me quite possible."

I look at the Unification Stones again. They are now so close that I doubt it will be much longer before they are connected. Maybe within the next ten minutes at most.

"Tell us your plan, Apakerec," I say, looking at him again. "All of us are listening."

Chapter Twenty

After explaining mine plan as best as I could, the four of us split up without another word. J997 and Lanresia headed for the Xeeonite Unification Stone, whilst Kiriah and I headed for the Delanian one on the other side of the Portal. All the while, the Founder and the Head continued their epic battle, but 'twas unimportant to me at the moment.

As Kiriah and I walked, I quickly reviewed the plan in my mind. 'Twas a rather simple plan on the face of it, but it could just as easily fail, so I had to review it to look for any possible flaws that might fatally affect its success.

The Head had explained to me earlier that it had been due to J997 and me touching the Unification Stones simultaneously that had started the reunification process. She had explained that it was because I was a native of Dela and he a native of Xeeo that it worked out that way.

But I thought, what if the reverse 'twas true? What if Kiriah and I, as natives of Dela, touched the Delanian Stone at the same time as J997 and Lanresia, who were natives of Xeeo? Might it possibly reverse the process, maybe even end the reunification process entirely?

'Twas no certain plan to work, especially considering how little I understood about these Stones. Still, it was infinitely superior to sitting around and watching the Head fight the Founder for the future of our worlds. And if it failed, I could at least go to the Gods' Abode knowing that I tried to save our worlds.

Even as we walked, however, I looked over mine shoulder at Resita. He was still lying where we left him, but Lanresia had assured me that he would be okay, as all of our enemies were now dead. Still, I did worry for his safety, though I put it out of mine mind for now as Kiriah and I made our way to the Portal.

Thus far, neither the Head nor the Founder seemed to suspect that anything was amiss. They were so engrossed in their conflict in the air that I thought the worlds could have ended around them and they still would not have noticed. It did make me wonder about their past, but again I thought not too deeply about it, for mine current preoccupation was with mine plan and whether it would work or not.

I did, however, look to see if Lanresia and J997 were in their positions yet. They were almost there, but the battle betwixt the Founder and the Head took place closer to Xeeo's Unification Stone, so they had to be careful to avoid getting hit by a stray energy blast of some sort. Still, I was confident that they would make it in time.

As Kiriah and I drew closer to the Portal, however, the immense power radiating from the Stones did begin to affect me. It did feel like a powerful heat wave washed over me, but Kiriah and I pushed forward, not allowing the Stones' power to overwhelm us. The energy beam connecting the two Stones was loud and appeared lethal, but we were thankfully not in danger of walking into it due to how high above the ground it 'twas.

Mine sister and I did pass through the Portal without difficulty. As we did so, I saw mine sister's head turn to look at Sura's body, which lay on the ground where Kalcan had killed him. She choked next to me, but she did not stop or break down. That did make me glad, for I had worried that she might lose herself when she saw Sura's corpse.

The two of us then stood in front of Dela's Unification Stone. 'Twas still a massive stone, but I cared not to admire its strange, otherworldly beauty. Instead, I looked through the Portal, trying to see if J997 and Lanresia were yet in place.

Thankfully, they were. The two stood side by side in front of Xeeo's Unification Stone, holding their hands out to touch it. But not yet, for we had to time our touching the Stones so they would be in sync. The plan depended on our touching the Stones simultaneously, although again I still knew not if this would even work.

But I banished all doubt and worry from mine mind. I prayed a prayer to the Old Gods, asking them to aid us, to give Kiriah, J997, Lanresia, and me the aid we needed to help our plan work.

Thus, I looked at J997 and Lanresia again. The two nodded in our direction to confirm that they were ready to do their part.

And so, with a nod of our own, Kiriah and I raised our own hands and reached for the Stone. Simultaneously, I saw J997 and Lanresia performing the same movements.

And then our hands touched the Unification Stones at exactly the same moment.

Even though I had already touched the Unification Stone

before, I was not prepared for what I felt now. Immense amount of energy—pure skyras—flowed through the Stone's surface into mine body. It was almost too much. Mine innards felt like they were melting, my heartbeat sped up, and I sweated profusely. 'Twas as though my whole body was about to explode, but I did not remove mind hand, nor did Kiriah or J997 or Lanresia.

Not only that, but I felt a consciousness within the Stone that I had not felt before. It was as alien and strange as the minds of the Old Gods. I could feel it pleading with me and Kiriah to stop what we were doing, to spare it, but I did not listen to it. 'Twas like a wicked devil, attempting to make us stop our mission, but there was no way in all of the two worlds that Kiriah, J997, Lanresia, and I would cease our actions.

And then, just like that, the energy beam connecting the two Unification Stones vanished. With it went that consciousness that had been pleading with Kiriah and me, along with the overwhelming skyras energy within. We pulled our hands away from the Stone's surface, but 'twas a difficult feat, for our hands seemed to stick to the Stone's surface like it was covered in thickest honey.

We turned to see the Portal starting to close. Without the power of the Unification Stones to strengthen it, the Portal could no longer support itself. It started to close like the curtain of a theater, lowering down, gradually obscuring mine view of Xeeo. This did fill my heart with gladness, for it meant that our plan had worked and that the two worlds were saved.

But then, without warning, the Founder landed in front of the Portal on the Xeeonite side. His robes looked burnt and his face was bloodied, but he stepped into the Portal and held up his hands. He caught the top of the Portal and somehow managed to hold it up. 'Twas an astonishing and terrifying sight, for I had never seen a living being hold open a Portal like that before.

"No …" said the Founder. His words tremble, but there is a clear sadness and anger in them that I cannot deny. He struggled against the Portal, which was trying to close on him. "I will not let all of my years … my centuries … my millenniums … of work be for nothing. The worlds need to be healed … the Rock needs to be healed … we must all be brought together again … together again …"

The Head appeared behind him without warning and wrapped her arms around his waist. She then squeezed and pulled, saying, "Let go! You will die if you stand here! Your Mission has failed. Accept it. If you come with me, you can live."

"Never!" the Founder screamed, but in that moment, I thought I heard two voices in his scream; one human, the other robotic. "Kara, you must listen to me. I will return Fariah to what it once was. *We* will return Fariah to what it once was. Vyll and Carem still live within me. They only want what is best for all of us. You must aid me. There is still time."

"There is no time, Founder," said the Head, shaking her head as she continued to pull him. "Fariah is dead. The Rock is dead. You must learn to accept these truths and move on."

"Nothing is true if I do not say it is!" the Founder shouted. "Let go of me, you foul woman, let go!"

The Founder's body catches flame, like he set himself on fire. The Head lets go immediately, walking backwards away. The flame on the Founder's body burns away his robes and even melts the skin of his organic half and his mechanical half. 'Tis an ugly sight, especially when the combined stink of melting skin and metal flows into mine nostrils.

"I will achieve my destiny," said the Founder, his two voices now sounding distorted and frightening. His eyeballs appeared to be leaking out of his sockets due to the sheer heat of the flames that engulfed him. "We will be together again ... all of us will be ... it will be just like old times ... before the war ... just like in the picture ..."

The Founder sounded heartbroken and confused. In fact, I began to pity him. I had thought for a long time that he was a vile and foul being, worthy of nothing but the most gruesome of fates, but now I saw nothing more than a small, scared person who merely wanted his home back. It did fill mine heart with sadness. Kiriah was even crying again, but I knew not if she cried because she came to the same conclusion as I or if the stress of the situation had finally gotten to her.

"Just like old times," said the Founder, though he now spoke in a single voice that was a lot softer than his normal one. He smiled, which looked hideous on his melting eyes and face. "Kara, Carem, and me ..."

Then, without warning, his arms gave out and the Portal slammed shut on him and he was gone.

Chapter 21

With the Portal closed, the pit becomes dark again, but then the Head creates a glowing light in her hand. It gives us some illumination, allowing me to see burns and wounds on the Head's body and wings that I had not noticed before.

There is no sign whatsoever of the Founder. I turn my skyras sensors back on, because I believe it is safe to do so now with both of the Unification Stones off. All I sense is the Head's skyras energy now, which, while powerful, is not overwhelming for my sensors.

"What happened to the Founder?" asks Lanresia. She looks pale in the glow of the Head's light. "Is he dead?"

The Head turns to look at us. If I am not mistaken, tears are running down her face, but when she speaks, her words are quite clear and without emotion.

"Most likely," says the Head. "When the Portal closed on him, he most likely ended up in the space between the worlds. There is no way that anyone, even someone as powerful as him, could have survived that."

"I agree," I say. "Does that mean that Reunification is finished?"

"Yes," says the Head. "There are still agents out there, as well as other bases, but the organization only survived due to the Founder's leadership. With the Founder and the Elders dead, and Kiriah on our side, there is no one left to lead it. What will likely happen is that the surviving agents will go into hiding to avoid being arrested and most will hopefully try to forget about all of this."

"I will locate them," I say. I gesture at the top of the pit, which is not visible in the darkness. "I will go into Reunification's headquarters and download all of their files from their computers. With luck, they should have information on every agent and base that they have on both worlds, which I will be able to provide to the governments of Dela and Xeeo to use to track down and arrest them all."

"A good plan," says the Head, nodding. "Once you do that, then Reunification will truly be dead."

"What about the Foundation?" I ask. "Are you still going to run the organization, now that Reunification is gone?"

The Head shakes her head. "No. It is no longer needed, as you said, because Reunification is no more. I will make sure to contact the surviving members who are still out there and tell them that the organization is disbanded."

"What will you do after that?" I ask. I look at Lanresia and then glance over my shoulder at Resita, who appears to be unconscious, although it is hard to tell from a distance. "Where will you go?"

Lanresia places the tip of her gun against my head, her finger on the trigger. I freeze, because I know that even with my reflexes, I cannot act quickly enough to stop her from blowing my head off and destroying my memory and personality.

"Lanresia, what are you doing?" asks the Head. "Why are you threatening his life?"

"Because I failed to kill him the first time," says Lanresia. "Him and Konoa. I should have done it back then, but I didn't because I was weak."

"I *was* about to bring up that," I say. "But I can see that I do not need to now."

Much to my surprise, the Head actually giggles at my words.

"What?" I say. "What did I say?"

"Oh, it was nothing," says the Head. She shakes her head. "I think it's just the stress of the situation, but your sarcasm was funnier than I expected, I will admit."

"Funny?" I say, ignoring the tip of Lanresia's gun against my head. "I … am funny? But I did not even tell a joke."

"It doesn't matter," says Lanresia. "If we let you live, you'll just come after us and throw us behind bars for the things we've done. There is no way I am going to let that happen."

"Lanresia, lower your gun," says the Head. "I didn't ask you to kill Konoa and him. Just Kojama. You should let him live, because he helped save our worlds."

"But …" Lanresia frowns and looks like she is struggling to think of a counterargument. "But he is going to arrest us. Aren't you, J997?"

"By all rights, I should," I say. "You two alone have committed so many felonies that I doubt even the Database could count them all. That is not even counting what your fellow agents have done or the actions of your organization over the centuries. Nor should I forget how you two betrayed Konoa and me, which makes this matter all the more personal."

"See?" says Lanresia, looking at the Head in triumph. "He's going to arrest us. We must destroy him so he can't."

"I am not finished," I say. "As I said, I *should* arrest you, but in this case, I will not. Without your aid, the two worlds would not have survived. It would be foolish, in my opinion, to punish you two for crimes that are miniscule in comparison to the good that you have done."

"Now that is unexpected," says the Head. "And here I thought you J bots valued law and order above all else. You aren't afraid that the Database will punish you for letting us get away?"

I shrug. "The Database will probably not punish me very harshly once it learns how I helped save the worlds. I cannot, however, guarantee that the Database will leave you two alone. The Database already has downloaded most of the information I know about you two, and because you two have indeed broken many laws, it will likely send my fellow officers after you two."

"I see," says the Head. "Then it looks like we will simply have to disappear. Right, Lanresia?"

Lanresia looks at the Head in surprise. "We? I thought the Foundation was disbanded."

"Officially, it is," says the Head. "But you and I and Resita have to stick together if we are going to survive and remain out of prison. Besides, I still have things I need to do and I will need both of you to help me do them."

Lanresia lowers her gun from my head. She looks quite relieved at what the Head says, which tells me that she was dreading being on her own after all of this.

"Disappear?" I say. "To where?"

DESINENCE

The Head smiles. "Do you really think I would tell you that? I don't want the Database to scan your mind and find out where we are going and then sending some of your fellow J bots after us. But we might see each other again someday, if destiny allows it."

I do not understand cryptic talk very well, but I understand the Head's reasoning behind this decision. And I happen to support it.

So I nod and say, "Very well, then. Let's return to the surface. From there, we can go our separate ways … and perhaps, as you said, meet again at some point in the future."

PART FIVE:
DESINENCE

Chapter Twenty-Two

One year later ...

How wonderful did the city of Xeeon seem today! The sun, though shining hotly, did make me feel energized and happier than I had been in a long time. The crowds of people in the streets no longer seemed like a faceless mass to me. Instead, they did seem like an interesting group to watch. Even the massive telescreens above, which blared their advertisements as loudly and obnoxiously as ever, did not bother me quite as much as they used to. On the telescreen, I saw the news replaying last year's footage from the swearing in of Mayor Mackar, the new Mayor of Xeeon, who had won the emergency election held after Xacron-Ah's corpse had been found in the basement of an abandoned apartment building.

I sat in a chair outside of the Crossways Cafe, sipping the so-called 'genuine' South Delan tea that this place served. Whilst the tea still tasted as awful as ever, I did not mind it quite so much anymore, because I was in a good mood on this blessed day.

I was waiting for mine sister, Kiriah. I did not see her anywhere in the crowds, but knew that she would show up soon. She had agreed to meet me here at ten in the morning and it was five minutes 'til. Of course, I knew she wouldn't be late, for she never missed our meetings, not even for all of the two worlds.

And then I saw her. Walking down the street toward me, she no longer wore her red robes. Instead, mine sister wore a jacket and simple blue pants that made her look quite Xeeonite in fashion. She still seemed to prefer Xeeonite clothing, most likely because she lived in Xeeon now. She even had a scanner over her left eye, which she had once told me was useful for helping her scan things, but I understood little about Xeeonite tech and the usefulness thereof and thought that it looked more than a little funny on her face.

She waved at me as she approached and quickly took a seat opposite me, causing the chair to creak under her weight. Placing her handbag on the ground next to her, Kiriah said, "Rii, long time, no see. How have you been doing?"

I smiled. "Fine, sister. I have rejoined the Knights of Se-Dela. In fact, I was promoted to the Captaincy just this week. They were quite forgiving of me when I explained to them the reasons for my absence, though Sir Lockfried still had me run one hundred laps around Castle Una anyway. Though 'twas hard for me to get another day off to visit ye, for they seemed to think I would get involved in yet another conflict betwixt another two secret organizations."

Kiriah laughed at that. "Well, I can tell you that no secret organization has offered me a leadership position, nor have they brainwashed me into serving them."

"That is good and well to hear," I say. "But tell me, sister, what ye have been up to since Sura's funeral, as it has been too long since your last letter to me."

DESINENCE

Kiriah frowned when I mentioned our older brother's funeral. We had held it shortly after we returned from the Winterlands. 'Twas a private affair, held on our family property, where we buried him in a grave next to our parents. It had been a solemn day indeed, but I felt comfortable bringing it up around Kiriah, even though thinking of his death still brought pain to our hearts.

"Got a job as Mayor Mackar's secretary," said Kiriah. "He technically doesn't need me, seeing as there are machines out there that can do the job better than me, but he wanted me to work for him to repay me for helping to save the worlds. He also granted me a pardon for my crimes I committed while in Reunification. Says that I wasn't really responsible for them, seeing as I was brainwashed the entire time."

"'Tis good to hear ye have gainful employment, sister," I said. "I did worry for ye, for Xeeon is a big city and there are many dangerous people who live here."

Kiriah chuckled. "I can take care of myself, you know. I'm a good sharpshooter, so anyone who tries to mug me will be in for a nasty surprise."

She removed part of her jacket to reveal a skyras gun strapped to her waist. I grimaced.

"A gun, sister?" I said. "'Tis a rather brutal weapon, is it not? I could train ye to use a sword instead."

"Thanks, but I like my gun," said Kiriah. "Easier to carry concealed than a sword."

"If ye say so," I said. I then looked around and frowned. "Say, where is J997? I thought he was supposed to be here with us as well."

"He is," said Kiriah. She scratched the back of her head. "I mean, I invited him, but I didn't receive a reply. Figured he's probably busy chasing down Reunification's remaining agents or maybe he's—"

"Apakerec, Kiriah," said a familiar mechanical voice behind me. "Wonderful to see you two again."

I looked over mine shoulder to see J997 walking up to us. His metallic skin was clean and shiny in the sun overhead. Indeed, he looked far better than I had seen him a year ago, almost like an entirely new robot. He even had new red stripes painted over his blue ones, but I understood not what that signified, if anything.

J997 pulled up a chair betwixt us and sat down. He did look rather awkward doing that, however, as if he was not used to sitting down in social chats with friends.

"Glad you could make it," said Kiriah, smiling at him. "How have you been?"

"Fine," said J997. He gestured at his red stripes. "For helping to save the two worlds, I was promoted to Squad Leader. I am now in charge of two dozen of my fellow J bots, which means I have more responsibility now. Oh well."

"Have you guys tracked down all of the remaining Reunification agents yet?" asked Kiriah.

J997 shook his head. "No. We are getting close, though. In the past year, we've captured a dozen of them. Reunification was not a large organization, according to their files, but they still have agents everywhere that are very good at hiding. I imagine it will be a long while before we capture them all, but that is fine, because we have plenty of time in which to do it."

"That is good to hear," I said. "What of their bases? And the Foundation's bases?"

"Reunification's Xeeonite base has been seized by the Xeeonian government," said J997. "There is far more in there than you'd think. We're still shifting through the rubble of the lower rooms and finding more and more things. We have not been able to find the Foundation's Xeeonite base, however. But that is classified information I am not allowed to discuss with people outside of the force."

"I hope ye find every last one of those scoundrels and bring them before the law," I said. "Anyway, I am surprised that the Database did not delete ye for your running away."

"Once the Database saw my memories, it agreed to spare me," said J997. "Though now I have to stay connected to the Database at all times and I am no longer allowed to go to Dela even after criminals I am assigned to arrest."

"Let me guess," said Kiriah, "they don't want a repeat of last year, do they?"

"Yes," said J997, nodding. "It is somewhat inconvenient, but I understand the Database's reasoning behind it nonetheless."

"And what of the Head, Resita, and Lanresia?" I asked. "I have not heard from any of them since the Portal closed."

"Still missing," said J997. "As is the Destroyer, although we did find out that the Destroyer killed every last one of Reunification's Lizard-men before vanishing. We have no idea where any of them are. I have, however, set Konoa free, although it took me many months of convincing the Database that he was not a dangerous criminal before the Database agreed to let him go."

"What is Konoa doing now?" I asked. "I know him not very well, but I would still like to know how he is doing."

"He recently received his certificate for J bot repair and maintenance," said J997. "That means he is now officially licensed as a qualified J bot technician. He already knew how to do it, but now he can practice it safely within the law. Or he would, anyway."

"Would?" Kiriah repeated. "What do you mean?"

"Konoa left Xeeon to search for the Head and the other two," said J997, gesturing in a random direction, perhaps to indicate where Konoa had gone. "He didn't tell me why, but I believe he wants to avenge Kojama. I don't know where he is, either. After he left Xeeon, he completely fell off the radar, so he could be anywhere now."

"The members of the Foundation are certainly good at doing that," I said. "A little too good, I'd say."

"They have had years of experience in that area," said J997. "But I'm sure that Konoa is fine. He can take care of himself."

Kiriah then leaned forward on the table quite suddenly and said, "Rii, can I ask you something?"

"Ask whatever ye will, sister," I said. "I shall answer as best as I am able."

Kiriah nodded, but she looked a little sheepish for some reason. "Well, I was just thinking … Sura was the last priest of the Old Gods in our family, right?"

"Right," I said. "He was the last trained in the ways of the priests of the Old Religion. Why do ye ask?"

"Well …" Kiriah seemed embarrassed for some reason. "I was thinking … what if *I* became a priestess of the Old Gods?"

"Ye?" I said. "Well, I certainly would not object to it, though I am not certain I could help ye do it. Sura only learned because father taught him, but with neither father nor Sura alive anymore, I do not think it is possible for anyone to learn that discipline now. And why do ye want to learn it, anyway?"

"To make up for my past sins," said Kiriah. She leaned back and frowned. "After everything I did … I still don't forgive myself, even if I *was* brainwashed and even if the Mayor pardoned me. I turned my back on the Old Gods for years, but I want to return to them, and I thought that carrying on our brother's legacy would be the best way to do it. I've been thinking about this for the better part of a year now and I've decided to do it."

"A wonderful idea, sister," I said. "But as I said, I know not how to do it. Only a priest of the Old Gods can make someone else a priest. I am not a priest myself; therefore, I do not see—"

"There is someone who claims to be a priestess of the Old Gods in Yaroz," said J997, interrupting me rather rudely. "That's a city state to the northeast of Xeeon, about five hundred miles from here according to my internal map."

"Really?" said Kiriah, leaning toward J997 with a look of eagerness on her face. "What's a priestess of the Old Gods doing here in Xeeo?"

"I do not know," said J997. "I only know that the Database has records on her. She's an elderly woman who lives by herself in an apartment in Yaroz. You may wish to visit her sometime."

"I will have to," said Kiriah. She held up her wrist. "Can you send me her address? I'll have to visit her on my next day off."

"Certainly," said J997. He tapped the side of his head and the device inside Kiriah's wrist glowed. "There you go. I also gave you directions for how to reach her from here."

"Thank you so much, J997," said Kiriah, lowering her wrist. "But, if I may ask, why did you tell me about her? I'm not complaining, but just curious, because I didn't ask you to tell me about her."

"I want to help you," said J997. He gave her the thumbs up, which looked odd indeed coming from a robot of all beings. "Consider this my way of thanking you for what you and your brother did to help save the worlds."

"I will," said Kiriah, rubbing her wrist. "I will."

She looked at me. "Rii, will you come with me when I go visit her? Please?"

"Certainly," I said. "I, too, wish to meet another follower of the Old Religion. We will have to coordinate a day and time for us to go together, however, because today would not be a good day for me."

"Of course, of course," said Kiriah, nodding. "I will talk with the Mayor about giving me time off to visit her."

"And I shall speak with Sir Lockfried about getting time off on the same day," I said. "And then we shall go together and it shall be glorious."

Kiriah smiled. Even J997 looked pleased at our happiness, even though he was a robot who could not feel anything.

So I took another sip of my tea, already thinking of what Yaroz and the elderly priestess will be like and what I will need to bring when we go to see her.

THE END OF TWO WORLDS.

.

Afterword

Hello, my readers! I hope you enjoyed reading Two Worlds just as much as I enjoyed writing it. I did my very best to make it the best I could and I hope that that shows in all five books.

But yes, this is the final Two Worlds book. There will not be another one after this one. So for now, the adventures of Rii, J997, and the others are over for now.

You may have noticed, however, that I left a few loose threads in this final book. The reason for that is because I might return to the Two Worlds universe in the future if this series sells. Right now, its lack of sales mean that I will probably focus on writing other, more lucrative projects instead, but I might still return to the Two Worlds universe at some point in the future if I see an opportunity for a good series that will sell well.

In the meantime, in Januar 2016 I am returning to the world of Martir, the main setting of my Prince Malock World and Mages of Martir novels, with a brand new series called Tournament of the Gods. It takes place after my Mages of Martir series, but I wrote it in a way so that even people who have not read any of the Mages books will be able to understand it and follow along. Still, I highly recommend picking up the Prince Malock World novels and the Mages of Martir novels if you have not done so already, as Tournament of the Gods features characters from both and builds upon the events of the previous two series.

Tournament of the Gods Book #1, *Gathering of the Chosen*, is scheduled for release in ebook and trade paperback in January 2016. If you want to be the FIRST to know about the release of *Gathering of the Chosen*, then subscribe to my mailing list on my website at www.timothylcerepaka.com. Mailing list subscribers also get two free books, *The Mage's Grave* and *Reunification*, sent directly to their inbox. Not only that, but mailing list subscribers also get exclusive deals and can enter contests to win amazing prizes you can't get anywhere else. And I promise not to sell your information to anybody and you are free to unsubscribe whenever you like.

That's all for now. See ya,

Timothy L. Cerepaka

About the Author

Timothy L. Cerepaka writes fantasy and science-fiction stories as an indie author. He is the author of the Prince Malock World fantasy novels, the Mages of Martir fantasy novels, and the Two Worlds fantasy novels. He lives in Texas.

Go to www.timothylcerepaka.com to find out more and to subscribe to his mailing list to get two free books and to be the first to know about his newest releases.

Other books by Timothy L. Cerepaka

Prince Malock World:

The Mad Voyage of Prince Malock

The Return of Prince Malock

The New Era of Prince Malock

The Coronation of Prince Malock

Mages of Martir:

The Mage's Grave

The Mage's Limits

The Mage's Sea

The Mage's Ghost

Two Worlds:

Reunification

Alliance

Allegiance

Retaliation

Desinence

Standalones:

The Last Legend: Glitch Apocalypse

All of the above books are available in ebook and trade paperback wherever books are sold!